PRAISE FOR ANI
A CALCUL.

Shortlisted for the 2013 Philip K. Dick and
Kitschies Golden Tentacle Awards

"Charnock is a subtle world builder . . . for readers who want a smart,
subtle exploration of human emotion and intelligence, this is an
excellent choice." —Alix E. Harrow, *Strange Horizons*

"Charnock has fascinating, complex things to say about work, sex,
family and hope . . . What she shares with (Philip K.) Dick is the
ability to write unease . . . a very noteworthy book." —Adam Roberts,
author of *Jack Glass*, winner of the 2012 BSFA Best Novel Award

"This is a story beautifully and simply narrated, the language
economical but evocative, and it remains compelling without ever
resorting to sensationalism. A coming-of-age tale exploring what it
means to be human, it kept me gripped to the end." —E. J. Swift,
author of The Osiris Project trilogy

"This story puts us inside one of the most interesting perspectives I've
encountered in recent fiction. Jayna's perspective is so unique that I
would happily have followed her anywhere, and, as a consequence,
the cleverness of this plot almost snuck up on me. A smart, stylish,
emotionally compelling book with literary richness and sci-fi smarts."
—Susan DeFreitas, author of *Pyrophitic*

SLEEPING EMBERS
OF AN
ORDINARY MIND

SLEEPING EMBERS
OF AN
ORDINARY
MIND

ANNE

A Novel

CHARNOCK

Text copyright © 2015 Anne Charnock

Published by 47North, Seattle

www.apub.com

Amazon, the Amazon logo, and 47North are trademarks of Amazon.com, Inc., or its affiliates.

ISBN-13: 9781503950436
ISBN-10: 1503950433

Cover design by M. S. Corley

Printed in the United States of America

In memory of Mabel and Betty

My ears are wearied by your carping. You brashly and pub-
licly not merely wonder but indeed lament that I am said to
possess as fine a mind as nature ever bestowed upon the most
learned man. You seem to think that so learned a woman has
scarcely before been seen in the world. You are wrong on both
counts . . . I am a school girl, possessed of the sleeping embers
of an ordinary mind.

Laura Cereta
January 13, 1488

HISTORICAL NOTE

Antonia Uccello (1456–1490) is described on her death certificate as a *pittoressa*—a painter. Her father, Paolo Uccello, was a pioneer of linear perspective in the early Renaissance. None of Antonia's work has, as yet, come to light.

CHAPTER ONE

London, 2113

Toniah drops three jasmine dragon pearls into her tall porcelain mug. She pours water, just off the boil, spilling it as she glances across at her sister, Poppy, and Poppy's new boyfriend. They sit, staring ahead, both checking their retinal mail, at the end of the long kitchen table. Toniah grabs a tea towel to wipe the spillage, but she knocks the mug. It tips over and cracks. A surge of weak tea floods across the kitchen worktop, sweeping the jasmine pearls and flakes of breakfast cereal over the edge, onto the oak floor.

"Sorry, sorry. I've got it." She crouches down and wipes the cupboard doors.

Poppy groans. "Shame. Is it broken?"

Toniah stands and holds up a shard of Botticelli's Venus—her left eye and three locks of windswept golden hair. "My favourite mug."

"Meet Ben, by the way," says Poppy. He looks across at Toniah and smiles broadly. She smiles back at him.

She finishes mopping the floor, makes a second mug of tea and takes it to the far end of the table. She wonders if Ben has stayed over before. He looks brawnier than her sister's usual type. The way he sits, leaning forward with his forearm across the table, with his hairy hand splayed . . . he looks as though at any moment he might lean across, grab the opposite edge of the table and pull the whole thing over, crockery and all. Or, he might leap to his feet so that his chair shoots backwards and smashes against the floor. And as for his thwacking footsteps on the stairs last night—Poppy let him in sometime before midnight—he sounded like a damned yeti ascending.

A young girl throws open the garden door. "I've fed the—" She trips over the threshold, rights herself and continues, "I've fed the chickens." With hands on hips, she says, "They wouldn't come out this morning. I had to sprinkle grain on the ground outside the door and shake the container. Lazy things. They were still asleep on their perches." She kicks off her garden shoes, scrapes back a chair, making Toniah wince, and stretches across the table to grab her school reader.

"Done your homework, Eva?" says Ben.

"Course I have."

"Eva's very good with her schoolwork, aren't you?" says Toniah. Eva flashes a smile at her auntie and then at Ben. Toniah needs to get the lowdown on who's been coming and going while she's been away. This *Ben* acts as though he's stayed a few times; he knows Eva, and she seems at ease with him.

"Toniah, can you walk Eva to school?" says Poppy. "I'm working from home this morning."

"Sure. You stay in your pyjamas."

Eva giggles. "Slouchy sloth day."

Poppy kisses Eva on the head. "I'll get your sports kit ready." She heads off, up the stairs to Eva's bedroom.

"Auntie Toniah?"

"Yes?"

"The hens are pecking Agatha again. We'll have to put beak guards on them."

"Is Agatha losing any feathers?"

"She's getting a bald patch on her back. It looks horrible."

"Let's put her in a separate pen for now, and I'll give her some treats. I'm not sure I remember how to fit those beak guards. I'll have to ask your mum."

"She can't do it. She's hopeless. If you help me, I'll do it."

"Okay. Later, after work."

"Auntie?"

"Yes?"

"Your hair's a real mess."

Ben, still checking his mail, laughs and puts his hand to his face. Toniah can't tell if he's enjoying some private banter or if he's laughing at Eva's remark. His shoulders shake. Toniah can't help herself; she smiles. He seems like a nice guy. And it's true; she should use a comb occasionally.

Eva takes hold of the saltcellar and, fidgeting, turns it over and over without noticing the mess she's making. They're quite similar, it occurs to Toniah—Eva and this man. The way they take up space. Eva pushes her right foot against the crossbar of the next chair, tipping her own chair so that it balances precariously on two legs. And *him* . . . It's not that he's big, Toniah says to herself—he's probably only an inch or two taller than she is—but he's stocky. He'd stop a runaway horse.

He laughs aloud now. "Sorry. Long-running joke."

He makes Toniah feel like an intruder in her own home. He just takes over. He's so different to them. A square face, with big eyes and a full mouth, thick and dark wavy hair. There's nothing subtle about him. She can see why her sister finds him attractive.

Poppy reappears and deposits Eva's sports bag by the kitchen door.

"Who's picking me up from school?" Eva says to her mother. "You or Carmen?"

"Me, I expect. Carmen left before I was out of bed, but she'll probably finish work before me, so I'll check if she's—"

"But, Mum. *Who's* picking me up? I want to know."

"*I'll* pick you up. Sorry." Poppy looks across at Toniah and winks.

"I don't like surprises, either," says Toniah.

Ben looks confused. "I'll make some toast then. Um, I can walk Eva to school."

Poppy gives him a frown that states *no* and says, "It's okay, Ben. It's on Toniah's way to work."

"Where do you work? What's the job?" he asks, turning to her.

"I'm in restitutions . . . at the Academy."

His eyebrows lift slightly. He doesn't reply. Just stares at her.

———————

Ben wishes they'd let him stay beyond breakfast, but the arrangement works well enough. He recalls the last time he stayed over, about a month ago. He sat in the garden, making the most of a fine start to the day, and he watched Eva feed the chickens. He took the water feeder from her, cleaned and refilled it at the garden tap. It was pretty heavy for a young girl to lift. Poppy appeared at the kitchen door and shouted—quite curtly, he thought—"She can manage. She doesn't have to fill it to the top." Still, he didn't see the harm in helping the girl. But he has come to accept the situation—that if he wants family involvement, he'll have to look elsewhere. Maybe when his job becomes more settled, when he's working offshore for shorter stints, that's when he'll try a proper relationship again, something more than this intermittent arrangement with Poppy. He doesn't have time right now for anything more.

He knows he should scarper soon.

———————

Toniah helps Eva into her school cardigan and picks up her sports bag. Poppy goes to the fridge, slides out a lunch box and passes it, baton style, to Eva as they make their way along the narrow Minton-tiled hallway.

"Your meeting today, Toniah . . . hope it goes okay." Poppy puts her arms around her sister and pulls her in for a tight hug. "It's great having you home."

"Thanks."

Ben picks up his jacket and follows them down the hallway. Poppy stands back to let him pass, but her eyes are fixed on Eva.

He steps outside, and before he pulls the front door closed behind them, Toniah turns, touches his arm hurriedly and raises a finger to her lips. "Shh." She points to the hedge bordering the tiny front garden. They see a bubbling in the undergrowth. For Toniah, it sparks a recollection from years past. Three pairs of eyes fix on the shivering, leafy detritus.

"A mouse?" whispers Eva.

A wren hops out of the leaf litter and flies low through the slatted gate.

"I thought I heard wren song yesterday," says Toniah, delighted. "You hardly ever see them— they're secretive."

"I've never seen such a tiny bird," says Eva. "I'm going to tell class at show-and-tell."

"And there's something else you can tell them," says Toniah teasingly.

"What? What can I tell them?"

They step down to the pavement and all turn to the right. "I'm going your way," says Ben.

"What can I tell them?" Eva tugs at Toniah's sleeve.

"A long time ago," Toniah says, as though launching into a fairy tale, "a long time before I was born or before my Nana Stone was born, the wren was stamped on our tiniest of tiny coins, a copper farthing. It was the best coin we ever had."

"A tiny bird on a tiny coin," says Eva.

———◆———

At the school gates, Toniah stoops to kiss Eva's hair.

"So it's definitely Mum who's collecting me?"

Toniah aches. She's caught in a time loop. Eva is such a little worrier—so like Poppy twenty years in the past. Toniah learned to anticipate her younger sister's anxieties, and looking back, she wonders if their five-year age gap might have sapped Poppy's confidence; an older sister always knows best. In any case, whenever Poppy grew worrisome, Toniah had discovered, distraction was always her best tactic.

"Absolutely definitely. It's your mum. Look! Isn't that boy one of your friends? Now, run along and have fun." Eva dashes across to the boy, and as they walk along the school path—her auntie still watching—they bump against one another repeatedly, carelessly, as though personal space were an alien concept. Eva makes tiny hops— Toniah smiles and her eyes mist. She's telling the boy about the wren.

Toniah turns and sees that Ben has been waiting. Well, there's no rule saying he can't, she thinks. But she wouldn't normally spend time with her sister's overnighters. As for their housemate, Carmen, Toniah has only once met a woman who stayed over, and she might have been a friend, rather than a date.

"Going to the tube? I'm taking the Victoria line," Ben says.

"Northern line."

"So, you've finished your studies. Poppy seems happy to have you home," he says.

"I wasn't actually studying. I was doing a postdoc, writing up papers from my PhD research."

"Sorry, I—"

"That's okay. I'm still a researcher in this new job. More of the same."

"How's it going?"

"I'm having an easy ride so far. I'm still settling in."

She doesn't want to talk about her work. It's too early in the day to muster a defensive position, and she hasn't parsed her explanation as yet. In any case, she still feels awkward; she's unsure how she landed the job.

"You've been seeing my sister for a while?"

"On and off for the past six months. I'm in London for a month at a time. I'm mostly offshore."

"That must be difficult."

"Not so bad now—I've bought a small flat north of the river. Makes a difference having my own place to come home to. But I won't stick the job much longer."

"And then?"

"Who knows? A nice clean desk job, maybe. Like yours."

It's sticky underfoot, as always in summer along so many London streets. High above in the towering common lime trees, armies of aphids ingest the limes' sap and excrete sugary honeydew, which drops to the pavements, playing hell with the soles of workaday and designer shoes alike. At one time, Toniah knew which sections of pavement to avoid, but she's out of practice, having been away in Norwich working flat out for two years—bar a few long weekends. Their ripping footsteps turn them into cartoon commuters. "Shit!" says Ben, and Toniah allows herself to laugh.

In fact, she has an affection for the tiny aphid creatures. As a school girl, she collected the names of unisexual species in alphabetical order, from aphid up to zebra shark, in a lined red exercise book. Whenever she was teased about her family—because she and her sister looked so similar to their mother, and their mother was so similar to their grandmother—she'd spout off the names of unisex predator species. Hammerhead sharks and Komodo dragons were her favourite corroborators; they didn't need the whole boring boy-girl thing. But it was all bravado on Toniah's part.

Thankfully, it's easier for Eva. She's a third-generation partho, and it's not so unusual any more. Toniah is now happy to imagine that she, Poppy and Eva are pretty much time-separated triplets, though not identical. Apart from their facial similarities, they share a few physical quirks, including a bent little finger on their right hand.

———————————

At the top of the underground escalators, they go their separate ways, but Ben casts a look across his shoulder as he steps onto the Victoria line escalator; he catches a glimpse of Toniah. He feels envious. She'll return home to her sister and niece this evening. The thought of going back to his underfurnished apartment is chilling even on a summer's day.

———————————

The latest postgraduate intake, six researchers in all, congregates by one of eight sculptures in the neoclassical foyer. It's a life-size statue of Ayn Rand—not Toniah's favourite philosopher. She feels more comfortable by the neighbouring statue of Laura Cereta, the Italian humanist, a feminist of the early Renaissance.

They await the arrival of vice president Elodie Maingey. It's the first time they've met a member of the board, but everyone knows her lineage. The Academy of Restitution was the brainchild of her mother, who used her position as the American ambassador to the United Nations to promote the concept of women's restitution. During the past fifteen years, the worst oversights of male-centric historicism have been corrected. Toniah brushes the back of her hand against the brass folds of Cereta's robes. She hopes this morning's encounter with Elodie Maingey will either convince her to stay or convince her to look for another job. She still feels bruised, disappointed that a teaching post didn't materialize at her university department in Norwich. They had dragged out the decision, and she couldn't wait; she'd needed a salary, fast. Falling back on her sister for financial support wasn't an option. That wasn't the way they operated.

As the vice president approaches them, Toniah realizes that, subconsciously, she expected a tall woman. Elodie Maingey is slight and shorter than any of the new recruits.

She launches straight in. "I wanted to meet you all here instead of the conference room for a specific reason. Look around this imposing foyer." She carelessly sweeps her hand. "Isn't it *begging* for more sculptures? If you prove yourselves over the coming twelve months and take a permanent post with us here at the Academy, you *must think big*. That's what I want you to take away from our first meeting. Imagine. Any one of you, through your own research, could secure the overdue recognition of one woman's life's work. But you'll only achieve that"—she wags her finger—"through persistence. Dogged persistence."

She turns, walks ahead and, with a forward wave, evidently expects everyone to fall in behind her. Toniah is accustomed to a solitary working life and feels out of place playing follow-my-leader. It seems childlike. But she reminds herself for the second time today—the first time was when she climbed the twenty-one stone steps to the Academy's entrance—that well-paid jobs for art historians are as rare as hen's teeth.

⸻

They shuffle in and take seats around an antique mahogany table, positioned diagonally across the conference room; it's clearly the only way the table will fit. Historical rarity valued above common sense, thinks Toniah. She's quick to grab a seat facing the floor-to-ceiling window so she can look out towards Tower Bridge. Elodie remains standing.

"So . . . now that you've completed the Academy's induction process, let's consider how you might get started on the *real* work. Maybe you already have specific women within your sights from your previous research—women who deserve to be lifted out of obscurity. If not, you can take as your starting point one of the Posthumous Awards granted by your own professional organizations." She places her fingertips on the polished table and leans forward. "You see, my mother was a damned wily character. She wasn't out to chastise, because she knew that would be counterproductive. When she launched the Decade of Professional Reflections, she knew the professions would oblige. It was simple enough to acknowledge a few names—women who'd been *inadvertently overlooked*. Today, we are still building on those formal acknowledgments."

She clasps her hands together. "Now, let's face up to something." She slowly scans the faces around the conference table. "Some of you will discover over the coming year—and you may not care to admit it to yourself, but we will point it out for you"—she allows herself a smug twitch of her shoulders—"that you are *best* suited to deconstructing and trimming down the reputation of a man who has been unfairly elevated by past historians. On the other hand, you may find you're better at piecing together shards of information to revise and enhance a woman's reputation. We'll try you out in both areas, but you mustn't feel that one skill is more highly valued than the other, despite what I told you in the foyer. We need both skills, though we tend to keep the two missions in separate silos."

Toniah looks around at her colleagues, all smiling.

"Bear in mind, I would like each of you to play a substantial role in achieving a *Top Outcome* over the coming year. It's our aim to promote five Top Outcomes every quarter, coinciding with our appeals for donations."

There's a raised hand. "Do we have to stick to our specialisms?" Good question, thinks Toniah.

"In theory, you may roam outside your discipline. We like you to follow your instincts. It's not for the Academy's board to tell *you*, it's for *you* to tell the board."

Oh dear, thinks Toniah. That sounds a bit rehearsed.

"I'll speak to you individually over the coming weeks. I like to be familiar with your interests."

As they stand to leave, she says, "Toniah, I'll have a word with you now if that's convenient."

———————

They sit facing one another across the conference table.

"You mentioned in your application that you live in a parthenogenetic household."

"I wasn't sure about mentioning that."

"It didn't do you any harm. Put it this way: How much do you know about our funding sources?"

Toniah throws Elodie a quizzical look. "Just the public information— government sources, United Nations, charities, private donations."

"I'll elaborate. A significant and growing source of small private donations comes from individual parthenogenetic women." Her lopsided smile makes Toniah uncomfortable.

"I'm actually second-generation. My grandmother was a trailblazer in the 2040s," says Toniah.

"Well, your partho background helped the board to push through your appointment. Recruitment felt we had enough art historians."

"And, so . . . ?"

"So, you'll need to make a good impression if you want to stay at the Academy. Only two among the current intake will be offered a permanent contract, and we're under par in economics and medical science. What I suggest is that you have an immediate input on the Paul Gauguin project—there's a final assessment nearing completion. I want you to look over the paper before the team makes its presentation to colleagues in the department. *They'll* pick up any major issues before the paper goes to outside referees, but I'm curious to know your opinion."

"Gauguin?" asks Toniah, incredulous. Her palms feel clammy, and she wipes them along the arms of her chair. "Not my area by a long chalk. I'm Early Renaissance. And there's no doubting his contribution, surely."

"Excellent. You'll need convincing."

CHAPTER TWO

Shanghai, 2015

Toni dares herself to go outside, but she's caught by a queasy feeling—
she knows they'll all stare at her like she's suddenly appeared out of
nowhere, beamed down by aliens. So although she's itching to walk
along the Bund and watch the river traffic up close, it's easier to say,
Why bother? She has a fab view of the Huangpu River from her suite—
her own frikkin' suite!—seven floors up at the corner of the hotel. From
the side window of her bedroom, she can see the river flowing north-
west. From the front windows, stretching across the bedroom and sitting room, she can see the river sweeping north and then eastwards in a
deep loop to the Yangtze and the open sea. Her dad sketched a map of
the river for her, and she's committed it to memory. She never has any
idea which way she's facing. She feels, looking out of the front window,
that she's facing south, towards . . . where? Hong Kong? But apparently
she is not.

This is stupid. Halfway around the planet, and she's hanging around
her hotel room. She grabs her denim jacket, her *bespoke* denim jacket,
embellished with her own handiwork—flowers embroidered in the

armpits and red-headed woodpeckers along the sleeves—perfect for the Bund not simply because it's chilly in the late afternoon in spring but because fashion is a big thing in China. Her dad says people have their clothes made to measure in the market so everyone's more *individual*.

Toni thinks this is amazingly cool—everyone wants to be a bit different in the most populated country on earth. She walks along the darkened corridor towards the elevators and stops to snap a photo of these really weird glass boxes set into the wall along the corridor, like fish tanks without the water. Inside each glass box, there's a rock. Just a lump of grey rock. Small lights are inset into the tanks, and they shine downwards so that the cragginess of each rock is obvious. Is it art? She has no idea. She must ask her dad.

He said he wouldn't be gone for long. He's in a pre-meeting at his client's office before they visit the client's home town, Suzhou. That's when they'll get down to the details of exactly which painting he wants her dad to copy, at what size. Her dad refuses to paint actual size; that way, he avoids any dodgy business. He's a professional copyist painter, with the emphasis on *professional*; that's what he always tells people.

The hotel reception is on the second floor, and as Toni wanders past, all three reception staff look up and smile. She takes the elevator down to the ground floor, to a windowless mini-reception where another receptionist stands in semi-darkness at a high counter. He's stationed there so that when people walk in off the street, he can say, "Please take the elevator to reception." Toni reckons he has the most boring job on the planet. Does he think it's a good job? She has no idea. He says, "Have a good afternoon. Do you need a taxi?" She shakes her head. "No, thanks."

Toni texts her dad: *Gone out. On the bund.* He replies: *On way back, meet you opp hotel. Don't wander off.* She replies: *As if!*

She knows he'll be in a panic now. Out on the Bund, on her own; anything could happen. That's the problem now; he thinks anything *can* happen, as though once one bad thing happens to you, it's easier for another bad thing to smack you. As if when you're vulnerable, God decides to kick you while you're still down. But she doesn't believe in God, not since she woke up on her last birthday, her first day as a teenager. That's when she decided.

Anyway, she doesn't mind her dad's fussing, because she's just the same—only she doesn't say anything. It's like she expects a disaster with every ping. During the past two hours, she has imagined her dad falling down the stairs at the metro station and being trampled by the crowds. She has imagined him walking from the metro and *glancing* instead of *looking* at a busy junction and getting flattened by a motorcycle rickshaw driving on the wrong side of the road. It wouldn't actually kill him, but he'd definitely end up in hospital. And now he's rushing back. The roads are so dangerous here.

Toni comes to a conclusion as she waits patiently at the road junction outside the hotel. She should worry about bigger things instead of stressing about traffic accidents. She should upscale to the apocalypse.

So she crosses to the promenade, leans over the railing and imagines in the distance a tsunami sweeping up the Huangpu. Would it come from her left or her right? She can only imagine it coming from the left. But that's correct. It would come from the sea, from the left. In front of her, there's a procession of three open barges laden with pyramids of coal. Boxy Chinese characters are spray-painted in yellow across the coal. The delivery address? Or a Chinese proverb? Or "Happy Birthday, Mai Ling"? That's the name of her best friend in the denim-jacket-pimping embroidery group. The tsunami roars towards the Bund. She grips the steel railing, and the leading edge of the wave lifts the coal barges so they're half as high as the buildings of Pudong on the opposite bank. Yellow-coated coal pours as easily as cornflakes from a box.

Toni feels much better for that. The world looks super normal now.

Daylight is fading, and the digital advertising on the Pudong skyscrapers starts to pulsate: "Dunlop" to "Range Rover" to "I ♥ SHANGHAI." She wheels around, too quickly, for she now attracts attention. It's not as though she looks foreign; her hair is dark. But when anyone sees her ice-grey eyes, they seem to freak out; she must look like a ghost. Two girls with that Harajuku look—white net tutus, white lace-up high tops and preppy, tight sweaters—smile at her, take out their smartphones and snap her photo. She snaps them back. They're delighted. Toni could get used to this place with all the smiley faces.

With her back to pullulating Pudong, she takes in the sedate granite buildings ranged along the Bund—the near-uninterrupted vista of 1920s solidity—and she picks out the Waldorf Astoria where her dad took her this morning for a white-chocolate mocha in the Long Bar. So swanky, but in a dark-wood way, with huge, lazy ceiling fans.

Toni turns back to the Pudong skyscrapers, a cityscape built in the last thirty years on swampy farmland on the east bank of the Huangpu. Small passenger ferries ply across the river, miraculously avoiding the heavy traffic of barges and container ships. The biggest ships are guided around the tight loop of the Huangpu by tugs pulling on their sterns. Between the commercial traffic and the passenger ferries, a golden galleon twinkles its carefree way, seemingly indifferent to the possibilities of waterborne calamity. "300 Tourists Drown in Huangpu as Megaton Ship Rams Golden Galleon." Toni wants to be a reporter when she grows up.

She isn't the only person twisting back and forth trying to reconcile the two banks of the river. "Colonial Past Meets Confident Chinese Future." Toni wonders whether, if she travelled at light speed back and forth across the river, she would travel back in time. She read about an astronaut going into space and back at high speed. He lost a second, or something.

If she could go back in time and fix things, then she wouldn't be here now on a business trip with her dad. He'd said she could stay home with a friend, but she knew he wanted some company. In fact, he follows her around the house now, always sitting nearby. Even if he's doing some admin, he'll sit close with his laptop. She doesn't mind; it's good, really, but she knows there's something she can't ever say, and it hangs there. And she's never, ever, going to say it aloud to him, or anyone. She's sticking with his version. So she says the words in her head once more, hoping this will be the last time. She hopes she can throw the words in the river and lose them in, where, the Chinese Sea? Here goes, one last time: *He* should have collected the parcel. It was *his* parcel.

He would have driven a different route, or maybe set off a few seconds sooner, because her mum always opened the back passenger door to hang up her jacket on the hook, and she always checked the rear-view mirror before setting off, which he didn't. So even if her dad had stepped out of the house at the exact same time as her mum did, he'd have driven past the timber depot half a minute before the *wrong-place, wrong-time accident*—as her dad describes it. He never mentions the parcel; he just says she was driving into town.

———————

A few texts are exchanged, and as Toni makes her way along the Bund, she spots her dad. It isn't difficult, because he's taller than most people around him, and he's wearing an unnecessarily bright, red, flat cap. He had wanted Toni to buy a colourful hat at Heathrow airport, but she refused point-blank. "I'll find you," she said, "with that nuclear button on your head."

He hugs her. "It's getting dark already."

"I'm fine. Everyone's friendly."

"Don't accept any invitations for coffee or anything. You just don't know. We're new to all this."

"How did it go with Mr. Lu?"

"Great. Let's celebrate. I've found a restaurant." He points to a road leading away from the Bund. "Down there."

"Has he chosen a painting?"

"We've narrowed it to three, and he'll decide at the weekend. So . . . we're going to Suzhou tomorrow, and he's booked another hotel for us."

"It won't be as amazing as this hotel."

"I thanked him. I said you love it."

"What's he like?"

"Urbane, polite, knowledgeable."

"Urbane?"

"A sophisticated man about town. He's done piles of homework, too, which was a bit embarrassing. I had to pretend I knew as much as he did."

"And did you ask him my question? Why didn't he ask a Chinese artist to do the job?"

"No point. He wanted the Dominic Munroe signature on the painting." And in a deep, self-mocking tone, "Copyist to the English aristocracy."

"Do I have to meet Mr. Lu?"

"You should say hello if he drops by the hotel in Suzhou."

"Okay. If you think so."

"You'll like him. He smiles a lot."

They walk away from the Bund along East Jinling Road, which is lined by tall stone buildings. Electric scooters speed past them, and Toni points one out to her dad. A young man, an office worker in a grey suit and white shirt, sits forward on his scooter with two male passengers tucked behind him, riding pillion, wearing the exact same colour of suit and shirt. All three men are laughing, heads back. Toni and her dad twist around and watch them as they swing out into the traffic on Zhongshan East Second Road.

"Thank God the bikes are all electric here," says her dad. "Can you imagine, back in Florence, with this number of bikes?"

"At least you could hear them coming." She stops. "Dad, look at these shops." Haberdashery businesses occupy the street-level shops, all selling more or less the same textile accessories—reels of ribbons, decorative edging, fabric tape.

"Dad, I want to buy some embroidered tape. Will they sell just a few centimetres?"

"I doubt it. Looks like wholesale. Hey, I reckon we've time to go to the fabric market tomorrow before we catch the train. I've got the address. How about that?"

"Brilliant. I want to pimp another denim jacket, better than this one."

As they walk farther from the Bund, the pavement becomes more uneven, and the small textile businesses give way to bakers, tobacconists, silk-duvet fabricators, barbers. There's a rotten smell from a stinky-tofu stall, so they rush past, cut off right and pass through a forest of concrete pillars that carry the Yan'an Elevated Road.

"Here it is." The Shanghai Laolao Grandmother Restaurant.

Toni throws a worried glance at her dad.

"Don't worry. I checked online. They'll have a picture menu."

"And with your brilliant Mandarin . . ."

"Yeah, we'll be fine."

Her dad has learned how to say in Mandarin—which isn't a huge amount of use as people here speak Shanghainese—*One bottle of beer and one Coca-Cola, please.* They join a melee inside the restaurant entrance, and within moments they're pulled away by the manager, who seats them in a cubicle close by the entrance. A waitress immediately deposits a large, ring-bound, plasticized menu on the plain laminate table.

"Did you see her shirt?" Her dad tries to catch sight of the waitress. "Can you see? It's totally creased. Looks like it's been stuffed in a bag for two years."

Another waitress rushes past, wearing a similarly creased shirt of the same gunmetal grey. "How do they manage that?" says Toni.

They share the menu across the table and flip through the pages: two large pictures and four smaller pictures on each spread, with lists of the main ingredients alongside. They select four dishes that seem comparable to the dishes from Toni's favourite takeaway in East Dulwich.

"I think we'll be fine with that. No hens' feet," says her dad.

The waitress returns, and he places their order by pointing at the menu, then trots out his one and only sentence of Mandarin. Is it a man thing, Toni wonders, that her dad feels no embarrassment, *at all*, about his crap Mandarin? Or is it just him?

"So, how's your coursework coming along?" he asks.

"I did some easy stuff. I still feel weird with the jet lag."

"What about your history project?"

"I'm saving that. It's the one interesting thing I've to do this holiday."

"You'll find it easier when you start dropping some subjects."

"Can't wait to drop French. It's absolutely pointless."

"It's useful on holiday. Remember . . ." He has second thoughts about dredging up memories, even good ones.

"Anyway, I've got an app for French."

"That's no use for a conversation."

"There'll be an app for conversation before I finish school. You'll see."

The waitress delivers one dish of sweet cucumber—cut into sticks and coated in a clear sauce—with two sets of chopsticks and two bowls. She stands to attention and, without making eye contact, announces the dish. She makes a tick on the order list and departs. Toni and her dad wait for half a minute, but there's no sign of any other food. "I think we'd better start," says Toni.

"Tell me about this history project. Wars of the Roses?"

"No. Wrong one. Hundred Years' War. Joan of Arc, et cetera. Anyway, we've finished all that. We're doing, like, everyday history now. How the Black Death changed everybody's life for the better."

"If they survived?"

"Exactly." She worries a piece of cucumber with her chopsticks. "I asked Mrs. O'Brien about that."

"What?"

"Why some people survived and others didn't."

"And?"

"Some people were immune. She said there's some research being done about the Spanish flu epidemic after World War I, to find out why so many young adults died—it was unusual. She said it might help our understanding of the Black Death and how it lasted for centuries."

"More people died of Spanish flu than died fighting in the trenches."

"But it looked worse, didn't it? The trenches, I mean. All those dead soldiers in the mud."

He looks blankly at her, as if she's said something he can't assimilate. But then, "Remember that Paul Nash exhibition I took you to? His war paintings?"

"Yeah."

"You've reminded me—he was sent to Ypres, and he brought back a bunch of work he called 'fifty drawings of muddy places.'"

She pulls a face. "Is that some sick joke?"

"Classic British understatement."

Another dish. Beef in a thick sauce. Toni pokes it with a chopstick.

"Anyway, Mrs. O'Brien said this thing that freaked us out. She said that everyone alive today is a survivor of the Black Death. Of plague. Our ancestors were immune, so we are. I keep thinking about it, so I'm going to do a project about that."

The waitress returns to their table, and three male customers try to squeeze past. They laugh when they see the mountain of rice the waitress is carrying.

Toni's eyes are saucers. "Did we order all that?"

"I have no idea."

———————

They return to the Bund, now that it's dark, to see the full impact of Pudong reflected in the Huangpu. "It's pretty amazing, isn't it?" says her dad. "Can you see the tall black building with the gap at the top? They call that the Bottle Opener."

"It's . . . okay. But it's all adverts for stuff, isn't it? It's nowhere near as good as the view of London from Tower Bridge. We stood on the bridge after our school visit. It was really, really strange."

"What was?"

"Well, when you look from Tower Bridge, all the buildings look like paper cut-outs. The whole thing looks cut and pasted. It seems like too many amazing buildings are too close together; you can't believe it. And the Bottle Opener wouldn't look so special next to our Gherkin."

"But this is completely modern. I feel like China's *the place*."

She looks at her dad, and she can see Pudong flashing in his eyes. Maybe he thinks he's going to get piles of work from rich Chinese, so he *wants* to think it's a great place.

"I do like China," he says.

She sighs. "We've only been here two days."

"First impressions are lasting impressions."

She cringes. She didn't want to hear that. It reminds her of that total creep in Year 8. "You're all right, you are." That's what he said, like a gawping idiot, and she thought he was going to follow up with some specific compliment—about the school newspaper and the cartoon she drew, or about how she's friends with Mai Ling, who everyone fancies,

22

boys and girls both. But instead: "When I first saw you on the school bus, I thought you looked dead frosty. Real unfriendly and stuck-up." It was so, so unfair. He'd never spoken to her before, and he'd made up his mind she was a bitch. He didn't say *bitch*, but she knows that's what he meant. What cheek. He's not exactly God's gift.

Afterwards, she was mad at herself, because for a split second she'd anticipated a compliment and had waited to lap it up. She hates him because ever since that stupid nonconversation, she's wondered if she does in fact send out a negative vibe. And so she smiles when she has nothing to smile about, just in case someone thinks she's a bitch.

"So, depending on the *urbane* Mr. Lu—depending on the painting he wants me to copy—I'll be going back to Florence or Paris, or staying in London. Fancy another trip to Florence? I can try to sway him."

"When?"

"I could delay until the end of exams."

"Can I bring a friend?"

"No way! You can look after yourself, but I can't take responsibility for anyone else's kid. Two thirteen-year-olds—you'd be sneaking out and getting lost in a foreign city."

"Anyway, how long is the trip? I don't want to miss anything important. And I don't want to be on my own all day."

"Come on. I'll have my work finished by the time you get out of bed. By the time you've had breakfast, got dressed and read a book for an hour, I'll be back. And then we can have the afternoon and evening together."

"So I could bring a friend, if we did that. If we didn't go out on our own."

"I don't know. I can't promise to keep a proper eye on what you're doing. Got to be honest about that."

"Why not ask Auntie Natalie to come?"

"That's a thought. I could ask. If we rented a small flat, and Natalie just pays for her flight . . ."

"Go on, then. Ask her."

"Let me think about it. Anyway, Mr. Lu may choose the Uccello in London."

Toni can see her dad is tired. He gets saggy cheeks and puffy eyes. On cue, he says, "I'm bushed. Let's turn in."

She tugs at his arm. "What's the name of the sea this river goes to?"

"The Pacific, eventually."

"Oh. Not the Chinese Sea?"

"The Huangpu flows into the Yangtze, which then flows into the East China Sea. It's not like you to ask a geography question . . ."

CHAPTER THREE

Florence, 1469

"Study the drawing carefully, Antonia. Study it until your eyes hurt, and then tell me what you see." Paolo Uccello eases himself down onto the stone wall of his courtyard. A blackcap's warbling, from deep within a honeysuckle vine, pierces the low-toned midmorning hubbub from Via della Scala.

Paolo rests his hands atop his walking stick, leans forward and arches as best he can to stretch his spine. His black robe absorbs the sunlight; his stiffened back slowly soaks up the warmth. He murmurs an invocation to the Blessed Virgin and ascribes the sweet easing of his pain to her saintly intercession. With his eyes closed, and with the heat now seeping into his old bones, he recalls himself as a younger man in the Green Cloister of Santa Maria Novella—stripped to the waist, ready to climb the scaffold, ready to paint into the fresh wet plaster, on the cusp of producing a masterpiece.

And the full-size preparatory drawing for that masterpiece is now fastened to the courtyard wall of his home, where he awaits the opinion of a twelve-year-old girl.

He prays she'll see what he wants her to see. She rarely disappoints him, but he knows he's pushing her, perhaps too fast. Time is not on his, or her, side.

The past three years, going back and forth between Florence and Urbino, have left him physically drained. He accepted a commission from the Confraternity of Corpus Domini to paint the predella of a new altar, and although the work was modest in size, it was too tempting to turn down. He'd already had long-standing offers of work in the homes of two wealthy families in the city, and he decided he could easily flit between the various sites. And the deal was agreed when the confraternity graciously offered to pay for his son's lodgings. Thus, Paolo and Donato embarked on a demanding series of commissions—a last exertion before Paolo's retirement and a good opportunity for Donato to gain experience.

The master painter now pursues his private studies—some say obsessions. With his savings and the rents from his land in Ugnano— bought piece by piece during the most lucrative years of his art making—he has no need to take on new work. Peace, if not solitude, at last.

The girl sits on the floor, hugs her knees and continues her inspection.

"I want you to tell me the story, Antonia, and I want you to . . . *read* the picture."

Does she understand? God certainly gave her the talent to draw, more so than her brother. But can she take that next step? If she proves herself, here, now, he will spend more time with her while he can, even at the expense of his own studies. She has a true eye for composition, which is difficult to teach, but does she have an instinct for storytelling, which any great painter must possess?

She twists around, her face flushed red. "Is this a test, Father?"

"Just study the drawing and tell me what you see."

"It's the story of Noah and the flood."

"That's a title for a picture. Tell me the whole story, as I've taught you before. Remember my painting of Saint George and the Dragon and how I explained it to you? It wasn't only the story of a knight slaying a beast, was it? There were hills in the background, neatly tended with straight furrows. Remember?" She nods. "So, just as George slew the dragon, the farmers tamed nature."

"Ah! I understand. I'll try again."

How he wishes he could take her to the cloister to see the frescoes, to see how he translated this drawing into an understated yet powerful depiction of the flood. The understatement was achieved through colour, by using terre-verte as the dominant hue. If she could see the cloistered walls, she might understand why his name—her name, after all—was revered in Florence, despite, as many saw it, the oddity of his work.

She points. "On the left, there's a strong wooden box. That's supposed to be the ark, and it's in the sea, by the shore." He cringes at her plain speaking. *Supposed to be.* A child's candour. "It's a *huge* box, without windows, and it reaches as far as the eye can see, towards a stormy horizon. Bits of broken branches and leaves are swirling in the air." She indicates the storm with her flailing arms.

"Never mind the dramatics."

"Sorry . . . Well, there are two men fighting in the foreground. I think they're fighting to get into the ark before it sets off into the storm. And there's a man trying to climb up the ark. But you know, Father," she says, twisting around again, "I don't think he'll keep his grip. And there's a boy in the water, blowing water out of his mouth. He must be drowning . . . but he looks quite calm." Another rebuke.

She continues, "A naked man is climbing into a barrel, but that won't save him, I don't think, unless God admires his spirit and decides he will live. Father, there are people on the shore weeping. There's a drowned infant, a drowned child and a drowned dog. Oh, it's such a sad picture."

"Go on."

"It's so strange. On the right-hand side of the drawing, there's another ark. It must be the same ark, because Noah only built one. This second ark has landed on dry ground. The flood has ended. There's a man—Noah—leaning out of a window halfway up the ark. A dove with an olive branch in its beak is about to land in his palm. Father, he survived. And all the beautiful animals of God's kingdom—"

"Do you think a cockroach is beautiful?"

She laughs. "Not to my eyes. But every creature is beautiful to its mother and father, surely, and to Jesus. Anyway, all the creatures must be inside the ark. Noah will let them out, and they will multiply until the land is filled again with all God's beauty."

"Don't race ahead, Antonia. I asked you to describe the picture, but you're telling me what you see with your mind's eye. So, tell me more. You haven't finished, have you?"

He watches her as she looks to and fro across the surface of the drawing, and his thoughts slip back to the time long before he left for Urbino, when Antonia was six years old, or was she seven by then? He encouraged and helped her to draw. Though it was a game to her, she took to it so easily. He drew animals—hounds, horses and dragons; yes, dragons were always her favourites. She rested her hand on his as he dragged the charcoal across the paper. With gentleness, he also taught her how to hold a stick of charcoal, and with his hand enclosing hers, he'd make sweeping gestures. He always instructed her, "Pretend your arm is asleep." And she would laugh at the very idea. But by relaxing, she would *feel* the drawing, experience the performance—so much more than a mere movement or twitch of the hand, it's a gestural movement that demands effort from the whole arm and shoulder and the muscles of the chest.

All these years later, he can still hear her say, "Another dragon, Papa."

Paolo straightens his back, bracing himself for more criticism.

"You made a clever picture, Father. It has two stories—one from the past and one in the future. You want to show the happy ending. An artist who wasn't as clever as you"—she twists around again and grins—"he would paint two separate pictures and place them side by side." The little monkey, he thinks; she already knows how to flatter. "But you found a way to tell the whole story."

She stretches her arms and clumsily climbs to her feet. "But I'm confused about this well-dressed man in the foreground. He can't be Noah, because he has no beard. He's looking to the right, at something beyond the edge of the paper, and he looks amazed, as if he's seeing the Garden of Eden. But he isn't smiling; he looks so serious. Maybe he's seeing the difficulties lying ahead of them. But then . . . the way you shaded the drawing . . . it seems the sun is shining on his face."

"Why do you think I've done that?"

She takes her time, for she wants to please him. "I think . . . it's your way of saying that the future is sunny, that everyone will prosper in this new land. Maybe this man *is* Noah, and you're showing him as a young man."

She has caught him out again. He recognizes his failing—the identity of the man is far too ambiguous. With hindsight, he knows he should have included the man's wife.

"That's an interesting supposition, Antonia, but you're incorrect. Noah has taken one human couple on the ark, and this white-robed man is the husband. However, you are accurate in deciphering his expression. He's filled with trepidation. His faith is wavering, even though he knows Noah has saved him for God's divine purpose. So he is trying to control his fear. Now, look again!"

She hesitates, her eyes wide, unblinking, as though she were trying to absorb the image whole. "I know it's a drawing, and it's made with charcoal. But I feel I'm looking at the real ark with my own eyes. It's as though I'm standing there on the shore."

"Bravo! And how have I achieved that?"

"I think I remember—you said something before, talking about another picture . . . your battle picture of San Romano. You make everything shrink, don't you? There are invisible lines that tell you the size of things in the distance. So, in this drawing, people who are standing at the far end of the shore are drawn much smaller than the ones standing close to us."

"Who do you mean when you say *us*?"

She pauses, grabs her arm behind her back and makes a half courtesy, and then jumps twice. She's struggling for the correct words. Paolo holds his breath, and then she turns and announces, "I don't mean *us*. I mean the painter. You, Maestro."

Excellent. "So, Antonia, when *you* stand in front of the picture, what do you see?"

"I see what you saw. But, you weren't really there, were you?"

He laughs. "No, of course not. I had to imagine the entire drama and then draw as though I *were* stood in front of all these figures and the two arks. As though I *were* on the shore."

"So clever," she murmurs.

"And in the coming weeks, you will learn to apply your own imagination. I'll instruct you."

"Are you sure, Paolo?" says the woman sitting on the shaded side of the courtyard. Her voice is so thin, Paolo is surprised her words reach him. He hauls himself to his feet and turns to face her. She holds a needle and thread in one hand and a half-finished piece of embroidery in the other. He wonders if these are props, part of a pretence that she's feeling well enough today for some handiwork. She has dark circles around her eyes. "What about her studies, her Bible?" the woman says.

"Didn't you hear her, Tomasa? She knows her Noah." He smiles at his wife. "But, I concede, she certainly needs to know more. Artists must be better versed in the scriptures than their patrons. She must study hard on her own—she applies herself well enough—and I'll teach her my artist's trickery."

Antonia follows her parents' conversation, knowing not to interrupt.

Tomasa tips her head to one side. "She makes a good likeness, that's true. But where will it lead?"

"Off you go," he says to Antonia. "Read again about old Noah and his ark, now you've shared my vision."

When she disappears from view, he says to Tomasa, "It's not unknown." He lowers his voice. "Think of Caterina dei Vigri in Bologna, God rest her soul. Her essays and her paintings are well known, and no one doubts her piety. We should entertain higher ambitions for Antonia."

"No one doubts Caterina's piety because she founded a convent for the Poor Clares. Mark my words, she will be pronounced a saint one day." Tomasa makes the sign of the cross. "I understand what you're saying, Paolo, but if Caterina dei Vigri, bless her, had married instead of entering the cloister, no one would know her name today. She'd have been too busy looking after the domestic affairs of her family. She might have died in childbirth."

He's barely listening. "And, do you know that women are now attending the university in Bologna? More's the shame for Antonia that I'm her sole tutor."

After a few moments' silence, she says, "When I last visited the convent, my aunt said there's always work in the scriptorium for a neat hand. I told her we can afford a good dowry for Antonia. We can secure a good marriage for the family. Well, that's true, isn't it, Paolo? We can afford far more than the spiritual dowry for a convent."

"Patience, Tomasa. I'll speak with Donato on his return; he and I will make the decision, together."

He removes the drawing from the courtyard wall, rolls it and walks stiffly to his study on the south side of the courtyard. His study is now home to his archive of sketches and preparatory drawings, dating back nearly forty years. They cover all his major painting commissions and even his early designs for mosaics and stained glass. What to do with it all? When he vacated his workshop, three months into his retirement, he burned the scrappier drawings. He now spends an hour each morning leafing through those he saved, attempting to establish some order.

He feels he ought to separate his own drawings from those of his assistants, but the truth is, he enjoys seeing all the works together for each commission, especially as he rarely sees his completed works. Many of his frescoes are in private chapels; his paintings are in the grand rooms of palazzos. Even some of his church commissions are hidden from public view. For him, these sketches and drawings are more personal, even more valuable, than the carefully executed final works. They trace the development of each commission and allow him to relive his decision-making. Standing now before a stack of drawings for *The Flood*, he travels back in time, inhabiting his younger body, his sharper mind. He will use these drawings to teach Antonia what an artist should discard in the quest for a perfect composition.

He still misses the old workshop on Piazza di San Giovanni. It fills him with pride—which has given rise to several admissions at the confessional—that he, Paolo Uccello, son of a barber-surgeon, ran a workshop on the main square of Florence. It's a year since he surrendered the lease, and as much as he misses the workshop, he misses his daily walk along Via della Scala, across the Piazza Santa Maria Novella and along Via dei Banchi and Via dei Cerretani. He always took the same route. The fixed routine helped him to trample the spiky irritations he felt most mornings, caused by the minor drama of an oversleeping servant, a reminder from his wife to pay a bill, a slipped roof tile in the night, a dead chick in the courtyard causing Antonia to cry . . . household trivia. With each steady stride from Via della Scala, his responsibilities and distractions seemed to diminish, so that by the time he reached the workshop, he was no longer someone's husband, someone's father. Just Paolo.

There was no point in keeping the workshop, he tells himself. It would be an affectation. How could he call himself an artist if there were no assistants, no patrons, no commissions? He'd be a pretender, stalking those cavernous rooms. But whatever anyone says, the work he's doing now is no less considered for being unpaid.

As the bell rings out from Santa Maria Novella at midday, the servant girl brings to Paolo's study a wooden plate with spiced beef and polenta. He eats his meal alone at his table, another routine that frees his mind. A line drawing hangs on the wall facing him—a copy he made of Donatello's *Miracle of the Repentant Son*, the original being a bronze relief for the high altar of Sant'Antonio in Padua. Paolo hung the drawing in his study many years ago as an act of humility—he felt he should remind himself daily that for all his achievements, it was this image that changed the course of his professional life. In tribute, Paolo knowingly borrowed Donatello's composition and applied it to his fresco of *The Flood*. He decides he must explain all this to Antonia, as she, too, must always acknowledge an inspiration clearly sent by God.

He drains his glass. It's not an everyday glass; it's a gift from a Venetian client, and the outer surface is decorated with enamel and gilt. He's determined to use this gift every day, while he's well enough and strong enough not to drop it. As his fingers trace the enamel relief, he wonders, were he to die in his sleep this afternoon, would it be so bad? After a long life, with two children surviving infancy? Donato is on the verge of adulthood, after all, and Antonia . . . Well, whatever life brings her, which might be less than he hopes, she must simply offer it up to God.

He pushes himself out of his chair and gathers up Antonia's latest sketches of Clara, their cook. He decides that Antonia should start a portrait of her mother. She knows how to handle egg tempera, though she's had precious little practice. He'll have to push her—she must learn quickly, before she leaves this household.

How he wishes for her sake she'd been a boy. He admits, with regret, that if fatherhood had come to him earlier, even in his middle years, he'd have found little time for the girl, if he'd noticed her at all. A late fatherhood was a precious gift, doubly so with Antonia, who was born after two years' resurgence of plague and who had survived her own brush with that deadly disease. God surely has plans for the girl.

CHAPTER FOUR

London, 2113

Aurelia Tett, project head for the Gauguin reassessment team, has a larger-than-average cubicle. It's so spartan that Toniah decides the woman's not an academic, though she knows she shouldn't jump to conclusions. Tett is engrossed in a projected spreadsheet, so Toniah knocks, in the absence of a door, on the cubicle wall.

"Ms. Tett, I've been asked to see you by Elodie Maingey . . . I'm Toniah Stone."

Tett turns her head away from the spreadsheet, but her gaze, and attention, only follow a couple of seconds later.

"Oh?" She retracts her thoughts. "Ah! About Gauguin?"

"Yes."

"Tremendous. Welcome to the Academy. Take a seat." She casts another glance to the spreadsheet, highlights three cells and blinks off the projection. "And it's Aurelia."

"Thank you. But . . . Aurelia, French modernism isn't my area. I mean, naturally, I know the essentials, but I haven't researched late nineteenth- or early twentieth-century art since my undergraduate days."

Aurelia gives a dismissive wave, but Toniah is insistent. "My area is fifteenth-century Italian—the quattrocento. Are you sure you want me involved?"

"It's good experience for you—to see the end result of a long-term investigation."

"So it's primarily a training exercise?"

"In part. There's something in it for us, too. We generally have at least one beta reader who is disinterested, before we go to our academic referees. These papers can create quite a commotion, so it's best if we prune out any ambiguous statements. That's where you can help. Indicate any areas of confusion. Insert comments and questions. Also, anything that sounds too contentious from a generalist's point of view. We'll take it from there."

"Will my comments be anonymized? I don't want to irritate any staffers—I'm scarcely a month into the job."

"Send your comments to me. My eyes only."

"I think it's only fair to tell you what I've already told Elodie—that I can't see how Gauguin can be demoted."

"Oh, really, Toniah. That's not the spirit."

"His Polynesian paintings . . . they established primitivism as *the thing*. Picasso took it further, granted, but Gauguin was recognized in his own lifetime. I mean, if you asked any gallerygoer—"

"Any reputation is a fabrication. Believe me," Aurelia says. Toniah frowns at the condescension. "Surely, you've already seen how it works within academia? A young researcher—yourself, for example, Toniah—writes a paper that's published in a fairly obscure journal, and then a key academic, a serious influencer, picks up on a single observation you've made because it bolsters some minor point in her research, and *later* she includes a reference to *your* paper in the tiniest of footnotes in a triple-A-rated journal."

She's on a roll. "Then other academics feel obliged to credit your paper, probably without even reading it, simply because the key influencer has considered it worthy." She smiles sweetly. Another condescension. "Success is a sticky material; it traps new successes. And, of course, it's the same for artists, in any era. If you were an artist, Toniah, success would depend on . . . let's see—which curator becomes a fan, if that curator gains advancement, which reviewer writes about your work, how many mentions you score in zines and five-star-impact conversations. And *then* who buys your work, who off-loads your work, which public galleries exhibit your work."

"But in my own area, in the early Renaissance—"

"Same thing, different waypoints. Any would-be artist had to be apprenticed to a master artist. How did that happen? Family connections, of course. And those connections also landed important church commissions."

"I accept that. But it's the work that matters. If the Academy is presenting Gauguin as an unsavoury character, I have to tell you that I don't think that approach is defensible."

Aurelia smooths her hair as though stalling. "We don't need to do that, Toniah. He stole his ideas. Read the report. It's in your inbox already."

The rest of her day is as familiar as any day in her old postgraduate office: she stares at a display hour upon hour, reading, highlighting, tagging. But this new office environment is a slick corporate equivalent of her old shared office space. She's doing her best to subvert the new straight-line aesthetic. Already, she has thrown off her cardigan—it lies in a heap at the entrance to her cubicle—and she has kicked off her shoes. They lie where they landed, cross toed.

When she first arrived at the Academy of Restitution, she resisted the unspoken intimation that she'd arrived among the anointed ones. The tokens are all there. She has her own desk instead of hot-desking at the university. She has a pass for the department kitchen, with its neatly stocked snacks and shining glassware. There's a free in-building sports centre, a jogging track on the roof and a free nursery—not that she needs one. From day one, she has kept her ego tightly tucked in. However, she does hope the Academy makes good on its promise of well-funded research trips. It was so bloody annoying she didn't get the trip to Florence last April—such a missed opportunity.

A few pages into the Gauguin report, she gleans the overall approach to this particular piece of revisionist art history, and she feels itchy. They're digging into his relationship with another male painter, Émile Bernard, twenty years his junior—both were members of the famous artists' colony at Pont-Aven in Brittany during the 1880s. While a painters' colony by the seaside sounds idyllic to an early twenty-second-century mind-set, Toniah knows the reality—a hand-to-mouth existence, freezing cold lodgings in winter, paintings often bartered for food and beer. She has always been surprised that bar owners back then were prepared to accept what must have seemed like slapdash daubings, often on poor-quality supports—even on hessian sacking. All experimental. Why would a bar owner do a swap?

Maybe Gauguin et al. refined their sales pitches in these bar-room negotiations, to the point where they could convince anyone that their artistic quest was genuine and heartfelt, that their search for something raw, emotional and unleashed was a worthy cause and would be recognized, eventually. *If not this year, then next*—she can almost hear Gauguin's voice. But he, as much as anyone in the group, struggled to move beyond impressionism—the most tame and polite of revolutions in her view. She agrees with the report that these Pont-Aven artists *all* flailed around until Émile Bernard demonstrated a flash of genius—*Breton Women in the Meadow*. And how many people have even heard of him?

Toniah pulls up the painting. Supposedly, it depicts local women at the Feast of Penitence, but it actually looks like a bunch of women having a picnic. She remembers, with a thrilling stab in her chest, how this small painting arrested her, in spite of the crowds, on her first visit to the Musée d'Orsay in Paris. She's sure she made a line drawing in her student sketchbook. She'll try to dig it out at the weekend. It's probably in the attic.

She wonders if Bernard *and only Bernard*—with his training as a stained glass maker—could have made this leap: abandoning perspective, simplifying the women's forms, painting heavy black outlines around flat colour—twentieth-century cartoonish to a modern eye—with the squishiness of paint to satisfy an aesthete's eye. It was a short step, a decade later, for Maurice Denis to announce the briefest of manifestos: modern painters must remember that a painting is a flat surface with colours arranged in a certain order.

By lunchtime, Toniah has skimmed through the full report. She'll make detailed comments later, but for now, while the material is fresh, she writes three sentences—one to encapsulate the main message and two to record her initial gut instinct:

Gauguin purloined the breakthrough of his younger collaborator and took the credit for forging a new path away from both realism and impressionism.

Gauguin was incapable of making the breakthrough. Without Bernard, he'd have faffed around with impressionism for many more years.

The Academy's argument will stand or fall in front of the paintings. The paintings are all that matter, and she'll look at them after lunch. She creates a new project and downloads the images:

Bernard's *Breton Women in the Meadow.*
Gauguin's *The Vision after the Sermon.*
Bernard's *Christ in Gethsemane.*
Gauguin's *Christ in the Garden of Olives.*

She's pleased the report doesn't demolish Gauguin's character. If it took that approach, the team would be attacked for its prurience. Everyone knows he abandoned his wife and children and cleared off to the South Seas to paint images of Polynesian women. Somewhere along the line, he contracted syphilis. But you can't damn him for his promiscuity without damning most of the male population at that time.

Syphilis—the focus of so much panic as the nineteenth century turned to the twentieth. Infected men bringing syphilis home to their wives and children, infants losing their eyesight. Toniah recalls the 1916 black-and-white photograph by Paul Strand of the ragged, blind beggar woman in New York, staring without seeing to the left of the camera lens, with a handwritten "BLIND" notice hung around her neck. Was her blindness an inheritance? Toniah can no longer look at the photograph without this question in mind.

Poor old Émile Bernard, she thinks. He didn't help his own case. He abandoned his experiments. He retreated into realist painting and set off to Cairo to produce mediocre depictions of concubines and harems. He knew Gauguin had recognized his breakthrough and run with it, gained the recognition. Bernard must have been seriously pissed off.

———————

There's one perk of working for the Academy of Restitution that Toniah would hate to give up—the rooftop jogging track. Not only because it frees up her evenings for slobbier pursuits. She'll never tire of the views across the city, along the Thames; and to the north, where the Thames basin rises to Hampstead Heath; and to the south, to Crystal Palace.

She loves this release from close reading. Her steady jog, unconscious and uncomplicated, allows her to think more freely, less attached to the facts, about an alpha male artist working in his garret—no exaggeration—whom, she suspects, if she were ever to travel back in time, she would actually find annoyingly attractive. She can't imagine

Bernard would be fanciable. Plainly, it's irrelevant, but, she reckons, progress sometimes requires a measure of ruthlessness, and that kind of drive in a person has its attractions.

When does that happen? she asks herself. A true professional friendship—a mutual master-and-pupil relationship—as enjoyed by Gauguin and Bernard. How does that healthy, supportive competition transform into a dash for the finishing line? Something fired in Gauguin's brain, and he sprinted. Was there a moment when Bernard realized he had lost?

Toniah stops and sees her more ambitious alter ego racing ahead.

Gauguin's killer instinct seems alien to her. Her priorities have always been quite simple—to pay her own way, to be independent, to have an interesting job, in that order. That's the way she was raised; it's the partho way.

She walks to the edge of the track and leans on the railing. She's niggled by Aurelia's remark about sticky success. Is it truly a matter of luck? And what if her greatest achievement, her own place in the canon of art history, is one day contained in a mere footnote? A seven-point Times New Roman acknowledgment for a life's work.

And what does it matter?

———————

There's nothing in the world Toniah enjoys more than this: studying paintings, looking for connections, spinning a plausible story. She feels like a forensic scientist picking over the evidence set out by the Academy. She swivels in her chair in the centre of her cubicle and assesses the images encircling her—Bernard, Gauguin, Bernard, Gauguin.

The Vision after the Sermon was Gauguin's reply to Bernard's breakthrough painting, *Breton Women in the Meadow*. That's the way they worked; they shared their experiments and bounced ideas off one another, each trying to build on the other's work. And so, in 1889,

Gauguin and Bernard decided to paint the same subject, and the resulting canvases were *Christ in the Garden of Olives* by Gauguin and *Christ in Gethsemane* by Bernard.

Toniah sees a connection. She enlarges Bernard's soldiers in his Gethsemane painting. She delves into the Louvre database and, in familiar territory, fifteenth-century Italian, she pulls up Paolo Uccello's *The Battle of San Romano*—one canvas from the original triptych, the three constituents of which are still scattered across western Europe.

Fancy that, she thinks. The soldiers' armour is exactly the same. She inspects the painting's history, and there it is: acquired by the Louvre in 1863, when Bernard was living in Paris.

Toniah can feel a footnote coming on. Bernard must have studied, even copied, the Uccello before going to Pont-Aven. So maybe there's some early-Italian influence in the mix, as well as the influence of his stained glass.

She sighs. It's so easy in academia to keep doing this—keep adding refinement upon refinement about artists who are already known so well. Why is she getting excited about Paolo Uccello having an influence on Bernard?

She blinks off all the images. Sod Paolo Uccello. And sod Gauguin and Bernard, for that matter. It's Uccello's *daughter* she's holding her breath for.

She feels a surge of euphoria, but it's tainted by a stomach-churning sense of frustration that she didn't get to Florence for the big news. She missed the conference and the thrilling announcement that an Antonia Uccello painting *may* have been discovered. The first ever, and it was found *not*, as one might have expected, in a private collection, but in the overflow storage of a provincial Tuscan museum. Toniah brings up the conference proceedings and enlarges the painting: a portrait of a woman, supposedly at prayer but caught as if in a daydream.

"Who are you?" she murmurs to the woman in the painting. "And what is your connection to the artist?"

"Talking to yourself, Toniah?" It's Aurelia Tett. She cocks her head. "That *doesn't* look like a Gauguin."

———————

Poppy leaps up when she hears the front door open. "Well, how did it go?" she calls towards the hallway. Toniah appears at the kitchen door, throws her jacket on a chair and smiles. "Let's have a cup of tea, and I'll tell you everything."

All Poppy wants to hear is that Toniah loves her new job. Please. Only good news. To Poppy, it doesn't feel like a real home with only Carmen, herself and Eva. And much as she loves Carmen's company, it's far more calming having her sister around. It would be so brilliant for Eva, too, if Toniah stays.

"Don't worry. It all went fine. Though . . . a bit disconcerting at times," says Toniah. Poppy's stomach churns.

They take their drinks to the garden, where Eva is crouched on the ground inside the pen. She's watching the hens sitting under the mulberry tree, their favourite place for dusting themselves with dry soil. They feel safe under a tree, safe from predator birds. It's one of the reasons their hens are such good layers; they're less anxious than hens in a run with no shade. And they're crazy about the mulberries.

"Don't get too close to them, Eva. You'll start sneezing," says Poppy.

"Five eggs today. I think they're happy," says Eva.

"It's a wonder the eggs aren't purple with all the fruit they're eating," says Toniah.

"So, go on," says Poppy. "Tell all."

"I met the VP. She made a big deal of me being partho."

"You told them?"

"Why not? I thought it might sway the decision, and it seems it did. She's put me on a big project, and it's interesting."

"So what's disconcerting?"

"First impressions, that's all. It's less academic than I'm used to. It feels a little cavalier—the attitude."

"But it's still research."

"Sure, but the agenda—"

"Well, obviously, there's an agenda. You knew that when you took the job." Poppy bites her bottom lip.

Toniah touches her arm. She leaves her hand there. "So, tell me about this guy Ben. We walked to the tube station together."

"He won't be coming over again."

"Why not? He seems sweet. Good-looking."

"He wants a bit too much, you know. Wants to hang around and get involved. I told him—Eva and I are happy as we are. She doesn't need a dad. Anyway, he's a bit too serious for me. More your type."

"Thanks a lot. I'm the boring older sister, am I?"

"You know what I mean. All the time I've known him, I've thought you'd be a better match. So . . ."

"So . . . ?"

"I don't mind if you want to see him."

———

Toniah is soaking in the bath, and she can hear her sister telling a story to Eva in the bedroom across the landing. By following the intonation and the back and forth between them, she's trying to identify which storybook they're sharing. It's an old favourite, judging by the quick interplay of voices. As she narrows down the possibilities, she hears the front door being pushed open and then shut, the door bolt rattling in its sheath. Toniah towels herself, throws on a robe and hurries down the stairs. "Hi, Carmen. We saved you some food. It's plated up in the fridge."

Carmen has flopped on the sofa, but she's so tiny that the sofa seems to be barely dented. She's always so beautifully dressed, and the deep-blue dress against her black skin and against the yellow sofa instantly brings to mind a painting. Toniah can't get away from Gauguin. His Polynesian Mary, exhausted after the birth of Jesus. *Te Tamari No Atua.*

"Brilliant," says Carmen. "I'm glad you didn't wait. Sorry I didn't message—I was running late."

"A late property viewing?"

"No, it wasn't work. I went to the clinic."

"Oh? You feeling all right?"

"Not the medical centre. I went to the baby clinic."

Footsteps on the staircase. "The baby clinic?" says Poppy as she appears in the kitchen.

"Yes. Don't look so surprised, the pair of you. You should see yourselves. It's about time, isn't it? And you know how bloody broody I am."

They sit around the kitchen table, and while stabbing at her salad, Carmen deals calmly with her interrogators. They're thrilled, of course, but Toniah senses that Poppy is holding back. She'll want to know about the financial implications. How much will the treatment cost? Will Carmen return to work full time? Will she be able to afford her rent, or will they need to rent out the smallest bedroom for a few months?

"What are your treatment options?" says Toniah.

"It's likely to be a two-egg process, one more mature than the other. I told them I've joined a partho household."

"So they didn't discuss donor semen or artificial Y?" says Toniah.

"No. I just said I'd prefer to go partho."

Poppy presses her hands flat between her knees and leans forward. "And what about the baby's gestation, Carmen? Have you discussed that with the clinic?"

"That was one of their first questions. Needless to say, it's cheaper if I carry the pregnancy, assuming it all goes smoothly. I don't think I can afford an artificial womb—I don't want a loan that's bigger than absolutely necessary."

"But if you have any pregnancy complications, you could be off work," says Poppy tentatively. "You'd better check your maternity terms." Toniah tries to catch her sister's eye. Warn her, with a small frown, to ease off. "It could be a false economy," says Poppy. "And . . . you're so tiny, Carmen."

"More's the reason to go partho. I'm less likely to have a big baby."

Poppy sits back and pushes a hand slowly through her hair. Toniah can see she's trying to calm herself.

"Eva's going to be excited," says Toniah.

"That's true," says Poppy. The frown lines between her eyes begin to dissipate. "She'll have chosen a name by the weekend." Her face relaxes, a mirror to Carmen's and Toniah's easy cheerfulness.

"Just wondering, Carmen, did they ask any intrusive questions at the clinic?" says Toniah.

"Yes. When we discussed an artificial womb. Put me off a bit. They said they'd need next-of-kin details, and more than one, preferably. In case I died . . . or absconded."

"You're joking," says Poppy.

"Seriously. It must have happened. So I told them I'm gay and I'm not in a settled relationship, so I'd have to give my sister's name, and . . ."

"My name as a backup?" says Poppy.

Toniah is wide-eyed.

"Anyway, it won't come to that. I'm carrying my own baby."

CHAPTER FIVE

Suzhou, 2015

In the manicured grounds of the Garden Hotel in Suzhou, Chinese instrumental music twitters from speakers hidden aloft in the cherry blossoms.

"Why don't we do this, Dad? Have music playing in our trees?"

"Maybe it's only for the cherry blossom season."

"It's so sweet—kind of silly."

"It's very calming."

Each specimen tree is labelled with its Latin name and the year of planting.

"According to the labels, all these trees were planted around forty years ago," he says. "Did that coincide with the end of the Cultural Revolution? What were the dates, Toni?"

"Er . . . mid-1960s to mid-1970s." She looks up at him. "Did you do *any* homework for this trip?"

"Didn't I mention? I'm delegating history to you. I had to research Mr. Lu's paintings and make all the travel arrangements."

They pass by a young Chinese couple who are taking close-up photos of the deep-purple blossoms that sprout along the main branches of one curious tree.

"You'd think they'd be used to cherry blossoms," says Toni. She takes her own phone from her pocket and, holding it waist-height, turns and surreptitiously takes a photo of the man and woman, who are still looking up with their phones held high.

"Come on, let's not dawdle. We've got an hour before the Master of the Nets Garden closes," says her dad. "You're not too tired, are you?"

"No way. This might be the one time in my life I come to Suzhou."

How amazing, knowing the name Suzhou, and knowing how to pronounce it, perfectly. Sue-Joe. It's easy to remember—she *has* two friends Sue and Joe. They took her to Hyde Park with a bunch of other friends when they were trying to cheer her up. It suddenly seems ages since that trip. Hyde Park, with all its giant trees, now feels a little foreign amid all the pretty blossoms.

What's cool is this: her favourite place in the whole world is Venice, and Suzhou is called the Venice of the East because of its canals and waterways. Two Venices on one planet. It doesn't seem possible. Suzhou might even be the *better* Venice; it has famous gardens with the maddest names, which she memorized because she can't rely on her dad to remember the must-see sights—the Master of the Nets Garden, the Humble Administrator's Garden, the Lingering Garden on Tiger Hill, the Pavilion of Dark Blue Waves.

Why don't we have any good names? she thinks. What have we got? Hyde Park, St. James's Park, Green Park—a bit like saying Yellow Desert. Clapham Common, Kew Gardens. C-minus for poetic effort.

The high arched entrance to the hotel is set back from the main street, and in its shadow stand three taxi drivers smoking cigarettes. One of the drivers, evidently reluctant to go back behind the wheel, half-heartedly waves for her dad's attention. She and her dad press on. Toni takes hold of her dad's jacket sleeve as they reach a cycle path that's choked with scooters and cycle taxis. It's separated from the main road by a line of trees, their trunks painted white. Having dodged their way between the cycles, they wait for a break in the car traffic.

"Where's that music coming from?" Toni peers down the road and laughs. A street-cleaning vehicle emitting electronic Muzak is edging towards them, its rotor brushes clearing the gutters. Her dad chuckles. "Sounds like a Chinese version of 'Greensleeves.'"

"A singing street cleaner."

They dart across the road towards the My Hero Chicken takeaway, which sits at the end of a block of gaudy shop frontages at street level, at odds with the traditional timber-framed architecture above.

"This way," says her dad as he walks towards the cobbled alleyway at the side of My Hero Chicken.

Toni takes his hand. "Is it safe?"

"It's fine. I've checked the street map, and we're a minute's walk from the garden entrance. I think those are tourist stalls ahead."

Toni stops and takes another photo. "I think it's washing day," she says. Ahead of them, above their heads, two sweatshirts—one red, one white—hang in T-shapes, a wooden pole threaded through the arms. The ends of the pole rest on the roof gutters on opposite sides of the alleyway.

"Could be a sign," he says.

"A sign?"

"For a laundry. Maybe there's a laundry service somewhere along here."

"Are you joking?"

He shrugs. "I'm guessing. There's no way of knowing."

The stallholders are already packing away their souvenirs—decorated fans, silk scarves, bookmarks, landscape paintings with calligraphic inscriptions, baseball caps, T-shirts. They call out, trying to guess the nationality of the passersby. Toni waves back.

"Hey, Dad, they're selling terracotta warriors—are they near here? Can we go and see them tomorrow?" Toni pleads.

He laughs. "Selling a terracotta warrior in Suzhou is a bit like selling a Leaning Tower of Pisa in London. I did actually check out the warriors: they're hundreds of miles inland. Maybe a thousand miles."

"So why are they selling them here?"

"Saving us the journey?"

The alleyway opens out into a stark, white-walled courtyard. Towards the far right corner stands a solitary black-barked tree in naked, terrified silhouette. Four yellow scooters are parked behind the tree; her dad takes a photograph. On the left, towering above them, is the ornate wooden gateway to the Master of the Nets Garden.

They buy tickets at a small kiosk inside the entrance and wander, as though stepping through a secret doorway, into a fairy tale. They hear a soundscape of flowing and falling water and stand transfixed, trying to assimilate a tight vista of craggy limestone rockeries, lush but controlled flora and narrow pathways, one of which leads over a zigzag stone bridge to a small pavilion. Toni and her dad approach the signpost by the bridge: "To the Waterside Pavilion of Washing Hat-Ribbons." They look at one another with raised eyebrows.

"You'll have to rename your garden shed, Dad."

Whitewashed walls separate one section of the garden from another, but latticed openings provide teasing glimpses of far pavilions, shocking-pink cherry blossoms and bulging purple magnolia buds.

"Can I explore on my own?"

"Go on. But—" She's already off.

Toni follows the brick path—inlaid with pebble mosaics of fish and chrysanthemums—crosses the bridge and starts to climb a craggy outcrop towards a viewing point. She notices that the miniature mountain is made from large limestone rocks cemented together. That's a bit naff, she says to herself. And standing at the top, looking across the Master of the Nets Garden, she remembers their Shanghai hotel—the glass tanks with carefully lit lumps of grey rock. Why do they like making little landscapes? She recalls making her own gardens as a small child, in baking trays, and for a moment captures the smell of wet black soil. And she remembers her mum helping her to make a fence with spent matches and wire.

From this high point, Toni can see the garden's white perimeter wall; it's high, with no window openings. She can't decide if the garden feels like an oasis or a prison. It depends what's outside. Maybe, she wonders, the Master of the Nets was afraid of someone or something. Was he afraid of dangers that lay beyond the garden? Maybe this was the only safe place in Suzhou, and people were . . . Toni can feel another apocalypse taking shape.

Flesh-eating creatures, half-human, clamber over one another in a heaving mass—she has seen the movie—so that one, just *one* of them, can scramble high enough to leap over the wall and . . . That's it. The Zombie Wars of Mainland China. The Master of the Nets was the last survivor in Suzhou, and at the end of the war, he set out across China—with only his walking stick and the clothes he wore—to find other survivors, to start the world all over again.

Picking her way down the cemented outcrop, she feels proud of herself; she's imagined something seriously worth worrying about. It's all a matter of perspective. There's always someone worse off, unless you're a zombie.

She steps through the circular opening to another courtyard within the garden, and when she looks back across the tiny lake, she sees her dad. He's taking photographs.

He must love it here, she thinks. She can imagine the kind of photographs he's taking, because she knows he sees things that no one else notices. That's what her dad always says: the artist sees things that *normal* people are in too big a hurry to see. That's his job, he says: to help people to see better.

Toni sits on a smooth boulder, folds her arms and watches him. His photographs, she decides, will mainly be close-ups—for example, photographs of the floor. He likes photographing floors. Not the predictable things like the fish mosaics; that's what everyone else will photograph. No, he'll find some random arrangement of pebbles with a discarded cigarette butt. And he'll definitely photograph the latticed openings in the plain white walls . . . with something jutting into the picture—a bare branch or three angled tree trunks. He won't be able to resist taking a snap of the old couple chatting in the Waterside Pavilion of Washing Hat-Ribbons. She noticed them holding hands and whispering to one another. Her dad won't ask their permission; he rarely does. He claims he's not being nosy or rude. He calls these photos "celebrations of passing intimate moments." Not that she believes everything her dad tells her.

She decides to explore the far reaches of the garden, follows a path through a stand of young green bamboo. She finds, to her complete bewilderment, the best thing *ever* to photograph. How unbelievable, she thinks, that she found it before her dad. She steps closer and inspects the bamboo. Chinese characters have been carved into the tall, woody stems. The characters are so clear—pale brown against the smooth, hard green. Absolutely bloody amazing. She takes out her phone and takes seven photographs. This is *the* most fabulous thing in the entire Master of the Nets Garden, and *she* found it.

He likes her photographs of the bamboo graffiti.

"What do you think the writing says?" asks Toni.

"Peoples' names? 'Toni was here,'" he says.

"It could be a line of poetry."

"What makes you think that?"

"Well, this garden is special . . . and Chinese people are more respectful. They wouldn't *do* gormless graffiti."

"I'm not so sure about that. Anyway, these might be political slogans."

"Or secret messages."

"Well, it's interesting, isn't it? If you exhibited this photograph in a gallery in London or New York," he says, enlarging a section of bamboo on her smartphone screen, "people would ask exactly these kind of questions. Assuming they couldn't read Mandarin. As the photographer"—he turns and raises his eyebrows at her—"*you'd* have to decide whether you wanted people to guess what the characters say, or whether you should translate the words and then use the translation as a title for the photograph."

Her dad says bizarre things like this all the time. It's like he's trying to make her brain think like his artist's brain. She doesn't know what he's on about half the time, and she's learned to just say hmm—without even rolling her eyes.

"Hmm. Well, I'd like a painting of the bamboo graffiti. Make me one, hey?"

"Why paint it? Make a big print from the photo."

"You copy other peoples' paintings. Why not copy my photograph?"

He pulls a face as though he's smelling milk, suspecting it's gone sour. There's clearly some big artsy conflict going on in his head.

"Okay. I'll do it."

"Good. And I'll tell everyone that the characters are coded messages."

He laughs and puts his arm around her. "Come on, they'll be closing soon. We don't want to get locked in."

Coded messages, Dominic muses as they leave the garden. The ways kids think . . . He recalls, momentarily, his own childhood excitement over a secret spy headquarters hidden at the back of a tailor's shop, at a time when a coded message involved winding a strip of paper around a pencil.

There's a more adult interpretation of *coded message,* one that's taken on a mutated meaning. He feels a shiver of recognition as he hears again the police officer who asked Dominic to formally identify the body. *It's not a child-friendly environment.* He was home with Toni at the time—she'd stayed home from school—and although he knew the morgue was an inappropriate place to take a child, the police officer correctly intuited that Dominic needed everything spelled out. He was in shock. And down at the morgue—the memory is always at the edge of his consciousness—a white sheet covered Connie's body; her neck and face were uncovered. He couldn't believe there was anything wrong with her. The morgue assistant left him alone, and Dominic wishes now that he hadn't lifted the sheet.

———

Dominic takes a bottle of wine from the room's minibar. It's not surprising Toni has crashed, he thinks; she struggled to stay awake through their room-service dinner. They had an early start this morning, and everything here is different. That's it, he says to himself; it's the incessant lack of familiarity that's so exhausting.

Toni lies curled on her bed, and scattered around her on the bedcover are small paper and plastic bags that contain the small treasures she discovered in Shanghai's South Bund Fabric Market. Hand-embroidered tapes, painted buttons, metallic thread.

He wonders if the fabric market will be the highlight of Toni's visit to China. It wasn't what he expected; he'd thought they'd find themselves in an open-air market with semipermanent stalls, rather like Shepherds Bush or Borough Market back in London. In fact, the South Bund Fabric Market turned out to be a three-storey building with escalators—a down-market shopping mall, each floor packed with small shops selling fabrics, scarves, bags, belts. The tailors' shops displayed sample suits, dresses, skirts, shirts and winter coats on hangers. Shoppers merely pointed at the design they liked, and then they were measured. Or they took a garment for copying. For Dominic, the charm of the fabric market lay solely in seeing Toni's excitement. But a flash of panic did occur—when she ran back through the market to find the button shop, he thought he'd lost her.

For him, the big eye-opener today was the rail system. China knows how to move people. Shanghai and Suzhou railway stations were the size of airport terminals. There were two departure lounges for every train—one for the front half and one for the back. And the platforms were as wide as airport runways. In their first-class carriage on the shiny white bullet train—he chuckles quietly as he relives the journey—the overhead TV monitors were showing Mr. Bean's trip to the Launderette. All the passengers were laughing out loud. Occasionally, the show was interrupted, and the driver appeared on the screen with a view of the track ahead. He would turn to the camera and, wearing white cotton gloves, make a clenched-fist salute whenever the train reached maximum speed. Dominic had needed to remind himself more than once that he was in China, not Japan, because in his imagination, Japan had always offered the default vision of the future. He wonders how China will cope when all this new infrastructure needs replacing in a hundred years' time, just as London is now struggling to replace Victorian water mains, sewers, bridges, tunnels.

Mr. Lu bought the train tickets for them in advance and, fortunately, explained how to decipher the printed information. Dominic smiles when he recollects Toni's rebuke: *Jeez, Dad, I don't know why you're panicking so much. It's all in the guidebook. There's even a photo of a rail ticket with every bit of information explained.* One sight had stopped them dead: a man in iron ankle shackles being escorted by two police-men through the Shanghai terminus.

The door is wedged open to his adjoining bedroom, but instead of settling down next door with his glass of wine, he slumps in the arm-chair by Toni's bed. He doesn't dare close his eyes; he knows he'd sleep only until the small hours. He'd wake up confused, and he's had enough of that. In those first months, he'd wake in the night and feel a surge of relief, believing he'd woken from a nightmare. Connie hadn't died. One time, he dreamed he heard the clinking of a cup being stirred in the kitchen below, and he rushed down, believing that Connie couldn't sleep and she'd decided to make a cup of tea—he was halfway down the stairs before the truth of the matter felled him.

No more daytime or early-evening naps.

It's a godsend to have Toni's company, but at the end of the day, he misses the lazy exchange of stories with Connie.

He hopes this trip to China will draw some sort of line, that China will become a new landmark in Toni's life. In his life, too. Not that any landmark could ever dwarf Connie's accident. But at least they'll have something else to refer to as a time marker—in their thoughts, that is. He wants Toni to think to herself: I did such and such after I went to China. Instead of: I did such and such after Mum died.

———————

He lies in a deep bath with his wine-soaked thoughts, imagining himself laid out on a slab. He takes another mouthful of wine and reaches up to place his glass on the marble sink. He's afraid that if he closes his eyes he'll see Connie's trauma wound, the cleaned-up aftermath from being impaled on, what? A timber pole? He didn't ask the mortuary assistant what *exactly* had skewered her. He'll never tell Toni, or anyone else, about the injury. He doesn't want anyone living with the mental image of her impalement, the *blunt-force trauma*, as stated without elaboration and printed in plain Helvetica in the autopsy report. He simply says that she died from internal injuries.

He peers down at his own body—unscathed, unmarked by any past injuries. Connie once commented that men could exit this world with their bodies perfectly intact, pure as snow almost, having none of the damage that women routinely incur in childbirth. She didn't say it with any edge of bitterness. Toni's birth had been reasonably straightforward. He'd only said that once, though, in Connie's company. She'd replied, "Not from where I was looking."

CHAPTER SIX

Florence, 1469

Paolo sits at the plain, paper-strewn table in his study and assesses his previous day's work—a half-finished pen drawing of a small garden urn. He placed the urn on a low wall in the courtyard so that when he sat down to start his sketch, his eye level was close to the centre point of the urn. In addition, he positioned the urn on the shaded side of the court-yard to avoid the visual distractions of flickering and static cast shadows. This allowed him to focus on a searingly complex mental task—namely, to imagine the walls of the urn as a series of hollow building blocks. His drawing thus comprises the penned outlines of all these tiny blocks; the blocks that form the back of the urn can be seen through the hollow blocks that form the front.

By embarking on this some-would-say foolhardy project, he hopes to reveal how a symmetrical object manifests within a perspective draw-ing. How much distortion has to occur to make the urn look *real*? It's a painstaking task, but if he doesn't do it, he asks himself, who will?

His patrons and admirers appreciate this eccentricity—his love of perspective—which everyone can see in his work. But he knows that for some people, his style is seen as intrusive, cold, too clever by half.

There's a second eccentricity that is not universally admired. It arises from his early training as a sculptor in Lorenzo Ghiberti's workshop. He can't help it—he sees the world with a sculptor's eye. So when he applies paint to his panel or canvas, and imagines a strong light raking across his scene, he paints abrupt edges to the shadows. Most of his contemporaries would *blend* into shadow to suggest the subtle change of curvature in a horse's neck or a man's naked torso. *Uccello paints badly chiselled sculptures rather than flesh-and-blood people.* Paolo closes his eyes and grinds his teeth. That fool of a silk merchant—whose comment reached Paolo through a mutual friend.

He does admit one professional regret. He wishes he'd made more work, more paintings, because he has experienced no better feeling in his life, no other comparable sense of euphoria, than the feeling at the start of a grand commission, when he conjured a vision, or at least some premonition, of the final outcome.

He has never been daunted by the size of an undertaking. He methodically planned his preparatory sketches, dozens of them for each commission. Many were drawn from observation—the flaring nostrils of a startled and rearing horse, a soldier's helmet lying on the ground, a hand gripping a sword, a woman shielding her face. Other sketches emerged from his imagination—a dragon's head, a lashing, spiked tail. These were but a beginning, and though many were sketched by his assistants, it was his own skill, guided by God's hand, that brought all these elements together in a composition that froze time at the moment of greatest drama. And all the while, as he journeyed from initial idea to final composition, he deftly balanced his expansive self-confidence with essential, flattening self-criticism.

He turns to the pile of sketches for *The Battle of San Romano* triptych and sighs heavily. Several of the sketches were useful for all three paintings, so which painting should he assign them to? He's now of a mind to archive all the drawings together, unsorted. What does it matter? They're of no interest to anyone other than himself. He pulls out a drawing that's larger than the others in the pile—it's the final drawing for what he regards as the best work in the triptych.

He smiles, pleased with himself. This will be Antonia's lesson today.

When Paolo enters the sala, he finds his wife cutting up some old, fine-quality curtains on the dining table. He's proud of his wife's care of the household, her diligence in making savings. She's cutting away the worn areas of cloth, and no doubt she'll find some new use for the salvaged material. Seeing her husband, Tomasa is quick to set aside her work. She takes a seat.

"Don't tire yourself," says Paolo.

"I'm tired already. I didn't sleep last night, Paolo." She shakes her head. "I believe I'll meet my Maker sooner than he himself intends if you don't start negotiations over Antonia. I can't get this worry out of my head for two moments combined. This year, it must be decided. Her childhood has passed—"

"You shouldn't worry."

She leans towards him and whispers, "What will you say if you receive a proposal in the coming weeks?"

"I'll say, 'Come back in twelve months.' They'll wait if they're serious."

They fall silent. He understands her impatience, but she should trust him.

She says, "I'm visiting the convent next week for the Feast of Saint Martha to see my aunt. I'd like to take Antonia. My aunt misses her—she was so happy when Antonia boarded there for her schooling.

And Antonia hasn't been back to the convent since you took over her studies."

"Yes, take Antonia with you. Take some extra treats for their celebrations."

"Thank you, Paolo. I—"

"Make sure to tell your aunt that Antonia must visit the convent's scriptorium. Tell her I want Antonia to see their current commissions—prayer books, tapestry designs. I want your aunt to be under no illusion. I'd pay a good dowry to the convent if Antonia were to take vows, but *only* if they offer more than a life of cold stone and early-morning prayer."

Tomasa takes his hand and speaks slowly. "What about Piero di Cosimo's cousin? Don't forget, he's the eldest son."

"He's the cousin of a painter, but that doesn't mean he'd be sympathetic to Antonia's talents. Once she's inside her husband's household, I'd have no say in the matter. Tomasa, listen to me. It would be far better, *if* she were to marry, for her to have a rich husband who would pay for an army of servants. With a rich husband, I could insist during negotiations that Antonia would always have her own private study, or at least a bedchamber that's large enough for her painting studies."

"So do you *want* her to marry, Paolo?"

He walks over to the window and gazes down into the street. He can choose whether or not to answer his wife's question. "I've ordered a wooden chest from the cabinet-maker who supplied the workshop. I've specified the best quality. It will be Antonia's dowry chest, and I'll decorate the panels myself."

"At last." She tips back her head and sighs heavily. "I have the linens for her wedding trousseau. I can half-fill the chest already. But you haven't decorated any furniture in years. That's work for an assistant."

"Ah! But a dowry chest painted by Paolo Uccello"—he turns and smiles to his wife—"will help any negotiation, don't you think? Whether I'm haggling over a husband or negotiating with your aunt's abbess."

Antonia sits by a niche in the wall of her small bedchamber, her prayer book open in her lap. There's a small painting hanging inside the niche. It's an image of the Madonna with her infant child, and in front of the painting there's a scattering of pink petals, which Antonia collected from the courtyard. When she hears the servant girl's footsteps on the stairs, she knows her father is ready to teach her again, and as the girl calls, "Your father—" Antonia is out of her chair and racing down to his study. As she hurries, two stairs at a time, she wonders how many girls on the long Via della Scala are allowed, as she is, to enter their fathers' studies.

She trips at the entrance to the room, rights herself. "What are we doing today, Father?"

She finds him reaching up; he's tacking a large line drawing to the shoulder-height wooden shelf that runs the length of the room. "It's one of your battle paintings," she says, excited.

"It's the final drawing for the painting. Now, I don't want to talk about the story in this work. This test of observation is different from the lesson on Noah and the flood. In fact, for today, you must *forget* the subject. I particularly want you to see the arrangement of things."

Antonia's jaw drops. "The arrangement . . . ?"

With the drawing secured, he turns and stares at her, hard. "A painting is just an arrangement of things. Understand?"

"But who did you paint this battle for, Father? And where is the painting now? Is it somewhere grand? In a palazzo?"

"It belongs to the banker Lionardo Bartolini, and it hangs with its two sister paintings in his palazzo on Via Porta Rossa where it meets the Via Monaldo. Close to here. But I tell you, Antonia, wherever the painting hangs, now or in the future, I am in command of whosoever casts an eye towards *The Battle of San Romano*."

She presses her palm to her forehead. "How do you *command* someone when you're not *there* in the Bartolini palazzo?"

"Prepare to be enlightened. Pay attention, child. I want you to close your eyes, and open them only when I say so." He takes a seat by the drawing and faces into the room. He wants to watch her eyes, to follow her gaze. "Now open your eyes and study the drawing."

After some moments, he forces a frown, because he doesn't want Antonia to sense his delight. She's under his spell. It's not easy for an old man to control a young mind, but he has done so. The question is, can she slow down and work out *how* he is controlling her?

"Close your eyes again."

"I haven't finished studying."

"Close your eyes!" She does so. "And when I tell you to open them, I want you to tell me, straightaway, what you look at *first of all* in the drawing. What takes your attention first?"

"But I look at all the picture, Father."

"No, you don't. Believe me, you don't. Now open! Speak, what do you see first?"

"A knight on a horse. It's rearing on its hind legs."

"Where is it positioned on the drawing?"

"Slightly left of the centre."

"And what else makes you notice this knight?"

"His huge hat."

"Good. And what next? After you see this knight on horseback, what do you notice next?"

"I look at the far right of the drawing—there's another knight in armour on a horse. His horse is rearing, but not so much as the first one."

"And what connects the two knights on their rearing horses?"

"Connects?"

"Is there something in the painting that joins the two knights?"

"Ah! Let me see. There's a lance."

"Describe it."

"The lance," she closes her fists tight, "is almost horizontal, and the two ends of the lance join—"

"Yes. I connected the two knights on horses by a lance. The butt of the lance is precisely positioned close to the horse's head on the left, and it reaches as far as, and beyond, the other knight."

"It was a near miss, Father, wasn't it? He's lucky he isn't impaled, and look at the barb on the end of that lance."

"Never mind the story. So . . . You're looking at the right side of the canvas at the knight who has had *a near miss* . . . Where do you look next?"

Paolo understands her hesitation; it's less clear in the drawing than in the painting. "Trust yourself, Antonia."

"I'm looking away from the battle, at the hills higher on the canvas. There are foot soldiers in the fields. They're tiny. One is running with two spears, another has a crossbow over his shoulder, and another soldier is loading an arrow into his crossbow. Is that right? Am I looking at the right things?"

"Just carry on. Where do you look next?"

"That's easy. The fields stretch from the top right of the drawing to halfway across the picture. There!" she says, pointing. "I see the big, swirling flags of the Florentine army, and there are many, many lances pointing skyward. They're held by all the knights behind the leader of their army—"

"Yes, behind the man with the big hat on the rearing horse. Exactly. So, remember this, Antonia. You started by looking at the man with the big hat on the rearing horse, and your gaze has moved in a circle around the picture, back to where you started."

"Oh."

"What's the matter, Antonia? You sound disappointed."

"I think I am. It's such an exciting picture, with the Florentine army charging into the enemy. But you're telling me that there's another story, I think. The story of how the drawing is made."

"Not how it is made, but how it is composed."

"So you thought carefully about how to . . . compose the painting before you . . ."

"Of course. Do you think that an artist imagines the final painting in an instant? That the painting composes itself through a moment's inspiration? The artist must have a strategy every bit as cunning as that of the commander of a great army. Like Niccolò da Tolentino, here, in this painting. Remember that!"

She looks back to the drawing. "You're right, Father. You guided my eyes. I had no idea you could do that."

"And the lesson is not over yet, because there's something else that connects all these points on the drawing—the rearing horses, the lance between them, the soldiers on the distant hills, the swirling flags and the lances pointing skyward . . . In the painting, I applied the same colour to all these elements. They're all white, or close to white. There's a yellow cast to the white."

She stares. She lifts her outspread hands to her cheeks. "Father, that is so clever. And it would be so plain to see if I were standing in front of the painting . . . But did the soldiers really wear yellow-white hose?"

He laughs with a slow shuddering in his chest, which prompts a coughing fit. Antonia pours ale from the pewter jug on his table.

He repeats her words, "'Did the soldiers really wear yellow-white hose?'" He laughs again. "It's a fiction, Antonia. I can make the soldiers wear any colour that suits my strategy. And now, you can perhaps understand that my greatly esteemed, but guileless, patron is entirely under my control when I present my finished work. He sees what I want him to see, as surely as if I'd set off firecrackers across the painting. So, what do you say to that, Antonia?"

She hesitates. "But why do you want to be in control?"

65

He seems stumped. He looks up for several moments. "I'll answer your question with another question. What's the point of making a large painting if people only look at one small part of the composition? They won't feel excited, and they won't read the whole story."

"Did Lionardo Bartolini like the way you told the story?"

"Well enough. He insisted on one change, when he saw the early preparatory drawings, but that usually happens."

"What didn't he like?"

"The lance. Originally I had the lance impaling the knight, through his chest."

"He wanted the lance to miss him?"

"That's right. It didn't affect the composition, so I agreed."

"I'm still confused. I only ever think of the story when I look at a painting."

"If you want to be an artist, Antonia, you must think like one. For me? It's all about bringing together the many individual elements. That's why I left my bed early in the morning for so many years, and why I worked long hours, with so many years spent away from home. Do you think I care about Niccolò da Tolentino and his army? I'll paint anything for the right coin. I care that the Florentines defeated the Sienese, of course, but the story doesn't excite me. It's the *painting of it* that excites me and keeps me awake at night."

———————

Antonia slips into the kitchen in the late afternoon and sits in a chair under the window. A sheet of paper rests on a board in her lap. She holds a stick of red chalk in one hand, and she grips the board tightly with her other hand. She glares at Clara, who is preparing the family's dinner at the large table in the centre of the kitchen.

"Clara, Father has set me a difficult task for tomorrow. I have to make a likeness of Mother. So I'd like to . . ."

"Yes?"

"Practise. I need to practise. So . . . may I draw you again?"

"I've got a meal to prepare."

"I'll try to draw you while you're working."

"When I'm skinning this rabbit?" she says, gesturing with her knife.

"Yes. You'll be stood in one place while you do that. Can I sit closer?"

Clara gestures with her head, and Antonia pulls her chair across the kitchen. With her foot, she drags a stool out from under Clara's table. It's Antonia's own stool, kept in the same place since her childhood, when she spent so many hours in the kitchen during her mother's bouts of illness. And now, she uses the stool as a footrest so that her drawing board sits higher in her lap.

There's no need for Clara to pull her face like that, just because she's using a knife, Antonia thinks. She struggles to capture Clara's grimace. After several attempts and repeated smudging out, she says, "Can you keep your face relaxed while you're cutting?"

"It is relaxed."

Antonia feels she ought to be able to draw anything in this room from memory, even Clara, but she's learned that her memory is fickle. When she lies in her bed at night, she can conjure the kitchen smells so easily, but she can never fix the detail she needs for a drawing.

"It's so difficult, Clara."

"It must be my ugly face. Here, let me look." She comes around the table, wiping her hand down her work smock, and stands behind her young mistress. "I look like a man."

"I'm sorry." And they laugh. Clara touches the backs of her fingers against Antonia's forearm and rubs gently. She raises her hand to her mouth. She kisses and makes the sign of the cross. Clara's superstitious impulse has been normalized by repetition. All the servants in the Uccello household know how close the family came to losing Antonia to the plague. They believe she passed over, that she reached Saint Peter's gates, that her return to them was due to the sincerity of their prayers. She came back and brought good fortune, not only for the family but for all the family's servants.

Antonia doesn't mind Clara's superstitions. At least Clara no longer asks which saints she met at the gates of paradise. The truth is that Antonia didn't see anyone or anything, and she wonders if she wasn't as sick as everyone thought. She'd love to tell Clara that she's seen paradise exactly as it's painted in the church of Santa Maria Novella. She loves the fresco, by Nardo di Cione, in the Strozzi Chapel—with all the saints huddled together, row upon row, with their haloes nearly touching. The saints look so pleased to see one another; many look around aghast—wide-eyed in holy rapture.

Even if she had seen paradise, Antonia believes, God couldn't have allowed her to return home with her memories. How could God test mankind if revelations were handed down so freely? Men and women must earn their place in paradise through faith.

Antonia wishes she *had* stepped through the gates, but she can't convince herself it happened. No, she didn't see the saints. Nor any thrones, nor angels. She didn't see her earthly family mourning by her bedside. She didn't gaze down from great heights.

CHAPTER SEVEN

London, 2113

"Please, Auntie Toniah. Let me go up with you," says Eva, pleading.

Toniah pulls the extending attic ladder down to the landing. "Okay. You can stand at the top of the ladder and take a peek. Put some shoes on." Eva rushes to her bedroom. Toniah calls after her, "I don't want you crawling around in the attic. I haven't been up in years—it may not be safe."

It's midmorning on Saturday, and classical music permeates the entire house from downstairs. Toniah would prefer something a tad more current, but Carmen likes to start the weekend with piano or clarinet. Today, it's a concerto that Toniah has heard several times since returning home—Clara Schumann's Piano Trio.

She's content to go along with Carmen's music ritual; it generates a genial current. A few bars of Clara Schumann transport Toniah towards sunny beach breezes, undermining any intention of tidying her bedroom or sorting her laundry. But this morning, she has a task that's not a chore; she wants to hunt out her student sketchbooks.

Eva reappears wearing black school shoes below blue polka-dot pyjamas. She steps onto the first rung of the ladder and twists around. "What's up there? Any of your old toys?"

"It's mostly junk. I need to go through it all."

Clearing the attic was one of many jobs Toniah's mother had repeatedly postponed. She eventually gave up any pretence that the clearout was imminent. She'd simply say, "I'll do that when I'm retired." Toniah can sympathize. For her mother, a teacher, retirement must have beckoned like a walk across open, rolling countryside. That's how Toniah regarded summer vacations during her undergraduate days, but somehow, summers soon became cluttered. From a distance, the future always seems serene.

The smell of dust and neglect seeps down onto the landing, and Toniah sneezes.

Her mother died before reaching her retirement, so the contents of the attic were never sorted. Toniah made one attempt, three summers ago; she lifted down a plastic container filled with framed pictures, hoping to discover photographs of Nana Stone—they had only a handful. All she found were cross-stitch samplers and a set of washed-out watercolours. Her mother had grown tired of them, presumably, but why did she hold on to them? Toniah dismantled all the frames and thought about saving the watercolours, but in the end everything went into the recycling bins. She felt disrespectful, as though she were labelling a part of her mother's life as inadequate.

It has become clear to Toniah in the years since her mother's death that household organization was low on her mother's agenda, perhaps because the requisite talents were sapped by her schoolwork. She had other priorities. It seems to Toniah that her mother dedicated herself to keeping in contact with everyone she had ever met—school and college friends, work colleagues who had long since retired. She kept conversations alive with local friends who had moved overseas, and even kept track of Nana Stone's ageing friends.

As Eva steps up the ladder, Poppy appears from the bathroom. "Hurry up, Eva. It's your swimming lesson, and I don't want to be rushing for the bus again."

"Do you need anything from up there, Poppy?" says Toniah.

"Nope."

Toniah notes the resemblance. Her sister is fixed in the here and now, just like their mother. She wonders if a longer view might give Poppy a sense of perspective; a bit harsh, she knows. But a feeling for history, even family history, can alter one's world view. She had hoped motherhood would give her sister a new sense of herself, create an aura of calmness; it was a romantic notion, perhaps. It has even occurred to Toniah—and the idea is solidifying—that Poppy rushed into motherhood, almost in desperation, as a way of shoring up their disintegrating family. Nana Stone dead, Mother dead two years later. Toniah could have returned home a little more often from university—she wonders if she let Poppy down by not doing so.

Eva pokes her head into the attic. "I can't see anything."

"There's a sensor inside the attic, near the hatch. Wave your hand around."

When the light comes on, Eva steps up. "It's a bit untidy up here."

"Don't go any higher."

"Right at the end, I can see some rackets, tennis or—"

"They'll be ancient, Eva. You won't want them."

"Yes, I will. Are they yours?"

"Probably. I'll try to reach them—but later, when I've found my sketchbooks."

Eva sneezes. She steps down the ladder. "Please bring them down. What's the point of keeping them up there?"

"I think your nana put them up there when Poppy and I bought our own rackets, more modern ones."

"Why didn't she sell them?"

"I guess she was busy, or she thought she might have grandchildren one day."

"So they're actually meant for me?"

Toniah laughs. "You're right. I suppose they are."

Toniah climbs the ladder, pulls herself into the roof space—rarely disturbed these past ten years. Such a waste. All their neighbours have long since extended their homes upwards into their attics. Toniah doubts she'll persuade her sister it's worth the expense or disruption. She'd have to drive the whole project herself, sort out all this junk. Maybe if she won a couple of promotions and Poppy advanced, maybe then they'd take out some more finance. They've already remortgaged to update the house since their mother died. It's a small mortgage, but Poppy regards it as a noose.

Toniah averts her gaze from the boxes of unsorted papers otherwise known as "the family archive." The archive isn't Toniah's designated responsibility, but she is the older sister. And she is, after all, the historian in the family.

A large suitcase has been pushed into the attic since Toniah last looked up here. Probably Poppy's and Eva's winter clothes. She shoves it aside and scans across the attic. No two boxes are the same size. Toniah wonders if she should buy some plastic containers. Then at least they could see the contents, and they could stack them, add labels. She's embarrassed by the lack of order.

Her oldest sketchbooks were packed in an empty duvet box, and she spots it halfway along the kinking path that leads to the eaves. She stoops to avoid the roof timbers as she makes her way along the attic, squats by the box. It's funny, she thinks, after all these years, she can remember the shape and backing of each of her student sketchbooks. The Paris sketchbook is square, and it's covered in a pale-green fabric, resplendent with swirling black doodles.

She empties the duvet box and there it is. She feels the stab, the thrill revisited, when she finds her sketch of the Émile Bernard painting.

Breton Women in the Meadow. A simple line drawing of Bernard's composition with her handwritten scrawl. She anticipates the words: *flat yellow, thick black lines, white headdress, seated figures float in space, no aerial perspective.*

She closes the sketchbook and sits quietly on the old chipboard flooring, feeling relieved and even pleased with herself—it took some pluck to come up here. And, with eyes closed, inhaling the disturbed dust, she imagines a doll's house with a small figure sitting cross-legged in the attic. She imagines three standing figures in the kitchen of the doll's house—two women and a girl—and four tiny plastic hens pecking by the side door. What a peculiar thing a home is, she says to herself.

More than once in the past few years, she's imagined coming home to find the attic stripped bare. She wished Poppy would simply do it, without asking. After all, there are house-clearance people, so-called estate-furniture specialists, who will do the dirty deed. Absent-mindedly, she opens the lid of a large, lopsided cardboard box that sits at arm's length. It's one-quarter filled with empty glass bottles without lids.

Whose crap is this? she wonders. Mother's? Nana's? She struggles back to her feet and edges towards the tennis rackets. Three of them, hung by their strings on square-ended nails—nails as old as the house. She reaches, grabs a leather handgrip, and she's back in school on a Wednesday afternoon walking across the top tennis court by the dining hall.

A second racket twists free of its nail and drops down. Stooping to pick it up, she sees a small leather suitcase, scuffed, missing its handle, and when she looks closer, she can see that some of the stitching has been mended with bright-yellow thread that doesn't match the original. She drags it closer and pushes the metal buttons beside the two locks; one latch flicks open. She lifts the stubborn second latch and opens the suitcase: a jumble of envelopes, flat peppermint tins, rolls of paper held by elastic bands. She sneezes. She can see her mother pushing this suitcase farther and farther back in the attic as she shoved more boxes up here. Toniah sees a graph: a linear relationship between the number of indecisive years and the distance from the attic hatch. When her mother was dying—she tries to smother the thought, but she gives in—did she lie there in hospital, at the very door of death, and think, Oh dear, I'm leaving the girls to sort out the attic.

Toniah shudders with silent laughter, and when she stills herself, she feels suddenly sickened by her own blatant omissions. The merest scintilla of curiosity would have surely prompted her to say, "Hey, Mum, tell me about your childhood with Nana Stone." Or, "Tell me, Nana, about your father." Toniah isn't even clear why her nana chose parthenogenesis. As a child, Toniah sensed a sad, almost angry vibe around Nana Stone's past. She recalls her nine- or ten-year-old self, conjuring a simple explanation: Nana Stone had been jilted at the altar. This satisfied a child's curiosity and also instructed her not to pry. Why would she want to remind Nana Stone of the worst day of her life?

What is clear in her memory is Nana Stone saying, more than once, "Don't talk to me about men."

———————

The piano concerto has been switched off. Carmen has left for her yoga session, and Poppy is racing around searching for Eva's goggles.

The Paris sketchbook lies discarded on the floor. The battered suitcase is open on the large square coffee table with its contents strewn and picked over. Toniah found a greetings card in one of the envelopes, and she rereads it for a third time. She can't make sense of the handwritten message, from Hildi, their old family friend, to Leah—that is, to Nana Stone. It's a thank-you note for a day they've spent *doing the galleries*, but the ending of Hildi's note is enigmatic:

I've been mulling over what we were talking about, and you know I'll always have your interests at heart. I just feel, Leah, you should be more open. You've done nothing wrong!

Toniah doesn't show the card to Poppy. Maybe later. She wonders if their mother ever read it. If she did open it, she might have glanced at the first sentence, assumed it was trivia and closed it again. Did she even open the suitcase?

"We're off. Back by lunchtime," Poppy shouts from the hallway. Toniah hears the front door slam, and in the silence, she can hear her blood circulating through her head. She closes Hildi's card. The picture on the front is one of those innocuous but seductive images that suggests to Toniah that the sender appreciates a certain type of art: nothing too challenging, a field of ripened wheat swaying in an imagined breeze, under a false blue sky. She slips the card back in its envelope, which is addressed to Nana at this house and makes Toniah feel like a squatter.

She walks over to the window and sees the bus pull up at the bus stop. All to a schedule; everything in the street is exactly as it should be. Eva will be on time for her swimming lesson, and they'll be home for lunch for Eva's Saturday favourite—hot chocolate with Welsh rarebit. Toniah has slotted back into the warmly familiar routines of the house. *You've done nothing wrong!* She feels she should quarantine herself with Hildi's puzzling note. Why share it until she can make some sense of this singular sentence?

She returns to the suitcase and kneels down for an item-by-item inspection. It all appears to be Nana Stone's stuff. There's an incense stick holder, a glass paperweight, a crab made from shells—surely bought by a child at the seaside—a pendant stating "First Prize," but for what? Tins, most of them empty. And tight rolls of papers, which haven't uncurled even though the elastic bands which once bound them are now desiccated. They're quaint paper receipts, and the ink is all but faded. Toniah smiles, remembering the story of Nana Stone returning faulty hair straighteners twelve years after she made the purchase, because she still had the receipt.

She picks up a small, roughly carved wooden box—a cheap jewellery box, most likely—turns it over, gives it a shake. There's no rattle.

She tries the lid, but it's locked, and she can't find a key among all the jumble.

The utility room by the kitchen, in contrast to the attic, is well ordered, and Toniah goes straight to the toolkit at the far end of the work surface. She stands the small wooden box on its hinged side, eases the sharp edge of a flat screwdriver under the lid and taps the end of the screwdriver with a hammer—small taps escalating to bigger taps and then a whack. The lid tears away from the flimsy lock. Toniah stares at the contents—a single small photograph, its colours as vibrant as the day the box was locked. It's a young Nana Stone holding an infant on her lap. A boy.

CHAPTER EIGHT

Suzhou, 2015

Toni and her dad appear to be the only westerners among the throng at the western buffet breakfast. She sidesteps along the line of hot tureens and lifts the lids, sagging with each revelation. Nothing quite looks like breakfast food. She's tempted by the boiled eggs in the final tureen, but she decides against them; they sit in a steaming black soup that smells of soy sauce. So she returns to their table with a plate of watermelon, three small egg custards in puff pastry and fried rice.

"Look over there, Dad," she whispers across the table. "That's the couple who were photographing the blossom trees yesterday."

The man and woman are sitting opposite one another and strike the same pose, as though saying grace. Their quiet contemplation is focused on their smartphones, held identically against the edge of the dining table. The man stands somewhat abruptly and leaves the restaurant. The woman leans across the table and grabs his phone. She holds both phones side by side and thumb-swipes across their screens, repeatedly.

"I think they've had an argument," Toni says, and she sets off towards the buffet as though eager for a second helping. She walks behind the woman, lingers to look over the woman's shoulder, sweeps past the buffet and grabs a banana, then rushes back to her dad.

"She's comparing photos."

"What?"

"They haven't had an argument. She's comparing his photos of the blossom trees with her photos of the blossom trees . . . Look how happy she is."

"Yes, you're right. She does look happy." Her dad smiles fleetingly. It's a weary smile, and Toni looks down at her plate and pushes her fried rice around. She can feel her face burning. She and her dad do this to one another all the time; one of them makes a chance remark, and it makes the other feel deep-down sad. It just happens, like they're on hair triggers all the time. In fact, her dad has done it to her already today, without actually speaking. She woke this morning to find he'd left his laptop open on the chair next to her bed—she could hear him in the shower—and his mail window was open. There was a message from their neighbour Anna Robecchi.

Not that she opened it—she'd never do that. And the message had no subject line; Anna must be a total computer illiterate. The question was: Why had she emailed when they were halfway around the globe? What was so important? Or had she dreamed up some excuse to send him an email? She's always dropping by the house. So blatant; so gross.

"Come on then, Toni. I want to be in the foyer at least fifteen minutes before Mr. Lu arrives. Can't risk keeping him waiting."

As they leave the breakfast room and cross the foyer's indoor stream, some twenty-five minutes early, her dad sees the concierge holding the hotel's entrance door open for Mr. Lu. "Blimey, he's here already."

Toni takes his hand, an instinctive move. She knows his attention is about to slip away from her. "Dad. Dad! It says in the guidebook . . . Chinese people are always early for appointments."

"Now you tell me."

"Well, read it yourself."

In his deep voice, with false seriousness, "Eh, none of that cheek in front of Mr. Lu. Chinese children are polite."

He doesn't hear her muttered rebuff: "I didn't read *that* anywhere." He's already striding ahead with his hand outstretched to greet Mr. Lu.

Toni is surprised; Mr. Lu isn't wearing a sharp suit. He looks like a golfer. Not that she's interested in golf. Her dad likes to show her the highlights on television—a hole-in-one, or a spectacular miss—probably because he and her mum used to watch golf together. So, Toni says things like, "That's amazing." Or, "That's hopeless." She hates watching the eighteenth hole, when the players wave their caps to the spectators and show off their white foreheads with no embarrassment at all. She always thinks, Idiot, keep your cap on.

"You must be Toni. I'm pleased to meet you."

"Thank you," she says. She checks his forehead.

From his soft briefcase he pulls out a small wrapped package. "You can open it now if you'd like to."

She deliberately takes the present with both hands—she read about local etiquette in the guidebook, unlike her dad—and carefully picks at the sticky tape, as she imagines a Chinese girl might do.

"You can *rip off* the paper," says Mr. Lu.

Inside, she finds an ivory-coloured cardboard box; the lid has a magnetic flap. On the lid, there's a drawing of a studious boy wearing a blue robe. He's pointing to a poster with a teacher's cane; he's instructing a cartoon Bambi. She notices that the poster is a miniature version of the studious boy in blue, teaching Bambi.

"They are aphorism cards. They have little sayings," Mr. Lu says, delighted. "Open it and read one."

The top card has a colour drawing of a baby-faced boy carrying a hoe; he's walking beside a river. "So cute," she says. Mr. Lu laughs. There's a block of Chinese characters with an English translation below, which Toni reads aloud. "'Weeds do not easily grow in a field planted with vegetables.'" Her mouth stretches and tautens; with the dread prospect of giggles, she clenches her stomach muscles and clears her throat. "'Evil does not easily arise in a heart filled with goodness.'" She doesn't dare look up.

"Well, there's food for thought," says her dad. He ushers Mr. Lu towards a seating area by the flowing stream while telling him about their trip to the Master of the Nets Garden. Toni wonders about asking Mr. Lu to translate the bamboo graffiti, but she decides she prefers the mystery of it all. And maybe he'll be offended if she brings some loutish behaviour to his attention, as if that were the most interesting thing she'd seen in China.

"Have you been to England, Mr. Lu?" she says, and she wonders what a real journalist would ask next.

"Yes, I took a business trip to London last year."

"And what did you notice? I mean, did anything really surprise you?"

"Oh yes. The bicycles. You see, in China, it's the poorest people who ride bicycles, and they pedal slowly, but in London, the cyclists ride *fast*. And I noticed at the traffic lights, they're eager to set off ahead of the buses. In China, cyclists always ride *behind* the buses."

"So you don't ride a bike?"

"No. But if I moved to London I would, because it's more fashionable."

Both men pull out their laptops, and her dad moves to the sofa to sit next to Mr. Lu. Toni, sitting opposite, knows the signal.

"Should I go back to the room?"

"Please, stay with us. We might need your opinion," says Mr. Lu. "I'm having difficulty deciding which painting I should ask your father to copy."

She wants to check her messages, but she thinks that would be rude. So instead, she opens the box of aphorism cards. She doesn't see why there's a Bambi; it's so Disney. She slowly sifts through the cards, reading each one carefully—she knows her dad will take ages—and setting aside the ones she likes best. There's one aphorism that sounds familiar: *The journey of a thousand miles begins with one first step.* Most of them are a bit boring and clunky: *If we are not attached to outcomes, then we will not suffer from the pain of fallen expectations*—picture of a boy caught in a rain shower. *In the face of adversity, be grateful, for such opportunities do not come by easily.* That's plain ridiculous. How could her mum's accident be an opportunity? Sadly, her favourite aphorism has the worst drawing—a boy dressed in grey, reading a book: *Every single day is like a blank page of our life.* She looks up at Mr. Lu. He senses her stare.

"Do you like them?"

She nods. "Do you read them every day? Like, one a day?"

"No, not at all. I like the sentiments behind them. That's all. They're based on Buddhist teachings, though I'm not a Buddhist."

"They're all written by the same man. It says on each card— 'Dharma Master Cheng Yen.'"

"She's not a *man.* She's a famous Buddhist nun who lives in Taiwan."

"She's not Chinese, then?" says her dad.

Mr. Lu smiles. "Yes, she is Chinese. Of course." Her dad looks vacant, confused; too late, he grasps his geopolitical oversight.

"In fact," Mr. Lu says, "Dharma Master Cheng Yen was inspired by three westerners—three Roman Catholic nuns. She was so surprised that the nuns were helping to build hospitals and schools, she decided to start her own charity to help society."

"What does this one mean, Mr. Lu? 'Every person we meet, every event we participate in, is a lively essay.'"

"Very appropriate. I think the translation is difficult. It means that every person we meet is the start of something exciting. A new chapter. Yes, *chapter* would be a better translation than *essay.*"

Toni doesn't read out her favourite card; she keeps it to herself.

"So it's one of Uccello's three battle paintings: this one at the Uffizi in Florence or this one at your National Gallery in London. Not the one in Paris." Mr. Lu clicks through the images. "Or, Mr. Monet's *Water Lilies* at the Musée de l'Orangerie in Paris."

"They're vastly different paintings," says her dad. "You should consider the mood you want to create."

"Well, it's for the boardroom, so maybe . . . I'm not sure. Is a battle scene asking for trouble?" They both laugh. "Or would Mr. Monet's lilies send everyone to sleep?"

"What do you think, Toni?" Mr. Lu turns his laptop around and clicks between the three images.

"No contest."

"So which one?" says Mr. Lu.

"The knights on horses, the battle. The one in London is best."

"I think you're right."

Toni isn't convinced that Mr. Lu is letting her decide. She thinks he had already chosen the National Gallery painting; he gambled that she'd choose the same one. She smiles all the same, because she's pleased her dad won't need to travel abroad.

Toni wants to go back to her room to sew embroidered tape along the shoulder seams of her denim jacket. But Mr. Lu has The Whole Suzhou Tour lined up, and it's crystal clear they won't be back for hours. As they walk towards his four-wheel drive, Mr. Lu asks her that predictable adult question. Namely, he wants to know her favourite subject at school. She tells him it's history.

"Have you read any Chinese history?"

"A bit, in the guidebook."

"Maybe you should start with what's around you and see where that leads." Which sounds to Toni like an aphorism. "You see, this hotel was once the home of Lin Biao, who was chosen by Mao Zedong as his successor. Later, it became a guesthouse for Communist Party officials and foreign dignitaries. Have you seen Lin Biao's official car? It's on display here."

"Is it green?" says her dad. "I saw a green car in an open garage."

"Yes, that's the one. Let's take a look."

"So what happened to Lin Biao?" says Toni, because she gets the impression there weren't many happy endings in Chinese history.

"He died in a plane crash in Mongolia. He was accused of plotting against Mao, and it seems he was escaping to Russia."

"So his plane was shot down?" says Toni.

"I don't think so. I believe they ran out of fuel. His young son died with him. You see, Lin Biao's wife and son were on the plane."

They walk over to the garage. There's a framed photograph of Lin Biao and a text panel. While her dad reads the text, Toni and Mr. Lu walk around the car, though Toni hasn't any idea why an old olive-green car might be at all interesting.

"So, that was a real disaster, wasn't it? For China. I mean . . . Mao losing his successor."

"Why do you ask?"

"It's my school history project—it's about big disasters like the plague, and famine, and wars."

Mr. Lu turns to her and frowns. "That's too serious." She doesn't reply. "The topic is too big."

She looks at him with an equally serious frown. "I know, it is. And I don't want the project to be all facts and figures."

"Then you should . . . write about people."

"Am I missing something?" says her dad.

She doesn't answer immediately, because there's a loud *clunk* in her brain as the penny drops. Then, sounding absent-minded, "Mr. Lu is helping me with my history project." She's not going to spell it out for her dad, but she'll get started on it as soon as they get back home to London, even before she starts on her new denim jacket. She'll make a questionnaire and send it to her friends, or maybe she'll post it online and let anyone join in. Anyway, she already knows the killer question: Do you have a missing side to your family?

———————

Toni awakens in the back of Mr. Lu's car when they arrive back in downtown Suzhou from their visit to Tiger Hill. She hears Mr. Lu talking about the battle painting, and he's saying he'd like something in the picture, actually *added* to the picture, to remind him of China. She knows her dad will hate the idea, totally hate it. Mr. Lu turns around and says to Toni, "Did you hear that? Your father is making a change to the painting to amuse me. What do you think he should include?"

"Er . . . how about the boulder at Tiger Hill?" She's sitting up straight, alert. "The one sliced clean in half by the famous swordsman." When she stood in front of the boulder, she had the uncanny feeling of history being mirrored on opposite sides of the world; the legend of the split boulder was so similar to the legend of the sword in the stone. Even if the legends weren't *exactly* historical fact, the story of the split boulder was way cool—an ancient sword, still buried, left undisturbed at Tiger Hill, and the mystery of how such a perfect sword was made so many centuries ago.

"I was thinking your father could change the fields in the background to paddy fields, rising up in terraces." Her dad's head is sinking into his shoulders, and Toni wants to burst out laughing. "But yours is a much better idea. Don't you think, Dominic? A boulder sliced in half would sit naturally in the foreground. Much more subtle."

Her dad twists around and winks at her. "Yes, as you say, it's subtle."

They turn into the Garden Hotel, and Mr. Lu starts talking about deadlines and payments. She thinks it's mad they've left the real business chat to the end of the afternoon when they're about to leave.

As she climbs down from the rear seat at the hotel entrance, she knows this is her last chance to ask her own burning question, and she knows, for sure, a real journalist would blurt it out. So she says to Mr. Lu, "I read something in my guidebook, and I've been thinking about it . . . All those Chinese people who died of famine when Mao ruled China . . . Does your family remember those times?"

She can tell that her dad is embarrassed. He's rubbing his face with his hand. But Mr. Lu doesn't seem to care. "Oh! Well, I have to say that my own grandparents were fortunate. They had good jobs, but everyone was affected to some extent. My father remembers, as a child, being very hungry."

Toni wonders if he's playing it down.

Her dad pushes open the hotel room door. "I'm amazed Mr. Lu gave up his whole day to show us around," he says.

"He had an ulterior motive, didn't he?"

"That's far too cynical for a thirteen-year-old."

"But it's true. He definitely wanted a bit of Suzhou in the painting."

"I don't mind. It's refreshingly disruptive."

And that's her dad putting a positive spin on things, she says to herself. He should be a politician. She drops onto the bed as he sits down at the lacquered desk. Toni knows that as soon as he opens his laptop, he'll check his mail. So, when he opens the lid, she watches his eyes. He looks at the top menu bar and clicks the Wi-Fi icon, and when a few moments later he glances down, she knows he's looking at the bottom toolbar to click the mail icon. She's tired, but she pushes herself off the bed and walks behind him. She looks over his shoulder. There it is, the same mail window; the new messages haven't downloaded yet.

"What's Anna Robecchi emailing about?"

Her dad doesn't answer straightaway. "What's that?"

"Anna Robecchi . . . what's she emailing about?"

"She's watching the house while we're away. Watering the plants and getting the mail from the letterbox."

"So why does she need to send a message?"

"Toni—"

"I mean, she can do those jobs without emailing you. Or has she done something stupid?"

"Toni, stop it. She's—"

"Dad, I'm sick of her checking on us. We don't need her help any more."

"Well, *you* might not, but I'm grateful to Anna. Especially when she brings one of her fruit crumbles. She knows I don't have time for baking."

"I don't like her crumbles."

"Yes, you do."

He turns in his chair and pulls her onto his knee. "Stop it, Toni. We're both tired out. Let's talk about it when we've had a rest. Come on! We've had a great day."

"She's always at our house acting like she's my—"

"Well, she's not your . . . Look, I can tell her I'm starting to make puddings . . . as a hobby. Or something." He tries to laugh. "I'll buy myself a baker's apron." But Toni won't smile. She understands it now— Anna Robecchi is a new blank page for her dad. It's all right for him. She rests her chin on his shoulder. Her tears fall inside his collar.

CHAPTER NINE

Florence, 1469

Antonia stands outside her mother's bedchamber and recalls a time when the door was always open. That is, unless her mother had visitors who had business to discuss or gossip to share—in which case Antonia would be shooed out and the door would be closed behind her. Outside of such occasions, Antonia could wander in and out of her mother's bedchamber at will. These days, however, she feels she needs a specific reason to enter, as though the effort required to push the door open has to be weighed against the triviality of her errand. Because why would she open the door just to look in, to see her mother, to wave—and wait to hear her say, "Hello, sweet one"—and then dip out of the room? The open door kept the insensibility of her childhood in play.

The door is now closed as a matter of habit so that her mother might catnap without being woken prematurely by noises from the kitchen. When her mother's enclosure became the norm, Antonia found herself in a limbo, having no careless contact with either of her parents. Her father worked at his workshop until late, and in any case, he worked away from home for months on end. But since her father's retirement last year, she hangs around outside his study. The door is usually open, and she often wonders if the house is too quiet for him after the noise and clatter of his workshop. He knows she's loitering, she's sure of it, because when she peeks around the door, he speaks to her as though he's picking up a conversation in progress. He'll say, "So, come here and look at this." Or, "There's something else I want to tell you."

Antonia can hear her mother and Clara talking on the other side of the door, and she wishes she could slip into the room unnoticed. She needs to consider where her mother should sit for her portrait, consider the light in the bedchamber, consider the backdrop. There's so much to think about before she can make a single mark. Her father's instructions make perfect sense when he's explaining them face to face, but as soon as she leaves his study, she feels adrift.

Forget the subject. That's easy to say. How can she possibly forget her mother? She sighs. Her hand is pressed flat against the door, and she steels herself to make her entrance. Instead of pushing, she leans forward and taps the door silently with her forehead.

At least she has grasped one important point from her father's lessons: making a drawing and making a painting are two separate endeavours. A drawing is merely a beginning. A drawing captures the detailed observations; it establishes the pose, the composition. Antonia hopes her father will not be angry with her, for she plans to steal one of his ideas. The portrait will show her mother looking into the distance, beyond the picture's edge, like Father's Noah. Noah worried about the future, just like her mother.

She enters the bedchamber. Her mother briefly glances over, but she doesn't falter in her conversation. She's reclining atop the bedcover, propped on cushions, while her maid and Clara sit on the bench alongside the bed. The maid is mending a shirt—no doubt one of Donato's, since her mother wants all his second-best shirts repaired and their cuffs embroidered before he returns from Urbino.

"How many sweetmeats should I make, mistress? One for each sister?" says Clara.

"More than that. The convent may have extra visitors for the Feast of Saint Martha, and on *her* feast day of all days, we should double our efforts. Make another pot of almond paste for some extra canisiones. And my aunt loves custard torta, so let's take twenty small ones—don't stint on the cinnamon. And two batches of rice fricatellae. But cut them into smaller pieces than you serve here. We don't want to be accused of culinary excess."

Clara laughs at her mistress's remark, for only a month ago, one of the city's wealthiest merchants, a patron of Paolo's, had received a visit from the sumptuary officer. Every citizen in Florence knows that this merchant has saved dozens of girls from destitution, paying their spiritual dowries so they could enter cloisters. Nevertheless, he was denounced over a banquet considered too lavish—denounced either by a guest or, more likely, by someone infuriated at not being invited.

"I've never known *any* of the sisters to refuse a fricatella, whatever the size," says Clara. She leaves the bedchamber with a long list of instructions committed to memory, and Tomasa dismisses the maid.

"Are you well enough, Mother, for this?" Please don't tire too soon, Antonia says to herself.

"I'm feeling much stronger today. Anyway, it can't be so hard, can it? Sitting and doing nothing."

"I can't believe you've never sat for Father."

"It's a measure of his success. Only a painter who's short of work has time to paint family portraits. In any case, your father didn't return home after a busy day at the workshop to start another painting."

Antonia sets down her paper, board and chalks. "I've been thinking about your pose, and I'd like you to sit at your small table by the window. I'd like you to have your prayer book open." She's embarrassed, ordering her mother around, but the pose is now fixed in her mind.

And so, her mother swings her feet slowly off the bed. She stands and straightens her headdress.

"Please, sit here, holding your prayer book as though you've been reading."

"I always kneel when I read my prayers."

"I don't want you to kneel, Mother. You'd tire too soon. Let's imagine you're studying rather than praying."

"Maybe I should truly read to myself while you're sketching; then I won't be bored and fidgety." She takes up her pose with seriousness writ across her face in frown lines and puckered mouth.

"I'm sorry. I don't want to be difficult, Mother, but I want you to look towards the window."

"How can I read if I'm looking out of the window?"

"Well, the story of the picture—"

"The story of the picture? What in heavens do you mean?"

"Father taught me . . . it's complicated. You see, the way he explains . . . there's the subject of the painting, which is you." Antonia can feel herself blushing at her own directness. "Then there's a story and . . . as well as the subject and the story, there's the composition."

"So what is the story for my portrait?"

"It's simple. You're studying your prayer book, and for a moment you look away, and you are lost in a private reflection. The painting will capture that moment. Anyone looking at the painting will wonder what you are thinking."

Her mother blinks at her, and after a long pause, she says, "Your father has never talked about his work to *me* in those terms. What is he filling your head with, at your age?"

"But will you look towards the window? Please, Mother. Look as though you are dreaming. I don't want you to frown."

"I think I should study a psalm for a few minutes to give me something to think about."

"You don't need to do that," says Antonia. She's alarmed that her drawing session will be delayed. "Think about something easy. Think about . . . Saint Martha. You know, the story of Martha and Mary. Think about how Martha did all the housework when Jesus paid a visit."

"'Paid a visit'? I'm sure Jesus didn't simply *drop by*."

"You know what I mean. Please, think about something pleasant and look out of the window."

"You'll have to be more patient than this, Antonia, if you want to be a painter." Her mother sits square to the table and holds the sides of the book with both hands.

"Place one hand flat on the prayer book as though you want to keep your place while you are contemplating your own thoughts."

"Like this?"

"Good. Relax your shoulders and, without twisting around, glance towards—"

"The window. Yes, I *do* understand."

"That's perfect."

Antonia steps forward to adjust her mother's simple white headdress, which covers all her hair and hangs to her waist. She adjusts the folds so they fall symmetrically around her still-striking face. It's so much easier to draw her mother than Clara, whose bone structure has long since disappeared beneath flushed and rounded contours. Antonia reminds herself that when she paints this portrait, she may choose any colour she likes for the headdress and the book's leather binding. And she'll add colour to her mother's complexion.

She sits down with her board and paper, and she pens several small line drawings with her quill. She needs to understand her mother's face—the length of her nose relative to her forehead, upper lip relative to chin, width of her mouth relative to the width of her head. Anyone who knows her mother will recognize even the slightest discrepancy. A portrait is far more difficult than any arrangement of bowls and pitchers. Who would ever know if a spout were too short?

But her headdress is too . . . boring—the folds are too symmetrical. So Antonia steps forward and adjusts the hang of the cloth and repeats the line drawings. It still doesn't look right. Antonia moves her chair a few inches to the left. That seems better, but she wishes her father were stood by her side. He could help her draw the edge of the table and the edges of the book. How do these angles work? She can't see it clearly.

Twenty minutes later, she pauses. "What are you thinking about, Mother? You're starting to frown."

"I'm not thinking about Martha and Mary. I'm wondering what your father thinks you'll do with all this drawing and painting. Any husband will need the patience of a saint to entertain such a distraction. And there aren't many patient men in the world."

"I could paint instead of doing needlework."

"That's all very well, but you can't expect a servant to do anything more than rough mending. A husband expects his wife to do the fine needlework, embroider the table linen and such."

"I'll have to find a husband who won't notice the linen."

"Antonia!"

"Sorry . . . Keep looking towards the window, Mother. I'm drawing your eyes now. Please keep your face calm."

Two minutes later, barely moving her mouth, her mother says, "One day soon, your father will make a decision, and you should be—"

"Mother, I'm trying to draw your mouth."

Her mother drops the pose. "Let's continue later. This afternoon, shall we?"

"I need the morning light throwing strong shadows across your face. So we must do this tomorrow at the same time. And the day after, too."

"If you insist, which *clearly*, you do."

Antonia rushes to plump up the feather cushions on the bed. Her mother lies down, lets her head loll backwards and closes her eyes as she speaks. "As far as I can tell, your father has taken no serious initiative.

He's either embroiled with his perspective or teaching you his artist's ways."

"Is it so urgent?" Antonia sits cross-legged on the bed beside her mother.

"Haven't you noticed? He's getting tired more easily, and we need him to be fully involved in any discussions. We shouldn't give this responsibility to your brother—which will happen, mark my words, if your father continues to procrastinate. As it stands, with your father's reputation and his mother's family name, we're in a strong position to negotiate any proposal. Apart from anything else . . ." She sounds weary. "I'll sleep better when I know everything is settled. We can't have you unbetrothed for much longer. If you so much as smile at a boy in church, the gossip will ruin your reputation, and the family name. For Donato's sake, we need you safely in another household or . . ."

"I know."

"Has your father mentioned your dowry chest?"

"What? No. What dowry chest?"

"My mother would turn in her grave if she knew how my artist husband approaches wedding negotiations. He buys a fine chest and gets out his paintbrushes. He should be talking to all his artist friends, his merchant patrons; he should be mentioning that you have reached the age where a proposal would be welcome."

"So Father *does* want me to marry?" Antonia kneels up on the bed and asks in earnest, "Did he tell you how many panels there are in the chest? Has he chosen the subjects to paint? I'd like—"

"Enough, Antonia! You're as bad as he is."

Paolo gathers Antonia's studies for her mother's portrait and spreads them out atop his battle sketches, still unsorted, on the table in his study.

"I have an old panel, already prepared with gesso. You can use it for your painting. So, let's look at these drawings of yours before you start mixing and splashing around with my pigments."

"I think I'll need your help with—"

"No need to speak. The drawings will say it all."

First he inspects the ink drawings, puts them aside. Then he holds up a larger drawing in red chalk that describes Tomasa without the use of line; it's a tonal drawing that shows her face in high contrast.

"You sat your mother close to the window?"

"Yes. I—"

He holds up a finger. "Not yet . . . You didn't *include* the window or any detail in the wall behind her?"

"No. Should I have done so?"

He doesn't reply.

"Are you satisfied with this tonal drawing? Are you intending to paint from this?"

"I think so. I like it." Antonia based the tonal study on the best of her small ink drawings, and it took two full mornings to complete.

"You know what's wrong with it, do you?"

"I know one thing that's wrong. The perspective of the table and the book."

He takes one of her small pen sketches, picks up a quill and dips it into his inkpot. He makes corrections.

"There's one essential piece of information—the level of your own eyes when you stand or sit in front of the subject. I can tell from your sketches that your chair was lower than your mother's, and your eye level would be . . . here. Yes?" He draws a small cross at the side of the sketch to indicate her eye level, and Antonia nods. "Now look what would happen if you sat on a higher chair, or if you were standing." He takes two more pen sketches, adds a cross on each for the new eye level and shifts the perspective.

"It's so much easier to understand when you correct my drawings, after I've tried and failed."

"Eye level is an important decision. So keep these corrections as a reminder. It affects your composition, and it changes your story and the mood. You see, it matters whether you look up to your subject or look down on her. But that's something you can consider in the future. For now, work from this chalk drawing for your painting."

She sighs heavily.

"Now, listen to me, Antonia. I wouldn't normally allow an apprentice to paint at this early stage in their studies, but I'll allow you to press on before you've mastered your drawing skills. We've done a few painting exercises together, so you know how to mix the pigment and egg binder. I'll show you how to use walnut oil another time. Don't rush your painting, or you will waste my pigments."

He wags his finger. "Impress me with your patience first, your skill second. Understand?"

She nods. "I'm confused about the story. Is it enough that Mother is looking upwards and to the side, that I capture her in a moment of contemplation?"

"Ah! Like Noah. Looking beyond the frame of the picture."

"Do you mind?"

"Artists are allowed to borrow. And, yes, that's enough. As long as your female subject does *not* look straight at you, Antonia. That would be too bold. That would be another story entirely."

"Would it?"

"Yes!"

"We haven't talked about composition either. Does it matter for a portrait?"

"Try to remember how I used colour—the yellow-white hose worn by the soldiers—and how I used the line of the lance in my battle painting. It's not so complicated for *your* painting, but you must aim, always, to guide my gaze around the picture."

Her shoulders slump.

"I'll give you a clue. A lance is a straight line, isn't it?"

She stares at her drawing, then looks up and beams a smile. "The folds of the headdress. I could make some small changes . . ."

"Good. You're learning to be strategic, but first and foremost, you must enjoy loading your paintbrush with paint and applying that paint with simple, unfussy strokes. If you don't, you'll never be a true painter."

She piles her drawings, stands to leave and recites to herself: The subject, the story, the eye level, the composition, straight lines, colour, patience. And she must enjoy applying the paint. She walks away from the table but stalls, and turns. "Father, may I ask . . . when will the wooden chest arrive?"

He bangs the table with his fist. "Is there nothing sacred in this house? Can't I mention the least matter without the whole of Via della Scala knowing my business by vespers?" He walks slowly towards her and places a heavy hand on her shoulder. "If you must know, it will arrive next week."

"Father, have you decided on the scenes you'll paint? And how many panels—"

"Off you go, now."

He watches her leave. Such a flimsy frame. Will she have the physical strength to be an artist? Maybe she'll only ever work on a small scale—portraits, still lifes, perhaps some furniture painting. He'll get her involved with the dowry chest. If he were younger, if he still had a workshop, he would set aside a room for her, and, behind the scenes, she'd assist him on his commissions. What's the best he can do for her now, in his dotage?

He can guide her towards sharing his opinion. He believes she'll welcome the decision he made some weeks ago—that her aunt and the abbess offer the best prospect. Marriage promises a life of frustration. A high-born connection of his kin or a self-important merchant's son would present one obstacle after another to her ambitions. Though

Paolo admits to himself that *he's* the one with ambitions for the girl. She's still a child; her mind is a sleeping ember.

CHAPTER TEN

London, 2113

The pub terrace of the Anchor is, unsurprisingly, packed on a glorious Saturday afternoon. Toniah spots a small table at the corner of the terrace with a fine view of the Thames. "I'll grab it," she says.

Ben emerges some minutes later from the bar with two beers, and she notices how small the pint glasses look in his broad-palmed hands. She wonders what it would be like having a man around the place, at home—not Ben, but a male housemate instead of Carmen. Or a male relative—someone who drops by unannounced, comes to birthday parties. And you always keep a couple of his favourite beers in the fridge, just in case.

He sets the drinks down carefully but catches the table leg as he sits down. Beer slops out and splatters across the table. "Sod's law," he says. As he attempts to wipe the beer away with the side of his hand, he asks, "Does Poppy know we're . . . ?"

"No. I didn't bother to tell her. She's busy."

"You don't think she'd be . . . ?"

She shrugs. It's sort of endearing, she thinks; he's the kind of man who can't finish difficult sentences. "Don't worry, Ben. We talked the other day, and she thinks we'd get on well. She knows I'm making an effort to meet new people." She tastes her beer, catching froth on her upper lip. "See, I've arrived back home, and most of my friends have moved away."

"I'm part of a strategy? Anyway . . ." He shifts his chair an inch closer to Toniah's. "I'm not sure I'll be visiting your sister from now on." He pauses and raises his eyebrows at her. "I guess I should tell Poppy first, but, you know . . . you're here." Taking a deep breath, he makes a further effort. "I don't think Poppy will be too bothered."

The pause is sufficiently stretched that each knows the other could say more but is holding back.

"I want something . . ."

"Something . . . ?" she says, coaxing.

"Um. When this contract finishes, I'd like something more than . . ."

Come on, she thinks. You can do it.

"Well . . . everything at the moment is on Poppy's terms, and that's been fine. But I reckon I'm more the family type, and that isn't part of the deal with Poppy." He sups his beer and leans back, looking more relaxed; the awkward stuff is nearly out of the way. "I wanted to explain." He laughs. "I've pretty much, you know, fucked up my social life with these contracts. Everyone assumes I'm not around, or they get tired of inviting me and getting the same old reply. I'm having a complete rethink now. I'm looking forward to being in one place for a few years."

"Good plan."

"How about you? Are you sticking around?"

"It's good to be home again. I'll have to see how this job works out."

She wants to mention the photograph, but why would she tell Ben, for heaven's sake? She only met him on Monday. And it's a bit heavy for a first date, if that's what this is.

They reach for their pints at the same moment, her little finger crooked, his straight.

"You and Poppy are quite different, aren't you?"

"Why? Did you expect a duplicate?"

"Not really. I've known a partho family before, and they looked pretty similar, too. I'm more surprised your characters are so different. You're—"

"Please tell . . ."

"How should I say it . . . ? You're calm, without being quiet. Whereas—"

"To be fair, Ben, Poppy is a busy mother, and she has a day job, too."

"You and Carmen help out, though, don't you? You take Eva to school and the like."

"Yes, and it's lovely. But Poppy keeps the schedule, makes sure the homework's done, makes sure there's a meal ready at the right time for Eva. Carmen and I can breeze in and out. But, sure, I'm an extra pair of hands, a free baby-sitter."

"It works well, then? The arrangement."

"It's fun. And I love Eva. I never feel lonely, and that counts for a lot, don't you think?"

"It does." He's nodding his head. "Absolutely, it does."

"So, if I've put your mind at rest about Poppy's reaction, I'm wondering . . . could we start seeing one another?"

"I'd like that. Not under house rules, though."

"That's easily sorted; I can come to your place."

"Damn. How dozy," Toniah mutters. She knew this was the stickiest stretch of pavement, but she finds herself ripping across flagstones while having no recollection of walking the last hundred yards. She looks up into the canopies of three lime trees, closely spaced. Those aphids don't let up.

It's Monday morning, and her head is thick. She had a late night on Saturday when she stayed over with Ben—she let Poppy assume she was staying with a workmate. At home on Sunday, she argued back and forth with herself over whether she should do an ancestry search on Nana Stone. When she woke this morning, her jaw was aching; she'd been grinding her teeth in her sleep.

She couldn't bring herself to do the ancestry search. It felt disrespectful; her grandmother evidently didn't want the family to know about the boy. The thing that bugs Toniah is that her grandmother's friends would have *known* the child, but no word had ever filtered down to Poppy or herself, or to their mother, presumably. At some point in the past, Nana Stone must have clammed up even among her friends, and maybe they knew better than to revive painful memories. Simply put, this little boy was left behind.

Toniah knows herself too well. She won't hold out much longer; she'll want to find some answers. The facts will be easy to uncover, no doubt about that, but she wants to consider the consequences before she starts digging. It's odd, she muses, that in her day job, she doesn't blink about unearthing the past. No one's going to get hurt. Whereas if she were to uncover a family secret—even though her nana is dead and the boy, too, most likely—she'd face a tricky decision. Would she keep the revelation to herself or tell Poppy? One day, Eva might need to know.

If she's honest with herself, she doesn't want to be disappointed by Poppy's reaction. She doesn't want to hear an offhand dismissal. She *knows* this photograph is beyond easy explanation. It was *locked* in the box.

In her own mind, the boy must be her uncle. If he were the child of one of Nana's friends, why would she hide the photograph? That wouldn't make sense. So the possibilities are reduced to two. Either the boy was Nana's son and he died, or the boy was her son and she gave him away. Could her nana have been a surrogate mother at some point? Was the photograph taken during a brief reunion? Toniah knows she's letting her imagination get away from her.

She sees a patch of water ahead where a resident has hosed down a section of pavement. She slip-slides across the paving slabs to clean up the soles of her shoes, stops and lifts her heel to see if it's worked. It hasn't. Skeletal leaves have already glued themselves to the gooeyness.

A maglev shuttle is pulling in as she descends the staircase, and she walks farther along the platform than necessary, towards a man who's holding a young boy by the hand—an unusual sight during rush hour. On boarding the shuttle, she takes a seat almost opposite them, two seats away. She wonders if she's getting broody. The man sits the boy on his knee, and Toniah is struck by how similar they are; their faces have an identical shape, and they have the same deep-set eyes. Yet the father's eyes are brown, and the boy's eyes are ice blue. And the boy's hair is a lighter shade of brown. She imagines this man and his son at home, sprawled out on sofas. It's a game she often plays on the shuttle. Commuters seem sullen when they're self-contained among strangers. Self-absorbed. Yet she knows each of these strangers would become instantly animated if a friend stepped onboard.

At home, this man would be laughing over a game with his son and the boy's mother. She creates the mother, in her mind's eye, based on the dissimilarities between the father and son; she'll have ice-blue eyes, blonde hair most likely, small ears. They sit together, the parents—in this imaginary sitting room—watching him play, and they play their own game of untangling their genetic reach. His mother claims his eyes, hair and high-arched feet; his father laughs and claims everything else. But then *she* claims the boy's calm temperament, which of course Toniah must accept in her daydream because she can't tell anything beyond immediate appearances, while *he* claims the boy's fussiness over his clothes. Toniah notices that the boy's socks are a perfect match for his T-shirt. What she finds fascinating is that a child can look like one parent but have the personality of the other.

If one day she decides to have a partho child, as Poppy did and as Carmen is about to, she'd miss out on this game of parental reach. It must be fun. She suspects if she loved a man, really loved a man—that is, if she were besotted (and she accepts that she may never find that man)—she'd *want* to know how their genes would mix.

For a moment she regrets offering to go with Carmen to the clinic this evening. It seems less of an adventure making a baby the parthenogenetic way. Two of your own eggs of different maturity—one converted to a pseudosperm—enough to create another little being, a baby girl, very similar in appearance to her mother, though not identical. Toniah doubts she loves herself enough. She takes a last look at the boy as he and his father leave the shuttle. Her heart beats hard.

———————

After two hours' immersion in the angst of the late nineteenth-century art world, Toniah dispatches her comments on the Gauguin paper to Aurelia Tett. She highlighted a few confusing passages and a handful of multiple-claused sentences that were almost impossible to negotiate. In an endnote, she added her own comments on the connection between the soldiers' armour in Émile Bernard's and Paolo Uccello's paintings. A bit embarrassing on reflection; her first contribution at the Academy is a clarification of how one male artist may have influenced another male artist. She felt it worth recording her observation, though, partly because she was proud of herself for noticing the connection. And you never know, she thinks; it might help to nibble away at a sacred tenet—that Japanese art and all those tribal masks leaching from Africa into private collections in Europe were the main springboards for modernism, for Picasso's cubist portraits, et cetera.

Toniah sighs and stretches. Maybe it's fanciful, she muses. She stares as if in a trance. The quattrocento has always been seen as a minor influence, but maybe its impact is simply less noticeable to critics, easily overlooked because of the era's familiarity. It sits within our own heritage. How could this influence compete when art collectors, artists and writers were agog over exotica? Japanese prints were flooding Europe from the middle of the nineteenth century, and the flattened space of those prints took *more* credit for kick-starting modernism than the flattened space of our *own* Italian paintings, by our *own* Christian primitive painters.

——————

After her lunchtime jog, Toniah decides to pre-empt Aurelia Tett delegating another project to her by making her own suggestion:

Aurelia,

I hope my comments on the Gauguin project are useful. Thanks for inviting me to contribute.

I'm turning my attention to the artists I mentioned during my interview for this post—those Italian artists of the early Renaissance who practised their art within nunneries. A painting has turned up in Italy that's quite likely to be attributed to Antonia Uccello, the daughter of the recognized artist Paolo Uccello. She is the least known of the nun painters. As this painting would be the first attribution to Uccello's daughter, I feel this offers the Academy a unique opportunity to revisit the early nun painters in Italy, some of whom are already reasonably well documented (e.g., Caterina dei Vigri, Maria Ormani, Plautilla Nelli, Barbara Ragnoni).

Regards, Toniah

She receives an almost immediate reply: *Thanks. Go ahead. A.*

She shakes her head. No small talk with underlings. She responds: *Thanks. T.*

At last, Toniah can slip back into the quattrocento. She pulls up the limited information that's currently available on Antonia Uccello, plus the image of the painting that's awaiting attribution and the all-important letter signed by the abbess of the convent of San Donato in Polverosa—found in a private archive nearly two years ago. The abbess is writing to one of the convent's patrons. This patron is a wealthy woman, a member of the Florentine elite; as evident from the letter, she has approached the abbess for advice regarding a commission she wishes to make for a portrait of her daughter. Toniah knows from her research that the convents were active in commissioning art not only for their own use but also for various churches in their environs. In the translated letter, the abbess writes:

You could consider our own Sister Antonia. She is a trained painter, and, as you may know, she is the daughter of the esteemed master painter Paolo Uccello. Sister Antonia has experience in painting portraits, and I can reveal her talents by way of a small painting that we hold here at the convent. It is a discreet and delicately painted devotional portrait, simple and humble. The only decorative element is a scattering of blue petals, which lie at the base of a plain crucifix within a niche. Your daughter could sit for the portrait here at the convent, which would alleviate your concerns regarding propriety and your daughter's security.

The description of the niche was specific and unusual, so the hunt began for this small portrait. It was correctly assumed that the medium would be egg tempera on wood—typical for a fifteenth-century work. And seven months after the art media first publicized the letter, a retired archivist—on hearing of the search at a lunchtime reunion with former colleagues—recalled seeing one such painting in storage during her service at a small museum in rural Tuscany. The museum rarely rotated its art collection, and according to its rather patchy records, the blue-petals painting had never reached the public galleries of the museum.

"Let's take a closer look at you, shall we?" murmurs Toniah.

What she sees is a searingly tender portrayal of a woman approaching her middle years. Or maybe she's older. Did the artist shave a few years off the sitter? It's fairly safe to assume so. The woman is lost in thought; it's dream-like.

What can be deduced by simply looking at the picture? Toniah asks herself. The sitter is wearing a plain headdress, so she's unlikely to belong to the highest strata of Florentine society. Maybe she's a merchant's wife who wishes to appear particularly humble, or she's an artisan's wife. Alternatively, this is an informal, intimate portrait—the sitter may be a member of the artist's own household, a servant or a relative. This would chime with the times, since a female artist would perhaps have difficulty finding sitters. How many men were willing to pay for portraits of their wives or daughters?

Certainly, a female artist would depend on the women around her as she practised her skills. Women were tied to the family home, especially younger women, who could venture out only with chaperones and maybe no farther than the church or a relative's home. Lower-class women had more freedom, whereas Paolo Uccello's daughter would experience many restrictions, as Paolo's mother, Antonia di Giovanni Castello del Beccuto, came from an old family of high social status.

Toniah decides to make a stab at this painting. The painter is Antonia Uccello, and the sitter is someone in her household. This woman may be a servant—after all, Antonia would have to practise on somebody—or she's a relative. Toniah's best guess is that the sitter is her mother, Tomasa di Benedetto Malifici, or an aunt, or a cousin. It's likely to remain a mystery, but she enjoys the speculation.

Putting the sitter's identity aside, she examines the painting's composition. These half-length devotional figures were becoming popular in the quattrocento. Toniah recalls a similar portrait—who was it by . . . Antonello da Messina? She pulls up his painting. *The Virgin Annunciate*. In this painting, the figure also gazes to the side, but downwards. Antonia's painting is slightly more audacious by the standards of the day—the figure is looking upwards, it's less humble, and it reveals a woman inspired by her reading. It's more inspirational, more uplifting.

Although the blue-petals painting is simple at first sight, Toniah can see the artist's mind at work. The line of the table's edge leads your gaze to the woman's hand, and from there, the folds of the headdress take you to her face. Her eyes are blue, and, no doubt by design, there's a niche in the wall on a level with her shoulder with a simple wooden cross and *blue* petals sprinkled at the base. That's clever. And then, the folds in the headdress lead you from the petals back to the sitter's hands. There's a strong contrast, a chiaroscuro effect, created by a raking light, which accentuates all the folds.

She makes a note: *A sophisticated composition, but the handling of the paint may be slightly less accomplished.* She would love to stand in front of this painting. Maybe she'll send Aurelia a proposal. See if the Academy might send her to Italy while she's still on a temporary contract.

———————

Carmen and Toniah meet in the plush reception of the gestation clinic attached to Guy's Hospital. Their tour starts in fifteen minutes, so they sit together on a sofa. Instantly, the latest news bulletins appear over their coffee table: the latest fine art auction sales for Toniah and a report on the London property scene for Carmen. They both wave the bulletins away. It seems absurd to Toniah to watch the news in this setting. Why would people focus on mundanities when they're thinking about bringing a child into being?

"I think I can afford this. I've been looking at the prices," says Carmen quietly.

"How much does it cost?"

"It's not straightforward. There's a basic package, but the options are so tempting. The sky's the limit. Tests for this, tests for that. But *then* if they find something wrong, or if something needs a bit of tweaking"—she shrugs—"it costs more."

"I *did* have colleagues at the university who carried their pregnancies, and they were mostly happy . . . Well, not exactly happy, but, you know . . . They survived." Which didn't sound as light-hearted as Toniah intended.

"I mentioned the idea to my boss last week. He looked at me like I was mad. I think he took it personally, like I was saying the company didn't pay me enough. Even the others, the other property agents, weren't too impressed."

"None of their business."

"Except they think I'd be having doctor's appointments all the time. And all those antenatal classes."

"Is that what they actually said?"

"No. Amy, the office manager, asked what I'll do about morning sickness. Would I be cancelling early viewings?"

"Oh. Very caring."

"They made me feel, you know, really skanky. Like I was letting the side down. I reckon they'd take me off the high-worth properties. Wouldn't want me waddling around like trailer trash."

"You could take them to court if they downgrade your job."

"No way. I'd never do that . . . I think I'll bite the bullet, take the basic package." She leans into Toniah and whispers, "But I'll tell them at work that I'm having *all* the extras." She laughs. "Just to piss off Amy— she wanted all the adjustments, but she and her fella couldn't afford it."

They stand in the viewing gallery above the second-trimester ward with a young administrator. In the dim light, they peer down through a tangle of tubes, which partly obscure a precisely ordered grid of "baby bottles," as most people call them.

"There's no need to see the first- and third-trimester wards," says the woman. "There isn't much to see in the first ward—the foetuses aren't visible from the viewing gallery. And in the third ward, the technicians are a little too busy for us this evening—I believe there are six foetus flasks being transferred for birthing. We schedule most of our births for the evenings—it's more convenient for the parents."

Toniah feels a shiver. *Our* births. The administrator talks as though the hospital has joint custody.

"Where do the births take place?" asks Toniah. In her mind's eye, she conjures a surreal vision—a bunch of technicians pushing the flasks across the car park to the main building of Guy's Hospital.

"In the birthing suites, alongside the third-trimester ward."

A technician passes through the ward below and is tracked by a pool of light. She stops in the middle of the front row of flasks. Eight rows of—Toniah counts up—twenty flasks.

"Why's the background lighting so low?" says Carmen.

"The foetuses are sensitive to light. We try to mimic conditions in an organic womb. We also play the voices of their parents, plus the maternal heartbeat, and any music requests—music that the foetus might hear if the mother were relaxing at home."

"You play this continually?" says Toniah.

"No." She laughs. "We switch off the voices and music at night-time and simply play the maternal heartbeat. We do *try* to keep every-thing as natural as possible."

Toniah hesitates and then asks, "Do the babies thrive the same . . . whether they have one or two parental voices?" Carmen looks at her quizzically.

"I wouldn't know; you'd have to ask a clinician." The administrator points their attention to a bank of screens at the end of the ward. "We monitor all the vital signs, around the clock, as well as nutrient levels, oxygen feed, waste removal. It's safer than a natural pregnancy once the fertilized egg has bonded with the womb lining—that all happens in the first-trimester ward. In here, our technicians monitor the data stream, *and,* for rows A and B"—she points to the authoritative serif capitals suspended from the ceiling—"they administer a range of interventions according to the optional extras selected by parents in their gestation contracts.

"Now, let me tell you about visiting hours . . ."

Toniah stops listening. She notices a foetus in the front row, row A. It moves as though it's shadow-boxing. She can't tell if it's a boy or a girl, but it has hair already. She remembers the photograph of the boy sitting on Nana Stone's knee. His hair was brushed back off his high forehead, like Nana Stone's forehead—and hers and Poppy's, *and* Eva's—but the shape of his face was markedly different, squarer, an alien intervention among all-too-familiar features.

"I'd visit the ward with you once or twice a week," says Toniah. And she imagines Carmen sitting in the second-trimester ward, her hand resting on the baby bottle—a modern-day Madonna and Child.

CHAPTER ELEVEN

London, 2015

Her dad coaxes the log-burning stove towards optimum combustion by cutting the cold air feed and increasing the hot air circulation. The flames no longer flicker. They roll around and lick the smouldering logs, a miniature aurora over a miniature landscape. It's the perfect welcome, Toni feels, for Natalie—her favourite auntie, her mum's younger sister. A fire makes a house feel like a home. Cosy.

He picks up the television controller from the coffee table by Toni's side.

"Don't change the channel, Dad. I'm watching that." She pulls out one of her earpieces.

"You're writing on your laptop and listening to music."

What's the point in stating the obvious? she thinks. "So? I'm waiting for the best bit when Amy Pond—"

"Is that homework, young lady?"

She tips her head to one side. "I'm doing something easy. As in *half-a-brain-cell* easy."

"So . . . listening to music, doing your homework, reading messages no doubt, watching television."

"It's completely straightforward. I'm making a questionnaire for my history project."

Toni rolls her eyes as her dad turns to leave the room. Multitasking—that's a major problem for her dad, she thinks. If she's in the car with him and they're listening to music, he actually turns down the volume when he starts a conversation. Even if it's just a question. Yesterday, on the way to school, he turned the volume down and asked, "Are you happy to have yesterday's leftover curry for dinner?" She said, "Yes," and immediately turned the volume *up*.

Her history project—now she's sorted out her ideas—will be a cinch. All she needs to do is ask her friends a few simple questions. The questions *must* be simple; if they demand more than thirty seconds' attention, her friends won't bother answering. And it's got to sound dramatic.

> *Do you have a relative who died in a major disaster or war?*
> *Did this relative die before ever having children? Please tell*
> *me his or her name, age (roughly) at death, how he or she died*
> *and one interesting thing that you know about this person.*

Is that asking too much? she muses.

She'll ask her friends to forward the questions to anyone they know in Costa Rica or India or New Zealand, or anywhere interesting—that is, outside England. Global reach will get extra marks—it's more data. It's not exactly scientific, but then this is a history project.

Toni looks up as Amy Pond says, "I think that's the first time I've laughed in thirty-six years." It's a brilliant line. Toni hits Rewind and presses Play again. She listens to Amy's laugh—the first in thirty-six years. It's so convincing. She wonders if she got it right the first time or if she practised thirty-six times. Toni laughs at her own joke, which she knows isn't cool.

"The Girl Who Waited"—it's the tenth episode of the sixth series, with Matt Smith, her favourite, as the Doctor—though he doesn't appear much in this episode. He's had the bright idea to take Amy Pond and her boyfriend, Rory, on a holiday to this planet Apalapucia. To Toni's eyes, Amy Pond is almost impossibly beautiful. And she looks convincing as a warrior with her shield and her club. If Toni could choose to be anyone in the universe, she'd choose to be Amy Pond.

Back to the project. Toni has already decided that she'll use the Historypin app to put all the dead relatives on a map and share it with everyone, including her teacher, Mrs. O'Brien.

On reflection, she realizes that most of these dead relatives will be men, because so many men died in wars. So she changes "died in a major disaster or war" to "died in a natural disaster, an accident, war, epidemic or childbirth." That makes it clear that Spanish flu is included, and all her friends have now studied Spanish flu. It could include being plain unlucky—death by lightning strike, crushed by a falling tree— but she doesn't want any car accidents in her project, so she deletes "an accident."

What else? Definitely photographs—because this app is all about pinning photos with a shortish comment. Pictures say a thousand words, et cetera. Is that another aphorism? she wonders. Probably not. Doesn't sound very spiritual, very Buddhist.

Toni knows she should give an example with the history questions, so she'll send out the invitation when she thinks of one. Maybe she should invent one. Also, she needs a good title for the project. "Dead Ends on Your Family Tree." "The Missing Families." "The Families That Never Were." Not bad. "Toni's History Project—Missing Persons." That's better. She jumps up from the sofa and swipes the air with an imaginary club. She's got it: "Toni's History Project—Persons

Unknown." Yes, then it's clear that she's really interested in the people who were never born, and it sounds a bit like *The X-Files*.

Rory's mad, and he's screaming at the Doctor back in his Tardis. This is the bit she's waiting for, so she pauses the programme, gathers herself for total concentration and presses the Play button. Rory shouts at the Doctor, "This is your fault. You should look at a history book once in a while. See if there's been an outbreak of plague or not."

That's it. She knew someone mentioned *plague* in this episode. The planet of Apalapucia is under quarantine because of a deadly virus, Chen-7. Anyone with two hearts, like the Doctor, will be dead within an hour. That's why Matt Smith is staying put in the Tardis. And Amy has accidentally stepped into an accelerated timeline, so there are now two versions of Amy Pond. One Amy is her usual gorgeous self, and the other Amy is ageing, fast. She's been waiting thirty-six years for the Doctor and Rory to save her, even though *they* think she's been waiting a few hours. Old Amy, all wrinkled but still lovely, is talking to Rory through the closed door of the Tardis. She tells him to leave her behind on Apalapucia. "Tell your Amy I'm giving her the days, the days with you."

Toni hasn't watched this episode since her mum died. Her stomach knots Poor Old Amy. She died before she had a child. A log slips within the stove, and the fire sparks. Toni decides to pin a picture of Amy in her project. She's a TV character, but Toni can borrow her; like her dad says, you can borrow anything you like these days. Anything goes. But where should she pin her?

Somewhere in Scotland; she speaks with a Scottish accent. She types a search question: *Where does Amy Pond live?* Answer: The *English* village of Leadworth. Is that a real place? Google Maps says . . . it isn't.

Toni does another search, this time on Leadworth, and the search result brings up a *Doctor Who* fan who has trawled—unbelievable—the entire British Isles on Google Maps and Street View to find Amy Pond's home as it appears in several *Doctor Who* episodes. In the real world, Leadworth is Llandaff—a village in Wales.

Toni pins Old Amy Pond in Llandaff and adds a few lines of text: *Old Amy Pond stayed behind on the planet of Apalapucia in an act of heroism so that Young Amy Pond could live out her life with Rory ("The Girl Who Waited," Episode 10, Series 6,* Doctor Who*)*. Teachers like references.

There's a mechanical screaming from the kitchen, and Toni knows her dad is blending the tomato sauce for the pizzas. It's her favourite meal, and she thinks she's lucky having a dad who makes home-made pizzas. She slams down the lid of the laptop, folds her arms and, between fingers and thumbs, pinches the skin in the crooks of her elbows until it hurts. She feels bad; if she had to choose between her mum and dad, she imagines she might have chosen her dad. She shuts her eyes and concentrates hard on her mum's prawn risotto.

The weird thing is, she didn't think about her mum too much in China. Now that she's home, she thinks about her all the time.

She leaves the sitting room and pulls the pizza toppings from the fridge. Pineapple, ham and mushrooms for herself, and ham, mushrooms and olives for her dad. Her mum liked anchovies, and there's still a flat tin of anchovies in the fridge. It's been there over a year, and neither Toni nor her dad has felt like moving it. Toni touches the tin for several moments, as she does every time she goes to the fridge.

Toni hears the back door open, and she spins around expecting to see Natalie, but it's Anna Robecchi carrying a dish.

"Smells good in here, guys," she says.

"Anna, you're too busy to look after us like this," says Toni's dad. Anna places the dish—baked peaches in custard—on the kitchen island and looks towards Toni, eyebrows raised, inviting a response.

"Look!" Her dad points to a hardback book on the island. "I've bought some pudding recipes. You've inspired me."

Toni is impressed. Her dad always uses the Internet to find recipes, so he's bought the book purely to make the point to Anna. And that's why he left it lying around; he usually keeps his kitchen tidy.

What's more, he wouldn't make the point if anything were actually going on between them. Toni feels relieved, but embarrassed, too. So, by way of apology to her dad, she says, "Thank you, Anna. Looks awesome."

Then her dad goes too far. "Stay and have pizza. Natalie's coming round in ten minutes. We'll make it a party."

"No. That's kind, but I've made plans. I can't stop."

He gives Anna a friendly hug, and she leaves.

He removes tea towels from three baking trays to reveal his pizza bases—he always lets them rise for half an hour after he's rolled them—and he starts to spoon on the tomato mix. Toni tears up the mozzarella into small pieces.

"That wasn't tactless, was it? I didn't sound ungrateful?" says her dad.

"You were fine."

She keeps her face down, hiding her blushing cheeks, and feigns total attention for her pizza construction.

———

Happiness is . . . Happiness is a lovely dinner with her dad and Natalie. Natalie raises her glass of wine and says, "To the chef. One of your best, Dominic." They all clink glasses—Toni with her sparkling water.

Her dad and Natalie are chatting about work. Toni's pleased she doesn't have to join in. She can look down at her plate and imagine her mum is sitting at the table—her voice was identical to Natalie's.

Natalie says, "I'm so jealous of your trip to China." It sounds, to Toni, as though her mum is talking to them from *the other side*. She imagines her mum would be fed up, missing the trip. But then, if she hadn't died, her dad would have made the trip on his own.

"Toni? I thought I'd look through some more of your mum's things this evening," says Natalie. "Would you like to help? There might be some clothes you'd like to keep."

She likes how Natalie barges in; doesn't worry about broaching things carefully. Some of her dad's friends tiptoe around her as though she's standing on thin ice.

"You've already had a sort-out, haven't you?" says Toni.

"I only went through the drawers." Toni knows Natalie means her mum's underwear and T-shirts. "She had a thing for multiple purchases, didn't she?"

Toni laughs lightly. "Three or four of everything, in different colours."

"I think she caught that habit from me," says her dad.

"Some of her nicer clothes could be collectibles in twenty years, Toni. You might wish you'd kept them. I'm thinking ahead. You know, the vintage of tomorrow."

"I suppose I could reuse any nice fabrics. Recycle bits."

Natalie grins, but her eyes fill up with tears. "That's a lovely idea. I hope you never throw away your DIY jackets. If you have a daughter someday, she'd love to wear them."

Toni's eyes widen. "I hadn't thought about that."

Natalie has this way of making her feel like an adult. When she arrived this evening, she took one look at the baked peaches and said, straight out, "We need to watch that woman next door, Toni. I think she's taking a shine to your dad." It made her feel better about making such a scene in Suzhou.

"Come on. Let's get started, then," says Natalie. "I'm kinda looking forward to finding all your mum's shopping mistakes."

Natalie peeked in Connie's walk-in wardrobe a few months back—wanting to spend a few quiet moments with her sister's clothes while Toni was out of the house. It certainly didn't look anything like this. The clothes are now organized by colour, whereas before they were grouped, as she groups her own clothes, by type—blouses and shirts, trousers and skirts, cardigans and sweaters, jackets and coats, with dressy clothes in the smallest section at one end. Dominic has evidently spent time setting out some colour palette. Black clothes transition through charcoal grey, light grey, purples—which always suited Connie—through to greens and yellows, creams and, finally, whites.

"Some nice clothes here, you know," Natalie says. "But your mum was taller and skinnier than me. In any case, I'm not sure your dad would want me walking around in her clothes. Might freak him out."

Toni droops, overwhelmed by the size of the task. "What will we do with them?"

"I'll help you pick out some future vintage. And you can look for anything for your denim projects."

"And the rest?"

"I can take them to a charity shop—if that's all right with you—but not around here. You don't want to see someone in your mum's coat, do you?"

"You decide."

"Okay. Leave it with me."

Natalie doesn't wish to drag out this task any longer than necessary. It's too difficult for both of them. She keeps a conversation going while they flick through the clothes, taking out items and laying them out on the bed.

"How's the school newspaper coming along, Toni?"

"Fine. I'm writing a report on China for the next issue."

"Big subject?"

They both laugh.

"I'm doing a history project first."

Natalie pulls out a Missoni wraparound cardigan. "Your mum always looked fabulous in this. She should have worn it more often."

"Okay. I'll keep it." Then, "Natalie?"

"Hmm?"

"Did anyone in our family, in the past—I mean in the last one hundred years—did anyone die like in an epidemic or a war, or was anyone struck by lightning . . . ?"

Natalie turns from the clothes rail, and they stand looking at one another for several seconds.

"Well, what about your mum? *She* died in a freak accident."

"I don't mean that. Did anyone die young, before they had their own family?"

She still looks serious. "Are you worried . . . ?"

"No . . . It's just a history project, and I thought I'd like to include Mum's side of the family."

Natalie places a hand on Toni's shoulder. "Okay. Let's see. Your grandparents all died in their seventies. But my great-uncle—your great-great-uncle—he died in the trenches in World War I."

"I didn't know that. Was he married?"

"He was engaged. Betrothed, as they used to say."

"So he didn't actually have any children?"

"No. Unless there's a family secret I haven't heard."

"Do you have a photograph of him?"

"Your mum had most of the family photographs, so we can ask your dad."

———

Why is it that some people have twinkly eyes? What exactly makes them twinkle? Are their eyes more watery than other people's? Or is it something about the way they smile?

Toni decides, looking with her dad and Natalie at the sepia photograph of Great-Great-Uncle Arthur, that his twinkly eyes and his kind but slightly lopsided smile go well together. It's a studio photograph. He's in his trim army uniform against a backdrop—a painted backdrop, probably—of cloudy skies. A dreamy background for a dreamy face, an almost heavenly scene, as though the photograph is preparing Arthur's mother for the inevitable bad news. A premonition.

This thought suddenly throws her back in time. She once asked her mum why she hadn't put any of her school photos in picture frames. Her friends had their school photos on display at home, but hers were all kept in a photo album. Her mum said she didn't like school photos because they were the photos the police publicized when a child went missing or was killed in an accident. They had a . . . Toni tries to remember. A morbid something? A morbid *aura*. And now, Toni sees the same morbidness in this photo of smiling Arthur.

"So have you visited his grave?" she asks Natalie.

"I'm not sure anyone has," says Natalie.

"What? Seriously?"

"I know. It sounds bad, doesn't it?"

"Back then, people didn't travel to France," says her dad.

"Unless they were fighting," says Toni.

"Exactly. No one in the family had the wherewithal," says Natalie.

"What do you mean? Where with . . . what?"

"They didn't have the *means* to travel. Basically, I doubt they knew how to get there. No one in our family had a car back then. When you think about it, coach travel to the continent didn't start till much later. People simply didn't travel . . . unless they were rich. To be perfectly honest," Natalie says, hesitating, "it probably didn't occur to anyone to visit the grave." Evidently, she herself is taken aback.

"My parents bought their first car in the 1960s—an old Lea-Francis," says her dad. "I don't remember it, but I've seen a photo. They wouldn't have felt confident enough to drive all the way to Dover, take the ferry crossing to France, and *then* find a small cemetery in the middle of nowhere. Cars were always breaking down. I don't know about you, Nat, but we never took holidays abroad. I went to Paris on a school trip. That's all."

"The same." Natalie is squirming. "You know, I've never heard anyone in my family express any desire to visit Arthur's grave."

"So he died for his country and was buried there, out in France somewhere, and no one has ever, ever been to visit him?" says Toni.

"I think the family simply accepted it wasn't going to happen," says Natalie. "It's like your dad says . . . Arthur died in 1918, and it was another fifty years before people started taking coach tours around Europe."

Toni sits cross-legged in bed with her laptop and tinkers with her history project. She adds more text to the About page, pins Great-Great-Uncle Arthur's photo and adds the story that Natalie told her:

Arthur was a good footballer, and he might have gone professional when he returned from the Western Front in World War I. In those days, footballers didn't earn much money, so he'd have returned to his old job in the post office and played football on Saturdays. He was betrothed.

She would like to ask her friends another question—namely, Have you visited your dead relative's grave? But she decides it's not strictly relevant. She'd like to know if other families are equally unimpressive, though. If Natalie and her mum's family had really wanted to visit Arthur's grave, they'd have found a way.

She hears her dad laughing with Natalie downstairs in the living room. They're good at cheering one another up. She hopes her mum doesn't mind them laughing so much. After a while, they grow quieter, and she wonders if they're now talking about something serious.

With Old Amy Pond and Great-Great-Uncle Arthur pinned, she saves her project and, from the drop-down menu, invites her friends on Facebook and her followers on Twitter to join "Toni's History Project— Persons Unknown."

This is a brilliant project, she decides. She leans back with her hands behind her head. It doesn't involve loads of writing, and it's all about personal histories. If more than ten people pin a relative on her world map, she'll count it a massive success.

CHAPTER TWELVE

Florence, 1469

Antonia throws her prayer book on her bed and runs out to the galleried landing. The sound of gritty, stabbing footsteps on the stairs can mean only one thing: Donato is home.

"At last," she shouts when she sees him halfway up the staircase. His hair is stiff with dust, yet he's more handsome than ever. Why did *he* get the beautiful hair?

"Where is everyone? There's a tired traveller here who needs a welcome."

The whole house comes alive with his warm, booming voice. Antonia ought to allow her father to greet him first, but she races ahead, and rather than embracing Donato, she collides with him, almost knocking him off balance at the top of the staircase. "We thought you'd be here yesterday, at the latest."

Her father emerges from the sala, arms outstretched. "You stayed longer in Arezzo?"

"Yes, Father. I planned to break the journey for two days, but then I met an old friend and—"

"Never mind your excuses. Your mother was worried, so you'd better make peace with her before you sit down." Her father and Donato embrace one another. "Go see her now in her bedchamber and then join me in the study."

"I'll tell Clara to prepare a plate of food," says Antonia. "I'll bring it to the study myself. And, Donato, Mother's been embroidering your old shirts, so make sure you notice."

Antonia enters her father's study with a plate of mutton and bread for her brother. She's delighted to find they're already talking about business; she loves to hear their tales of how they've negotiated commissions and won lucrative deals.

"So there's plenty of work in Urbino?" says her father.

Donato plants his hands on his hips. "Enough to keep me *and* three assistants busy for the next nine months. You wouldn't believe it. There's so much appetite in Urbino for the goods coming out of Florentine workshops. And with the Uccello name"—he grins at his father—"I'm guaranteed a warm and respectful welcome in any merchant's house."

"Well, that's pleasant enough to hear." Paolo's flat tone reveals his resistance to flattery. "A public commission of your own would still be a good thing. It would set you up for the long term. Let me speak with the confraternities and the Wool Merchants' Guild."

"Father, I can't match you. I don't want the world saying that Donato was the insipid follower of his father. There's good, well-paid work—small private commissions—that suit me far better. You know me. I'm an administrator at heart. You've always trusted me to organize your day-to-day arrangements. It's better that I go out and find the business and employ assistants to do the actual work. By this time next year, Father, I believe I could keep a workshop of five men busy just painting commemorative birth trays and small devotional images of the

Virgin and Child. You wouldn't believe how much money the new rich of Urbino are prepared to pay. All they want to know is what's fashionable, what's selling well in Florence. And with your name, I'll have no problem finding good assistants. I'm wondering, Father—"

"Slow down. You're full of schemes."

"It's a suggestion. That's all. I'd love to tell my patrons that while I'm away on business, *you* will keep an eye on my workshop. How would you feel about that? All you'd need to do is call by the workshop once a week. You'd like it."

"Donato, I've retired. I want to do my own work now."

"Please, a *half* day a week, when I'm travelling. Father, I'll have a wife and family to support one day, and the best way you can help me is to build the good name of my workshop."

Antonia knows better than to interrupt such a serious conversation. She hangs back, hoping neither of them will send her away.

"You know, Father, your experiments are a source of gossip and . . ." Donato hesitates and smooths back his thick, dirty hair. He starts again with more enthusiasm. "People talk about your predella in Urbino. There's such pride in the fact you accepted the commission, and they wish you'd accepted the commission for the altarpiece. But . . ." Antonia wonders what Donato is trying to say. "People are wondering what you do with your time now."

"Tell them I'm too tired for any more commissions. And *how* I spend my time in retirement is no one's business but my own."

He takes a deep breath and throws up his hands. "Very well, Donato. I'll help you. But I have this little one's studies to consider as well. Antonia, show your brother your portrait." He points to the small wooden panel that sits on an easel facing away from them.

Donato walks around the easel and stands stock still in front of the painting. He folds his arms. He takes two paces forward and looks closely. Antonia and her father join him.

"Well?" says her father. "Be honest. That's how she'll learn."

"It's strong and sympathetic at the same time. Father, did *you* work out the composition?"

"No, it's all her own." He looks down at Antonia, and they share a smile. "She needed a little help with the perspective, but we sorted that out in the drawings before she started to paint. See that niche? That's a compositional device she added without my prompting."

"You've handled the paint reasonably well, Antonia. It's a bit tentative and a little overworked in the folds." Donato points at the niche. "The blue petals are nicely handled."

"She shouldn't be painting so soon; she hasn't mastered her drawing skills as yet. But I'll teach her as much as I can. She has the basics, and she has a good instinct." He places his hand on her shoulder. "Mind you, she wasted a fair amount of pigment for this painting. Some would say it's better to waste a little than run short in the middle of your work, but personally, I believe it's a bad habit, best avoided." He strokes her hair. "Now run along, Antonia. I've other business to discuss with Donato."

She slumps out of the study.

Paolo waits several moments, and then: "I've ordered a dowry chest for Antonia from the cabinet-maker—she knows about it—and I've received a note that it's ready for delivery. I will instruct Antonia to repeat the portrait of her mother, and I want *you* to paint a self-portrait. Those two paintings will then form the end panels of her dowry chest. I'll paint the main panel."

"Does she know this?"

"Not yet. I wanted her to start her mother's portrait without feeling too pressured."

"So . . . have you made your decision about Antonia?"

Paolo sighs heavily, walks across his study and eases himself down into his chair. "Your mother is pressing me. Rightly so, for your sake. A younger sister can attract mischievous talk and rumour if her future remains unsettled. I've decided she'll take the veil. There's a practical consideration regarding the timing—I don't want her entering the convent at the onset of winter. She needs to go in the summer months."

"Which summer months? Next year?"

"This year. She'll leave this house before the end of August."

"That's only five or six weeks away." Donato stands in silence for several moments. "You know, I heard recently that the sisters at Le Murate's scriptorium are turning out extraordinary work. There's a waiting list as long as your arm for commissions."

"She won't be going to Le Murate, and not because of the expense. She's joining her aunt's convent. She schooled there. They all know her, and I can make sure she's treated well. I'll want assurances that she'll enjoy privileges. The abbess will agree if she wants to get her hands on the dowry chest one day."

"Assurances may count for little once your back is turned."

"You and I must insist on seeing her work regularly. Then we'll know how much time she's spending in the scriptorium and how much time she's wasting in menial work."

Donato returns to the easel. "It's much better than anything I did at her age."

Paolo remains quiet. He's had so many apprentices and assistants over his career, and he can recall only two or three who showed Antonia's early talent.

"You know, Father, I could steer small commissions her way, once she's proficient. The abbess could conduct the negotiations with my patrons. I could take a small fee, and I could insist that Antonia carry out the work. What do you think?"

"It's something to consider."

"But it's a shame she's the one with the ability, isn't it? You must be disappointed."

"I could never be disappointed with the girl. God allowed her to live, and in his mysterious way, he wants us all to find out why."

"Let's hope she and Mother take the news well. When are you going to tell them?"

"Soon. I wanted to wait for your return. I'll tell your mother in my own way, and whatever the reaction, I want you to show some enthusiasm for my choice. They'll be more receptive if they see that *you* share my vision. I've already exchanged letters with the abbess."

The servant girl enters and collects Donato's platter. "Tell the boy to take a message to the cabinet-maker," Paolo instructs her. "Tell him to deliver my wooden chest tomorrow morning. Early."

At dusk, Antonia joins her family in the sala, which is filled with the aromas of duck being roasted in the kitchen. Clara has prepared a special meal for Donato's return. Antonia finds her father raising his glass to Donato.

"So, Donato, let's toast your successful business dealings."

"And let's also toast my sister's success in the art of portraiture. Mother, you must be pleased with the likeness she's achieved, and such a harmonious composition. You have a talent there, Antonia," he says, teasingly. "I wish with all my heart that you continue your painting studies."

"She worked hard, but she was too strict," says her mother. "She knew exactly what she wanted, and I had to do exactly as I was told."

"An artist has to lay down the law," her father retorts. "And while we're talking about art—"

"We talk of nothing else in this household," says her mother.

"Well, be thankful Father isn't a baker, or we'd be talking of dough all day," says Donato, which makes Antonia giggle. How she loves having her brother home, and how he warms the house with his quips and makes her parents so happy.

"As I was saying," continues her father, "on the subject of painting . . . Antonia, your dowry chest will be delivered from the cabinet-maker tomorrow, and we should talk about the decoration. I have some ideas for the main panel, but I thought you might have a preference, seeing as you'll be living with this chest for all your days."

Antonia is aware that she's blushing. All eyes are on her. "I . . . I . . ."

Donato tries to help. "Come on, Antonia. You must have a favourite story—from a legend or from the Bible, or a romantic scene. Something dramatic to keep you entertained for years to come."

"It's difficult . . . Please, nothing frightening like monsters or those half-human, half-devil creatures I've seen in church."

"So you want a scene to send you pleasantly to sleep," says Donato.

"No. That's not what I mean. I'd prefer a peaceful scene, but something that's detailed and maybe a little bit funny."

"Ah! A family joke—so you'll recall us laughing together around this table."

"I think I'd like a painting with animals, lots of animals. And I don't mind if it's a Bible story like Noah's Ark or a scene . . . perhaps a hunting scene in the countryside."

"Let me see," says her father. He strokes his beard. "I painted a night-time hunting scene for Federico da Montefeltro two years ago."

"A lively *and* poetic work, Father," says Donato with enthusiasm. "Man's search for love and the soul's search for redemption. Brilliant colours against a dark background, with such excellent glazing. But don't paint a night-time scene for Antonia . . . Paint a daytime scene. Then you can show the birds in the trees and the sky. There'll be horses, hounds, a stag, of course, and hunters in fine clothes."

"Don't kill the stag or his doe. Show them escaping," says Antonia. "And can you paint some lady hunters, too, in their fine dresses?"

"That's *too* unusual," says her father with a frown.

"But no more strange than any Greek myth," says Donato. He rubs his chin. "I know. If you'd like to remember this very evening, Antonia, and this fine dinner . . . let's include Clara's face. She'll be a fine lady, hunting for our duck."

Above the laughter, her father says, "Well, then. I'll start the drawing for the main panel tomorrow, and I pray, Antonia, it meets your exacting demands."

———————

Paolo is already at work on the preliminary composition for the hunting scene when a servant knocks at his door. "Master, the cabinet-maker's boys are here with the chest. Should I tell them to bring it to you here?"

"Yes, and inform my wife of its arrival. She'll want to see it."

And so, when Tomasa walks into the study five minutes later, she finds Paolo inspecting the naked dowry chest, which sits brazenly atop his desk. When he sees her, he stands up straight and braces himself. He fixes his own stern expression. She stands in silence by his side, then dips her head and wipes a tear from her face with her forefinger.

"So, Husband, our daughter will *not* be getting married. You decided weeks ago, didn't you? That dowry chest is too small for the bedchamber of a well-married bride."

He doesn't reply; he's not obliged to.

"She's going to join my aunt, isn't she?"

Fifteen minutes later, when Tomasa has composed herself, she sends a servant to fetch Donato and Antonia.

Paolo waves them into his study, and without any preamble, he sets out his plan. "The panels are not fixed in as yet, Antonia. The three of us will take a panel each—the large front one for my hunting scene, the two smaller end panels for you and Donato."

"Are you teasing me, Father? Are you serious? I'm going to paint a panel for my own dowry chest?"

Paolo ignores her questions. "For the sake of your training, Antonia, you and I will prepare all three panels. We'll cover each panel in a piece of fine-weave cloth to deal with any knots, and then we'll apply at least four coats of gesso. You will learn how to make a perfect surface. I haven't prepared my own panels for a long, long time, but it's not something one forgets.

"Next, we will each draw our design and prick holes through the paper along the main features. You've seen me pouncing, haven't you?" She shakes her head. "Well, it's simple. You transfer your pricked drawing to the gesso surface by brushing charcoal powder over the holes. So your drawing *must* be the same size as your panel. Understand?"

"But I don't know what I'll paint. What should I do? I've never painted any animals, and mine would look so coarse next to your fine painting."

Donato opens the chest to check the hinges and smooths his palm across the underside of the lid. "A fine piece of carpentry."

"Antonia, you'll be painting your mother's portrait again. The last one counts as practice. Paint the same composition, and this time, I'll let you use my best brushes. You'll find them much better."

"Is Donato painting your portrait on the other panel?"

"You don't need the image of an old man." He laughs. "He's painting a self-portrait, so you'll always see your brother as he is today. You'll always have your mother and Donato to keep an eye on you."

Antonia frowns and twists a strand of her hair. "This chest is smaller than Mother's dowry chest. Is this the fashion now?"

"It's not a matter of fashion, child. It's a matter of what is most appropriate. So, come here. There's something we need to tell you."

———————

Antonia has stayed in her bedchamber all afternoon. She lies curled on the bed, her eyes closed, her mind racing. "None of them care," she says into her damp pillow. Her mother didn't seem upset by the decision. She seemed subdued but resigned. Donato didn't appear *in the least* interested. He simply stated, "It's a good decision, Antonia." Does he only care about himself? she wonders.

She hears footsteps and then a knock. The door opens.

"Are you asleep?" says Donato.

She opens her eyes, and he kneels by her bed. "Antonia, it won't be so bad."

"That's easy for you to say, Brother."

"Our aunt's convent is more open than many. It's not all prayer. They're in daily contact with the outside world because of their commercial work. And Father and I will make sure they understand that you've already had an apprenticeship of sorts. Believe me, you *will* be a painter, and this could be the only way. Mother says it's truly like a family. And they *all* know you."

"It won't be like this. It's so cold in winter, Donato."

"Listen. We'll make sure you have privileges. Father will insist. If the abbess wants that dowry chest, she'll have to agree."

"But can I keep the chest in my cell?"

"Of course . . . But it *will* pass to the convent, you know, eventually. The church takes a long view."

She covers her face with her hands.

"You'll be safer in the convent if the plague returns . . . and we'll all have the comfort of knowing that your devotions, your prayers, will make our family stronger."

"I know, but—"

"I've made a suggestion to Father. I told him he should sign over one of his Ugnano land-holdings to the convent. That way, you'll receive an annual annuity from the abbess to cover your personal needs—enough to buy extra food, oil, clothing . . . and pigments, of course."

She smiles, but her eyes fill with tears.

CHAPTER THIRTEEN

London, 2113

Toniah is pinpricked, deflated, when she arrives home and finds Poppy setting the table with their best cutlery and glassware. It's date night, as Eva calls it—their regular Thursday-evening dinner when they all endeavour to eat together. Toniah feels a pull-push; she loves Eva's enthusiasm for date night, but she's resistant to the growing obligation, the feeling she's being sucked into family domesticity before she's ready. This evening, she turned down the chance to listen to a guest speaker at the Academy. It wasn't art related, but all the same, it would be good to meet new people. She throws down her bag, creating an obstacle between the kitchen and living room space.

"Thanks for getting things started," Toniah says as she hugs Poppy. "I'll make a fruit salad when I've had a breather."

Poppy's embrace seems perfectly relaxed. Toniah is on alert for any hint of tension, because two days ago she told Poppy that she'd started seeing Ben. Poppy appeared almost thrilled, which Toniah found difficult to understand at the time. In retrospect, it all fits. It's as though Poppy has ticked off the last item on a list: Toniah likes her job, tick.

Carmen has applied for a gestation loan, tick. Toniah is hooking up with Ben, tick.

Toniah heads out of the kitchen, but hesitates in the doorway. She turns and says, "It occurred to me . . . I thought it might be nice if Ben joined us for dinner next Thursday."

Poppy's blank stare morphs into a grimace. "Why would we invite Ben?"

Toniah shrugs. She's tempted to back off—Sorry, bad idea!—but instead: "I thought, you know, it would be nice to have more male company. I liked my house share in Norwich—one man and three women."

"I thought you had problems with your housemates."

"That's not true. I was a bit narked with Linda; she was away a lot, but she didn't suggest swapping her big bedroom for a smaller one. I had no problems with Nick—he was a *great* housemate."

"But we all agreed we'd—"

"I'm only talking about Thursday evenings."

Poppy turns and busies herself at the stove. She tests a few grains of rice. Toniah wonders if the conversation has ended, but then Poppy blurts out, without facing her, "Why start now? I mean, first it's dinner, and then before you know it, he's staying for the weekend. You know the house rules: if you want to spend more time with a partner, you go to their place."

"Is that actually carved in stone?" She struggles to keep her composure; Poppy could at least look at her. "Where's the harm in trying something a bit different? And Eva likes Ben."

"He's just a guy at the breakfast table. I think she'd be confused if she thought he was moving in."

"I'm not talking about Ben moving in. For heaven's sake!" she says, trying to keep her voice down. Eva might be nearby. "Look at me. I'm simply making a suggestion."

Poppy turns, holds up her hands, palms facing her sister. "All right. I'll think about it."

"But, Poppy, it isn't for *you* to decide, is it?" She lowers her head, chin to chest, takes two steady breaths and looks up. "Let's have a chat with Carmen. I honestly don't see why Ben can't come for dinner and then stay over."

"The rules work well."

Toniah is wide-eyed. She can't believe how Poppy's digging in.

"We had a stable home life. That's not easily achieved, is it?" says Poppy. "I don't want a stream of live-in partners passing—"

"I don't take our happy childhood for granted. I really don't." Toniah notices her bag, picks it up and heads for the stairs. "I'll freshen up. We should talk to Carmen."

"Carmen signed up for this. It's what she wanted," calls Poppy as Toniah trudges up to her room, defeated.

Toniah stands by her bedroom window and looks across the patchwork of small back gardens behind their terrace of Victorian houses. Some of the gardens are better tended than others. It's dispiriting; the residents of the street can all see into each other's gardens, yet some people make no effort to improve their share of the collective view. For some, it's no more than a dumping ground; they've no sense of embarrassment. In all her years of idle gazing from this bedroom window, she has never seen any improvement in the next-door garden to her left—a grassy wasteland that's traversed every night by at least five neighbourhood cats. And while the cats mostly seem to avoid one another, at least once a week their nocturnal paths cross with screeching consequence.

Back in her old bedroom. Is this it? she asks herself. A good job, a house with a modest mortgage, a neat back garden framed by shabbiness, a quiet home life with an occasional sleepover boyfriend. She's in no hurry to feel settled—unlike her younger sister. Are the next five years—ten years, even—mapped out? She traces the figure *10* on the window, leaving an oily smear. Forever tiptoeing around Poppy. She's even tiptoeing around Nana Stone now. But why settle for half a story?

"What are you looking at, Auntie?" says Eva. She takes Toniah's hand. "Why are you frowning?"

"I didn't hear you come in." She smiles and picks Eva up, with some effort. "Had a good day?"

"Not bad. What are you looking at?"

"I'm keeping my eye on those chickens."

"You're spying on them."

"They're up to no good."

Eva giggles, and Toniah kisses her on the cheek. "I'm going to do an hour's work, Eva, and then I'll help with date night. Tell your mum, will you?"

"Okay." She squirms out of Toniah's arms and runs off, content to have an errand.

When Toniah hears Eva and Poppy chatting downstairs, she pads across the landing to the pine storage trunk, which contains a file of family legal documents. She kneels down, opens the trunk and roots out the file. She doesn't immediately flick through the contents. Instead, she closes the trunk and quietly slips back to her bedroom to sift through the file's contents in privacy.

She spreads out the paperwork on her bed—birth certificates for the family going back to Nana Stone, and death certificates for Nana and Mother. She takes a deep breath and reminds herself that Nana Stone made her choice; she hid the photograph. But Toniah decides she isn't going to her grave—and what's wrong with a little melodrama?—without knowing the truth about her own family.

***

Toniah finds it difficult to comprehend. This new information, her family history, has lain within her reach—and her mother's reach, for that matter—all these years. It was *there on the landing* all the time, awaiting discovery, requiring only a few minutes' further investigation. Maybe, she wonders, we're always trapped in the minutiae of daily life— constantly too distracted to think about the big picture. Yet it *is* important to her—to know where her family comes from, to know what *happened*, what events proved to be turning points.

All she had needed for immediate results was Nana Stone's date and place of birth, and her date and place of death. Toniah knew her birthday, of course, but she hadn't been sure of her birth year, which is now revealed on her birth certificate: 2014. Toniah rubs her face with both hands. Nana Stone was born in the centenary year of the start of World War I. She can't believe she didn't know that.

Toniah has now retrieved all the public registry records related to Leah Stone. There is one birth certificate and one death certificate that Toniah has never seen before. The birth certificate is for a boy named Maximillian. No name is recorded for the father. And the death certificate is for Maximillian, aged one year and two months. The cause of death is stated as influenza.

Maximillian. Why didn't we know this? she says to herself. Why did she bear it alone?

———

Toniah sits at the kitchen table with a cup of coffee and wonders if Poppy or Carmen noticed that she hardly spoke over dinner. They probably didn't; they were absorbed in choosing names for a baby girl, even though Carmen hasn't as yet started the treatment.

Poppy comes downstairs, having tucked Eva into bed. "Carmen says she's tired. She's going to read in bed and then turn in."

"In that case . . . come and sit down, Poppy."

"I'm sorry about earlier. I know I talk as though this is *my* house. I don't mean to. It's just . . . I have Eva to think about."

"I know. And I was tired."

"You took me by surprise. I'm not totally against inviting Ben." She busies herself, tidying away the spice jars and wiping down the glass splashback along the kitchen counter. Toniah thought she'd cleared the kitchen well enough, but Poppy always finds additional work.

"Actually, Poppy . . . Come and sit down. There's something I need to tell you." She sees her sister's face fall.

Poppy drops herself into a chair. "What? Has something happened at work? I thought you were quiet over dinner."

"No, no. The job's fine. Remember I was in the attic?" Poppy nods and frowns. "I found a photograph of Nana. There was someone else in the photo."

"What do you mean? Don't be so dramatic."

"She kept something from us." Toniah slides the photograph across the kitchen table.

Poppy reaches towards the photograph, but she falters.

"Meet Maximillian," says Toniah. "Nana Stone's first child."

Poppy murmurs, "So it's true."

———

They push aside the coffee cups and bring out the whisky bottle.

"To Maximillian," says Toniah. "The least we can do is wet his head." They clink glasses, but neither of them can raise a smile.

"Honestly, I didn't believe it. Not for a moment," says Poppy.

"And this conversation took place before I returned home from university?"

"Yes. Nana took a turn for the worse, so Mother told you to come home, and that was on . . . the Sunday. Then on Monday morning, Nana perked up a little when her friend Hildi came round . . . and that afternoon, I sat with Nana for a couple of hours. Like I said, by then she was rambling, talking complete gibberish. *Including* something about a baby boy. But she was exhausted. So . . ."

"Did you tell Mother?"

"No. Because Nana became lucid later in the day, and I asked her . . . I asked her to tell me about the little boy. I asked her what his name was, but she didn't know what I was talking about. So I decided to leave it alone."

"You could have told me."

The silence stretches, and Toniah pours another whisky.

"Was she trying to tell us . . . You know, before she died?" says Poppy.

"Probably. But if anyone knows the full story, it's Hildi. That is, if she's still alive."

———————

The nursing home, which overlooks a large South London park, is a gleaming Edwardian villa; original art-nouveau stained glass embellishes the wide entrance door and both bay windows. Toniah has always preferred Edwardian houses to the older Victorian houses in London's suburbs. Edwardian homes were built on larger plots of land, and their interiors are more airy, with generous entrance hallways, often oak-panelled. They're more welcoming than Toniah and Poppy's own Victorian house.

This particular Edwardian villa is close to Toniah's fantasy. She has long dreamed that one day she'll have her own study in the upstairs bedroom of such a house, overlooking such a park—a park with a wide blue sky and the sounds of children playing. She can imagine herself taking a break from her desk, jogging across the park, gaining the type of inspiration that a good jog can stimulate.

Today there's a game of football in progress in the middle distance. Toniah is surprised that the players' calls, and foul language, can reach them from so far away.

Eva has stayed home with Carmen for the morning, and this brief excursion feels like a treat—two sisters out and about on a Saturday, unencumbered. They may even grab time for a coffee before returning home.

They stand in the driveway of the nursing home, taking stock.

"It's not a bad place to end up," says Poppy.

They're ten minutes early, so they take a seat on a bench positioned under the canopy of a large ceanothus tree; cascades of blue flowers surround the two sisters.

"I feel bad we didn't know Hildi was in a home," says Poppy.

"Me, too. We let things slip, didn't we?"

"Well, it was a bad time for everyone. Her brother should have told us she'd moved here."

"He didn't actually know us, Poppy. Hildi just talked about him."

Poppy laughs, "That's right. The invisible . . . what was his name?"

"Peter. No . . . Pieter."

Every Mother's Day without fail, Hildi joined them at home for a special lunch. She didn't have children of her own, and Toniah is touched, looking back, that Nana included her in their Mother's Day celebrations. Hildi continued to join them after Nana Stone died, but her visits stopped once their mother died.

The senior care assistant leads them to Hildi's room. "She's expecting you, and she's fairly bright this morning."

"It's ten years since we last saw her," says Poppy.

"I shouldn't worry. Hildi has a loose grasp of past and present. She was a great one for posting videos, and she's reaping the benefit now.

She watches them over and over. And she paid extra for an avatar of her twin—"

"Pieter?"

"That's right. Did you know him?"

"No, we never actually met, but she talked about him."

"He died soon after Hildi came here. She sits him in an armchair all day."

"So she's not too lonely," says Poppy, hopefully.

"His conversation was limited at first—Hildi only had one recording. But she was stronger back then, and she told Pieter lots of old stories. So he repeats them back to her. He's a godsend, really."

The care assistant opens the door to Hildi's room.

"We have visitors, Hildi!" says the avatar. "We're so excited to have a visitor, aren't we, Hildi?"

Hildi lifts her head and smiles. Her hands are lifeless in her lap.

"Pull up some chairs," he says.

"I'll leave you to it, then," says the assistant, raising an eyebrow. "I hope Hildi gets a word in edgeways." She closes the door behind her.

"We're here to speak with Hildi," says Poppy firmly.

"It's such a fine day," he says. "And the forecast is for clear skies until Thursday, with possible thunderstorms on Tuesday." He laughs. "Two hot days and a thunderstorm. Isn't that right, Hildi? The definition of a British summer."

They pull up two chairs, and Toniah is tempted to place her bag on Pieter's chair, but she refrains. She takes Hildi's hand, and they sit quietly for a moment. She looks Hildi in the eyes to see if Hildi is registering who they are. "It wasn't easy to find you, Hildi. We had to trawl Mother's contacts, but in the end, we asked around in your old neighbourhood. The hairdresser told us where you were."

Hildi nods her head. "Well, it's a lovely surprise to see you both."

Poppy sits forward. "We wish we'd visited sooner but . . . Anyway, here we are."

"I'd know you anywhere," says the avatar. "I've seen seventeen photographs of Toniah and fifteen of Poppy."

Poppy throws a withering look towards Toniah.

"How is it here?" says Toniah.

"They're all very kind. And I have Pieter."

Poppy says, "Next Mother's Day, we could pick you up and bring you home for lunch. Like old times. And you could meet my little girl, Eva. She's started school already, and you've never met her."

Hildi smiles. "That might be too much for me. I'm an old bird now."

"Then I'll bring Eva next time."

Toniah worries that Hildi might tire quickly this morning, and wonders if they'll need to visit a few times to dig into Nana Stone's past. She jumps in. "Listen, Hildi, we don't want to tire you out, but we thought you'd like to talk about Nana Stone. You must have memories of happy times. We've brought some photographs."

"Excellent," says the avatar. "Have you any—"

"Pieter, now you've seen the girls, let me have a quiet chat." Hildi blinks him off. She tries to sit up straighter; Toniah rearranges the cushions behind her back.

"We never met your brother before now," says Toniah.

"A very kind man. He *always* has been," she says.

"How did you and Nana meet, Hildi?" says Poppy. She knows the answer, but it seems a good place to start.

"I met Leah at school." Her eyebrows begin to dart. "She was always the one getting into mischief."

Poppy brings an envelope from her bag and carefully empties out the photographs. She shows them in turn to Hildi, who nods at each one—photographs taken on Mother's Day at intervals across the years, with Toniah and Poppy inching from infancy to early teens.

"And we found one particular photograph we'd like to show you. We're hoping you can tell us something about it," says Toniah. The photograph is cupped in her hand. She offers it to Hildi. For a moment, Toniah believes Hildi has fallen asleep, but then she murmurs, "This was taken . . ."

"When was it taken, Hildi?" says Toniah gently.

She doesn't answer.

"Who is the little boy in her lap?" says Poppy.

Hildi's hands are no longer still. She smacks one hand with the other.

Toniah says, "We're sorry to spring this on you, but we think you're the one person who can tell us, Hildi."

"Leah didn't want to talk about it."

Toniah steels herself. "Can you tell us anything at all about this little boy?"

"He's her son, Max."

"But I don't understand, Hildi," says Toniah. "You've known this all these years, and yet . . . did Mother know?"

She shakes her head. "I loved the boy, but Leah wouldn't . . ."

"So you knew him, Hildi. But what I don't understand is . . . who was the father?" says Poppy.

"She didn't want a husband. She used a donor."

Toniah puts her hand to her forehead and sighs. Another incomplete story. It's Poppy who has the appetite for more. "Well, that's strange, Hildi. Why didn't Nana use a donor again? Why did she go parthenogenetic to have Mother?"

Toniah prays that no one comes in; she's embarrassed—grilling Hildi like this. Again, it's Poppy who nudges: "Why didn't she use a donor again?"

"She didn't want another boy."

No one speaks. In the absence of questions, Hildi eventually continues. "She said she couldn't love another boy as much as she loved Max. She only wanted a girl."

"And the way to guarantee that," says Toniah, disbelieving, "was to have a parthenogenetic conception."

"It was a new procedure then, Hildi. Wasn't she worried?" says Poppy.

"She was always the daredevil," says Hildi, with a tinkle of laughter. "She didn't give *two hoots*." The emphasis charms Toniah.

Toniah takes a tissue from her pocket and dabs the old woman's eyes. "Sorry, Hildi." There's a knock at the door, and a care assistant wheels in a trolley. "Tea, anyone? Where's Pieter? Was he talking too much, Hildi?"

When the care assistant leaves the room, Toniah says, "Hildi, I'd like to ask you something else. Nana used to say, 'Don't talk to me about men.' What did she mean by that? Did something happen?"

"That's probably . . . Yes, that's about her father."

"She never spoke about him."

"He walked out when Leah was eight years old. He didn't show his face again."

Toniah now wishes she hadn't asked. She prefers her childhood horror-fantasy that Nana Stone was jilted at the altar. The plain facts aren't half so satisfying.

Poppy brings out her photographs of Eva, but Hildi's eyes become heavy. Toniah glances at her sister. "I think we should perhaps let Hildi have a rest." She takes Hildi's hand. "We'd better go . . . But now we know where you are, we'll come back with Eva. And thanks for telling us about Max."

Poppy leans forward. "Hildi? Did Leah tell you anything about the donor? Did she have any information about him?"

Hildi's eyes widen. "Oh, we knew the donor. It was Pieter."

CHAPTER FOURTEEN

London, 2015

It's peculiar, to Toni's mind, that people travel across the world to visit London's National Gallery to see all the famous paintings—which were probably stolen from their own countries in the first place—but as soon as they see the copyist in the Venice room setting up her easel, they forget about the old paintings; they want to watch what she's doing. They probably think they'll learn how to do it, how to paint a masterpiece. But copying a masterpiece is not the same as painting the masterpiece in the first place. It's self-evident to Toni, but she thinks it's not clear to *some* people. They believe that if they had the knack and the correct equipment, they'd face only one simple question: What to paint?

Most people, she's convinced, would choose to paint a sunset. She knows she's being a bit harsh, and she tells herself to be a bit more . . . What's that religious word her mum used to use? Charitable. She should be more charitable.

When they arrived at the gallery, Toni asked her dad if she could go straight to the coffee shop. She remembered from her last visit that the coffee shop had an old-fashioned, steampunk feel—polished brass rails, black wall panelling and gaudy stained glass. But her dad wanted her to go with him to the Sainsbury Wing so she'd know where he'd be for the next two or three hours. She waved the gallery floor plan at him, saying she could easily find her way around, but he insisted. So she traipsed behind him through the Dutch rooms and now into the Italian.

She suddenly realizes that the oldest paintings, which are all Italian, are the brightest and happiest paintings. Perhaps Italians are more cheerful because of the better weather. She has a weather app, and she still has Florence as her first page; it's always sun, sun, sun, sun, sun for the five-day forecast. Well, nearly always.

They reach Room 54, and without pausing to look around, her dad strides towards the bench in front of *The Battle of San Romano* and sits himself down, right in the middle. He places his backpack to his left and pats the bench to his right. Toni sits with him, and they sit quietly. The painting fills almost the entire end wall. She can tell her dad is concentrating; he sits in a slouch—he doesn't care what he looks like—with his knees apart and his hands loosely clasped. His eyes blink rapidly. After a couple of minutes, he opens his backpack and pulls out a long tin, which holds his sketching pencils, putty rubber and a crafting knife, which he always uses to sharpen his pencils.

"What's the plan? Pencil sketches?" she says.

"Pencil for starters. Then I'll use pastels to record the palette of colours."

"So, no painting today?" She hopes not; she reckons he'll finish sooner if he sticks to pencil and pastel.

"Sadly, no one is allowed to use paints in the Sainsbury Wing, not even to make colour notes." He looks over his shoulder. "The gallery assistant might complain about the size of my sketchbook. You get the odd one who's a real stickler."

"There might be a poster in the shop for this painting? You could copy that."

"I've already bought it online."

"What? So why bother coming to the gallery?"

"I'm a pro. The colours are never right in a poster." He opens up his sketchbook on his lap. "And you definitely miss things."

"Why's that?"

"It's a bit of a mystery, really. I think the true colours change how you see the painting. So if the colours aren't exactly correct, you misunderstand the composition. And you always lose detail in the darker areas." Toni reckons if she keeps distracting him with questions, she'll never get away.

"And it's important to appreciate the size of the work, how it feels to stand in front of the real thing. Here's a good example. *The Battle of San Romano* nearly fills this end wall, doesn't it? It's a powerful statement. But look at that painting on the right—*Saint George and the Dragon*. It's small and feels more intimate. But if you saw them reproduced in a magazine, or online, you might think the paintings were the same size. Go and read the text panels for the two paintings."

She yawns as she wanders across to the battle painting. She reads the panel, turns, and as she walks along the end wall, across the battle scene, she pretends she's holding a lance and lunges. She reads the second panel by the smaller painting.

"Well?"

"They're by the same artist, Paolo Uccello."

"Surprised?"

"Suppose. He should have painted the dragon picture much bigger, don't you think, Dad?"

"It was probably made to measure, for a niche somewhere in a palace. And, interestingly, Andy Warhol appropriated that painting for a series of screen prints."

"Can I go to the coffee shop now?"

He hands her a pen, and she writes 54 on her wrist. She looks at him, raises her eyebrows.

"One hour," he says. He pulls some coins out of his pocket. "*Don't leave the building.*"

Typical, she thinks. The coffee shop is at the opposite end of the building. She wants to rush through the gallery rooms, but people are dawdling, and one elderly couple, Japanese, she thinks, comes to a halt right in front of her so that she almost crashes into them. They're holding black handsets, listening to the guided tour, and the recorded voice has, *evidently*, told them to stop and look at a particular painting. As she sidesteps, she notices the painting they're staring at, and she, too, stops in her tracks. It's a painting of stones and twigs. She dodges in front of the couple to take a closer look. It's like the grey rocks in the Shanghai hotel—the grey rocks in the glass tanks. She giggles aloud. Someone else thinks a rock is interesting. The title says *Rocks, Tree Trunks and Branches*, which doesn't seem right; it definitely looks more like stones and twigs.

She jumps two steps at a time down the long staircase to the ground-floor coffee shop and slips past a group of suited men, beating them to the queue. She orders a banana milkshake, and while she waits by the counter, her phone pings. It's a notification saying that Mai Ling has pinned a photo to the project "Toni's History Project—People Unknown."

That's the eleventh pin: target exceeded, total success. She touches the app icon, but it doesn't open; the free Wi-Fi is pathetic. She wonders if Mai Ling remembered to write one interesting thing about her dead relative. And it now occurs to Toni that her request for a micro-snippet of information is a bit rude. It shouldn't be possible, she thinks, to reduce a lifetime to a single sentence. What could she say in a sentence about her mum, or about her dad, or Natalie? One day, far in the future, someone might abbreviate *her* life. Toni Munroe . . . a renowned embroiderer of vintage denim.

She takes her milkshake to a long, marble-topped counter and perches on a bar-stool. She faces three large Georgian windows with wooden shutters folded back—the shutters match the room's head-height wood panelling, which is painted black. This would make a great movie set, she thinks, for a spy thriller. She's scanning the coffee shop, working out where two spies would make a live drop, when the hulking men in suits walk across the room with tiny cups of espresso and sit directly opposite her, blocking her view. She feels she's sitting in the middle of their group, but they don't seem to notice her—she's an invisible junior member of the species.

She frowns at her phone as though a crucial email has just *that second* landed in her inbox. But it's hard work maintaining the frown, so she pushes her phone into her pocket; it's not as though she ever receives world-redefining communications. She lifts the straw to the top of the milkshake and sucks off the bubbles. Maybe she'll ask her dad how many earth-shattering emails he receives in a year, but on second thought, she drops the idea. After her mum died, he didn't check his email for at least a month.

She's not sure why. It seemed to *her* that email would be the least painful way of dealing with people. But, oddly, her dad talked with any-one who telephoned—he didn't even let the answering machine take a message—even though he always cried when he talked about her mum. She overheard Natalie telling him to put an out-of-office notice on his mail. So Toni sent him an email to see what he'd written. He wrote that due to a family bereavement, he was taking extended leave.

It was all right for him. He made *her* go back to school even though the long summer holiday started only three weeks later. He said it would be best if she went back before the holidays, but she thought he was wrong about that. She should have stayed home to look after *him*. The house got into a mess, and she suspected he spent half the day in bed.

Anyway, she reckons that the subject of earth-shattering emails would make a brilliant feature article for a Sunday newspaper. She'd ask famous—no, she would ask *nonfamous* people—to recall the most important email they had ever received. "The Email That Changed My Life." She'd tell them she wanted happy stories. She'd pitch the feature as a New Year special, full of optimism for the coming year. In any case, why go out of your way to write sad stories? she says to herself. Unless it's a historical feature; then it's bound to be *all* misery.

Toni stands at the entrance to Room 54. She watches her dad at work and spontaneously feels the warmth of reflected glory, for two young men—art students, she guesses—are whispering to one another and taking sideways glances at her dad. Toni strolls past them, stands by her dad and puts a possessive hand on his back. "How's it going, Dad?"

"Fine. Not so difficult, this one. Uccello's approach is straightforward. It's just a coloured-in drawing. Not like the Venetian school."

"Hmm. How much longer will it take?"

"Bored already? Why don't you find a painting you like?"

As she leaves the room, she steals a backwards glance at the two students. They're looking at her. They must be wondering what it's like to have an artist for a father. She wants to tell them it's pretty amazing. Her dad takes her to loads of artists' studios. In fact, she doesn't know any other teenager who goes to open-studio weekends, and her favourite part is seeing her dad drinking beer from the bottle with his art mates.

What's more, he's made her realize that all these paintings are *her* paintings; all the big museums belong to *her*, and she can regard them as her own treasure trove. And years ago he taught her this: in a big gallery, you don't study everything. All you do is pick one painting in each room for a closer inspection.

In the next room she picks a small painting—the one that *isn't* a Madonna and Child. There's a man on a horse in a landscape full of animals—hounds, deer, stags, a heron, swans and two ducks. The stag has a crucifix growing out of his head, though Toni has absolutely no idea what the artist is trying to say.

The next room is utterly dismal. She sighs. It's a Dutch room, full of portraits of miserable people. She looks down at the wooden floor and moves on to another Italian room where the sun is shining in all the paintings. She's surrounded by bright blues, startling reds and happy, skipping angels.

However, in the far right corner, she sees a long, thin painting; it's like ultra widescreen, and it draws her in. To a scene of carnage: half-human, half-animal creatures are rampaging through a group of beautiful men and women who are caught unawares in the midst of a fancy picnic. The creatures are whacking the humans with clubs, biting their necks.

Toni steps forward to inspect the gore. Basically, it's a kidnap story—the naked women are being dragged away from their boyfriends and husbands. This is definitely the best painting in the National Gallery, she says to herself. Humans versus . . . What are they? She reads the title—*The Fight between the Lapiths and the Centaurs*. She hunts around the painting to see if there are any female centaurs. None. Why is it that women are always the ones being dragged off? Why aren't they the ones doing the clubbing and biting?

On a distant field, she spots a centaur dragging a man by his foot towards a cave. He must be a gay centaur, if there is such a thing . . . unless they're cannibals and this horror scene has nothing to do with sex. Toni decides the story would make a great movie, but only if the director insisted on having a few female centaurs. "Hollywood Cashes In on 500-Year-Old Painting!"

No, she says to herself. No exclamation marks in headlines. That's amateur!

Dominic packs away his sketchbook and texts Toni, telling her to meet him at the Portico entrance. But before leaving, he turns to take a last look at the painting from the far end of the room. He finds it difficult to comprehend the audacity, the sheer nerve, of the ruling Medici family in Florence. They admired this painting and its two sister paintings so much, they stole them.

That's what you call artistic appropriation, he says to himself. He imagines the Medici militia forcing its way into the residence of the Bartolini family, taking *The Battle of San Romano* paintings down from the walls. He wonders if the frames were damaged in the process, if repairs were needed. He imagines the militia marching back with the paintings through the streets of Florence to the Medici palace on Via Larga. Dominic decides that when he gets home, he'll find the address of the Bartolini residence online and follow the paintings' route on Street View.

Finally, plucking up the courage, he looks at the far right of the painting—at the glancing blow of a lance across the chest of a Sienese knight. Back in Suzhou, Dominic had willed Mr. Lu to choose *Water Lilies*.

The bus is packed on the journey home. Toni and her dad sit several seats apart until, three stops from their destination, the seat next to him comes free. She dives forward to take it. "I've been wondering," she says as she drops in beside him. "And I'm not being rude . . . I've been wondering why you don't make your own paintings instead of just copying other people's."

"Just copying . . . ? It's not exactly easy."

"I don't mean *just*." She taps his arm in apology. "But, you know, don't you have any . . . haven't you got your own ideas for paintings? You used to paint your own. There's that yellow and green one in your bedroom."

"The yellow and green one . . ." He frowns at her. "The abstract, you mean?"

"All right. The *abstract* in your bedroom, which happens to be mainly yellows and greens, by the way. Don't you want to paint more abstracts?"

"I haven't thought about it for a while."

"So you might?"

"If I ever retire, I'll do some more. I do *enjoy* copying paintings, you know. I'll let you in on a little secret." He leans into her. "It's a good feeling when you're good at something. It's good for the soul. And, here's the real secret—it doesn't really matter *what* it is you're good at."

"You're not disappointed, then?"

He shakes his head. "I have interesting clients. They usually pay on time. I like art history, and . . . I paint most days."

"That's all right, then."

"So what do you fancy for dinner?"

She shrugs. "And another thing, Dad . . . Have you ever copied a painting by a female artist?"

He looks out of the window for a few moments. He turns back to her. "No. I haven't."

CHAPTER FIFTEEN

Florence, 1469

Antonia leaves the confines of their home on Via della Scala and looks to see if the ground is wet, for it feels surprisingly fresh outdoors, as though a passing rain shower has narrowly avoided their own inner courtyard but doused the street and cleared the air of dust. However, the ground is dry, and Antonia realizes she has simply grown accustomed to the still air indoors.

She and her mother climb into the waiting carriage. It belongs to her father's cousin, who insisted—on hearing the news that Antonia's future was settled—that this feast-day visit to the convent of San Donato in Polverosa should take place in comfort and style. Antonia suspects this gesture is more than a treat; it's a reward. She and her mother each hold a basket covered in muslin to protect their sweetmeats from the summer's fattened flies. Antonia's mouth is watering, but she knows her mother would scold her if she tried to sneak a fricatella on the journey.

They emerge from the long Via della Scala into a grand piazza, dominated at the far, northern end by the newly finished church of Santa Maria Novella. The carriage rumbles across the cobbles of the piazza and cuts in front of the church. The Rucellai family paid for the completion of the church's edifice, and Antonia adores the small sculpted reliefs of billowing sails—the emblem of the Rucellai family—that stretch across the façade. She feels a great sense of pride, too, because Giovanni Rucellai himself commissioned several paintings from her father, before she was born. She strains to glimpse the baby-faced sun inlaid at the apex of the church—an innocent face that allows Antonia to forget, momentarily, the stormy sermons she hears within, week after week.

Beyond the church and the city walls, the carriage heads out on the road towards Pistoia, gradually climbing away from the city. It's just a half-hour journey to the convent, and Antonia decides, looking out across wheatfields, that if she had a choice of all the convents in Florence—inside or outside the city walls—she would choose the convent of San Donato in Polverosa, because it stands in the countryside where the air is clean, and in the height of summer, it is cooler than any convent huddled within the city.

Her great-aunt, Sister Giustina, has lived enclosed in the convent since the age of eight, and professed as a nun at the age of fourteen. Antonia feels sorry for her; she has surely forgotten everything of her childhood before the cloister. For her aunt, Florence is a city that exists only in her mind's eye, in images conjured by the letters from her family and by stories she hears in the convent's parlour.

The carriage reaches a rise in the road, and the convent's church tower comes into view. In the past, at the first sight of this tower, Antonia would be excited, eager to see her friends, since she had no young brothers or sisters to play with at home. She looked forward to their games, played in the cloisters and courtyards of the convent. Today, however, her stomach is knotted; this might be her last visit, the last time she'll be able to return home.

One of the carriage's wheels hits a pothole in the dirt road, and they jump in their seats. Her mother looks under the muslin to see if any of the canisiones have broken. But for Antonia, the jolt brings tears to her eyes. She takes her mother's hand and holds it tight. She doesn't utter a word, despite her mother's quizzical look.

———————

The gate officer at the convent admits them through the first set of heavy doors. They wait while she shuts the doors behind them and then opens a second set of doors into the convent. They are led to the parlour by Jacopa, a young servant nun, whom Antonia has seen often enough but has never spoken to. It was in the boarders' dormitory that Antonia learned from the older girls of Jacopa's circumstances—how she was admitted to the convent as a servant nun, with little chance of ever professing; she would never wear a choir nun's habit.

Jacopa came from an artisan family—mostly stonemasons—but her father, uncle and older brother died when the plague returned to Florence. Her mother had already died in childbirth, and so the girl was left destitute. According to the older girls at the convent, she was saved when her father's guild brought her plight to the attention of a wealthy Florentine merchant, who paid a small spiritual dowry to the convent to allow her admission.

"Tell Sister Giustina that her niece and great-niece have arrived," Antonia's mother instructs Jacopa when they reach the parlour door. Jacopa inhales the sweet aroma of almonds and sugared pastry, and for a moment seems reluctant to leave. "When you return, you must offer these pastries and treats around the parlour. At the end of our visit, take whatever remains to the refectory for the sisters to share."

Entering the parlour, they acknowledge three female visitors, members of the Lenzi family, who sit together with their cousin Sister Zanobia—a wealthy woman who took the veil two years ago on the death of her husband, Francesco Lenzi. Her piety was well known, and this tipped the balance when weighed against the prospect of burdening her brother's household.

Antonia tugs her mother's sleeve as a tall woman wearing white enters the parlour. An ornate brooch is pinned at her left shoulder. Her hair is plucked high on her forehead, and she wears a small turban-like balzo. "Ah! Tomasa di Benedetto Malifici. I see your daughter Antonia is still keeping you company," she says so that everyone in the parlour might hear. Antonia understands the implication of this remark, and she blushes. Maria degli Albizzi is suggesting that either the Uccello family is confident of securing a marriage for Antonia, or they're lax in delaying her entry to a convent.

"She's young for her age," says her mother.

Antonia accepts the slight, for she has no choice, and bows her head. She knows Maria degli Albizzi has steered commissions to her father's workshop. Only last week, Donato mentioned her name in the sala. Antonia steps back slightly, that the conversation might veer in a new direction, but the ploy fails.

"Let's hope the whole of Florence doesn't follow your lead," says Maria degli Albizzi, "or we shall be short of novices to pray for the salvation of our city."

Her mother winces. "We *do* have good news from my son, Donato," she says quietly. "He recently returned from Urbino, and he is now expanding his workshop under the guidance of his father."

"Then tell Donato to visit my husband. I'll tell him to expect a visit in the coming week. And Donato should bring examples of his work. I will look at them myself."

"You make a gracious offer, and our son will be grateful." She lowers her voice. "When Donato visits your husband, I will send a note for your attention regarding Antonia."

Sister Giustina enters the parlour. She waves discreetly to Antonia and walks as briskly as decorum might allow to greet her great-niece. "I've missed you, Antonia, so much. We all have."

Antonia whispers, not wishing Maria degli Albizzi to hear, "Mother has news for you. I shouldn't be the one to tell you." From her aunt's calm, smiling, incurious expression, Antonia knows the news has already reached the convent. Her mother joins them and places her hand firmly on her daughter's shoulder, as though cautioning her. "Antonia, take one of the servants as a chaperone and go to the church. Say your prayers to Saint Martha. Your aunt and I need to talk for a while."

Her aunt raises her hand to the servant. "Leave the baskets, Jacopa, and take this child to the church."

Jacopa covers the food carefully with the muslin and places the baskets on the table at the back of the parlour. She follows Antonia out of the room, and when they're out of sight, she nudges Antonia, dips her hand into the pocket in her tunic and reveals a fricatella. Antonia bursts into giggles; she's shocked more than amused.

"I'll save it for later," says Jacopa. She licks her fingers.

"You mustn't eat in church."

"I'm not *that* wicked."

They slip into the back of the church. Antonia kneels in a pew, and Jacopa kneels in the pew behind. It's Antonia's guess that Jacopa will not be saying any prayers.

On her occasional visits to the convent's church, Antonia has always wished she could kneel facing the large fresco by Cenni di Francesco on the right-hand side of the nave rather than the altar. Her great-aunt once told her that this nativity scene had been painted long before *she* ever arrived at the convent. Antonia convinces herself she's showing no disrespect to Christ on the crucifix when she shifts her gaze to the fresco. It can't be wrong, surely, to choose his nativity over his death as a source for her meditation. But she admits to herself that she's less interested in praying this morning than in reassessing Cenni di Francesco's work in the light of her father's lessons.

As a small child, still light enough to be held in her mother's arms during Mass, Antonia was captivated by this fresco. She looks at the bottom right of the picture, and her body shakes momentarily before she smothers silent laughter. For there, in the corner, Cenni di Francesco painted a white hound greeting a brown rabbit—an entertainment, Antonia is sure, to distract fidgeting and fractious children in the congregation. The hound dips its head and raises a paw. As she grew older, Antonia became distracted by other scenes within the fresco. All the figures, both men and women, appear to be gossiping as they lean into one another. Even the tethered horses and camels, their necks straining, seem to be sharing secrets. Cenni di Francesco surely loved God's creatures.

Antonia tries to work out why this fresco looks so different to her father's work. It seems so old-fashioned. If her father painted a nativity scene, he'd imagine he was standing right there in front of the manger with everyone gathered around Mary and Jesus. But in this fresco, people are in small separate groups, scattered across the picture. And near the bottom of the fresco, he has painted two nuns—painted in miniature as though he'd forgotten to put them in and had to squeeze them in at the last moment. She almost giggles again, for she can imagine the abbess standing behind the artist at work and announcing, "I believe this fresco needs some nuns."

One of Cenni di Francesco's tiny nuns has her arm around the other, and they're leaning their heads together, telling that secret again. In her giddy mood, Antonia looks across the whole fresco, and her shoulders shudder once again. The shepherds, stirring from sleep—woken in the night by an angel—are painted at the top of the fresco above the stable as though the past existed in the sky. Her father wouldn't do that. And there's a final curiosity. Cenni di Francesco painted all the figures wearing Florentine clothing rather than the long robes of Jesus's time.

Jacopa coughs. Antonia takes the hint. She closes her eyes, bows her head and recites three decades of the rosary; her lips mouth the words.

Antonia leaves the pew and genuflects in the aisle. As they re-enter the convent, Jacopa pulls her by the arm into a dark alcove in the passage. "Would you like some advice?" Antonia tries to pull away, but she relents and nods her head.

"If your family is thinking of dumping you here—" says Jacopa.

"That's not fair. If I end up here, they wouldn't be dumping—"

Jacopa rolls her eyes. "Well, that may be so, but if they do *dump* you here, make sure they send you with the essentials—the things I *didn't* arrive with. Extra blankets, silk or fine linen shifts for under your habit and a wool cape you can wear in winter in your cell. And a good pillow."

Antonia looks down at her feet. "I *will* be coming here, Jacopa, but don't tell anyone yet." She looks up. "And when I do come here . . . I'll bring something for you."

"You're a good girl. And I'll tell you another thing, for no reward. Keep away from the likes of Sister Umiliana and her flagellating cronies. Don't be taken in by all that show of piety—they're all *demented*."

———

When Antonia enters the parlour, she's presented with a scene as conspiratorial as Cenni di Francesco's fresco. She walks across to her mother and aunt. They stop their conversation.

"Come through to the cloisters, Antonia, through the boarders' doorway. I want to show you around the scriptorium. I'll meet you there, and your mother can rest here."

Although Antonia has sneaked a look in the scriptorium many times, she has never crossed its threshold. She makes her way alone through dark passages to the small courtyard where the convent's two main workshops face one another across the herb garden. One workshop for gold-thread making and embroidery work, the other for the rougher linen work carried out by the servant nuns. She rushes ahead to the Great Cloister, and there, at the entrance to the scriptorium, her aunt reaches out for Antonia's hands and kisses her forehead.

Antonia looks into her aunt's face and notices she's nigh on unwrinkled. Unlike Antonia's mother, she has no frown line between her eyes.

"So, Antonia, you're joining us, and I rejoice in this news. It's what I have prayed for. You may not thank me for those prayers just now, but a girl with talents could do a great deal worse." Antonia is wide-eyed. "You will enjoy *three* sources of consolation during your incarceration." Antonia feels light-headed on hearing her aunt's blunt words. "You will know that your prayers, as a bride of Christ, will sustain your family and our great city. You will always be protected here from the soldiers of invading armies. And you will take pleasure in using your talents, which Our Lord will countenance as long as you reject the sin of pride. A woman with a husband and children cannot hope for such things. Come with me, and I'll show you how my sister scribes devote their talents to God, and the abbess."

Several scribes' desks line the cloister walk. "These desks will remain here to make good use of the summer light, but as soon as we have three rainy days in succession, they'll be moved back into the scriptorium. And the communal calefactory next door, with its roaring fire, keeps the scriptorium warm through the winter.

"You'll find, Antonia, that some of the sisters who work in our gardens and laundry feel our scribes have an easy life. But you must know from your studies, here and with your father, that a mind concentrated for several hours is just as draining as any manual labour, even in winter."

"I'd prefer anything to freezing fingers, Aunt."

"When you become a novice, you'll have to call me Sister Giustina—but it doesn't matter for now." Antonia nods, and her head is swimming again. "Anyway, whatever talents we are granted by God, we must make the most of them, and we must offer our work back to him as a form of prayer. It doesn't matter if your talent manifests itself in the garden or at a scribe's desk. Having said that . . . let me show you the work of our illuminator, Sister Battista, and two of our best copyists. They've completed a Book of Hours for Maria degli Albizzi"—she lowers her head to whisper into Antonia's ear—"who, as you know, is seated in the parlour as I speak. So take care that you don't let her hear that I have shown you her book. She has seen the individual pages, but she hasn't seen the bound volume."

The scriptorium's arched windows face the cloister. On the opposite wall, there are smaller arched windows facing the street, but they're too high for anyone to see outside. Sister Giustina opens the doors of a wooden cupboard that sits at the centre of the scriptorium, and she brings out the new Book of Hours, wrapped in cloth. She sets it down on a lectern and turns to Antonia.

"Sister Battista painted the main illuminations herself. She directed two of our sisters in copying the Latin prayers and painting some of the simpler borders. It has taken them six months to complete the commission." She looks at Antonia, her eyes twinkling with mischief. "And she included her own portrait within one of the illuminations."

"Is that allowed?" Antonia is incredulous.

"It was our patron's idea, but the abbess prayed for guidance for a week before she agreed."

"But the sin of pride, Aunt."

"Sister Battista wasn't motivated by pride. That's all that matters in God's eyes. In any case, doesn't everyone know the paintings of Brother Angelico?" She gives Antonia a knowing look. "And Caterina of the Poor Clares in Bologna wrote essays under her own name. She was a painter, too, you know."

Sister Giustina carefully unwraps the cloth to reveal the prayer book, bound in red leather with a simple crucifix stamped into the surface and two metal clasps holding the pages closed.

"See, the binding is complete." She opens the book. Her hand shakes. "Here is one of Sister Battista's full-page illuminations."

Antonia is enthralled. Her hand reaches towards the page. She knows she mustn't touch, but she wants to feel closer to this small wonder. The colours are deep, brighter than stained glass in full sun, and the composition is complex and tight. On the facing page is the Latin prayer, which is wonderfully easy to read; the letters are beautifully rounded and even. Some of the letters are tall, and all the words are neatly spaced. It's so much easier to read than the northern fashion of lettering, which always looks so squashed and cramped to Antonia— no tall letters and everything pointy. Last week, in her father's study, she'd tried to read a book, from the University of Bologna, written in this ugly northern style. So many of the words were abbreviated—she couldn't make sense of a single sentence.

"It's the Suffrage of Saint Anthony," says Sister Giustina. Antonia looks back at the painting and finds it difficult to believe that a nun could paint an image of such brutality: a helpless Saint Anthony being beaten with clubs by four winged demons.

"See how much lapis lazuli has been used. Maria degli Albizzi has spared no expense." She turns the page. "Here, look at Sister Battista's self-portrait."

Antonia is disappointed. It isn't a full-page portrait. It's a small face framed by a nun's white cowl and black habit, painted below a block of Latin text. Sister Battista has made no attempt to compose her portrait, or to tell a story. Antonia looks up, but doesn't speak for fear of sounding unimpressed.

"Naturally, Antonia, you will start by copying breviaries and psalters for the convent's own use, and as you acquire more expertise, you'll illuminate choir books and books of sermons. But, imagine—one day, you might produce a Book of Hours as fine as Sister Battista's."

Her aunt narrows her eyes, evidently struggling to read Antonia's silence.

"Antonia . . . why do you believe you were saved from the plague? Surely, Our Lord wants you to serve him in a special way. How better than to serve him here in our scriptorium and make good use of the training you have received from your father?" Her attempt at mind reading continues. "You won't notice the simple food and the cold winters if you enter with the love of God in your heart. You will find a way to serve him that brings you peace and fulfilment. Life on the outside is hard in its own particular ways. There's no easy path. And believe me, it's a bored mind that makes a bright young woman feel like a pauper."

CHAPTER SIXTEEN

Winchelsea Beach, England, 2113

A slight westerly breeze blows across the beach, and the sea appears depleted of energy. The waves are mere ripples that dissolve into foam rather than break on the shore. Toniah looks along the coast from the top of the shingle beach. Five or so miles distant as the crow flies stands a block of concrete, which can only be Dungeness Fusion Power Station; it appears less brutal than Toniah expected. Strong sunlight reflects off its flat surfaces, giving the impression that the power station is painted white, which seems unlikely. To a time-traveller from the past, it would appear to be a fortress, defending the ancient trading posts of England's south coast, protecting its inhabitants from murderous incursions. And halfway between Winchelsea and Dungeness, at the far end of Camber Sands, stand the defunct wind turbines. They face into the wind, their blades no longer sweeping, awaiting their final decommission, their scrappage. They've served their purpose. The sands at Winchelsea are among the most unstable in the world, but coastal engineers have remained resolute, judging by the line upon line of timber groynes stretching from the highest terrace of the shingle beach down to the sea's shallows.

It was Ben's idea to make this day trip. He knows this stretch of the south coast from childhood holidays. Toniah stayed at his place overnight, and she had planned to set off this morning for Norwich to see her old housemates. She needed to escape the city, clear her thoughts. Ben persuaded her that sea air was the best medicine.

"If we turned back the clock a thousand years," he says, "we'd be standing in the sea. This shoreline has seen a lot of changes."

"What happened?" she says, surprised.

"Major flooding from the sea. Old Winchelsea and its harbour were inundated, not once but twice in a generation, and the settlement was rebuilt on higher ground. The king ordered it—I think it was Edward I—in the late 1200s."

"Why was the king so concerned?"

"Winchelsea was the main point of departure for France. After the floods, a new harbour was built, but it was smaller. Basically, this whole area went into a slow decline, and the wine trade with France petered out."

Toniah finds it reassuring that coastlines such as this still exist—gorgeously bleak, almost sublime, and underpopulated. Yet it lies just one hour from London.

"It's a wonder they bother," says Toniah. "You know, conserving these beaches. It must cost a fortune." The oldest timber piles have the appearance of burnt shards, disfigured yet seductive.

"Once you start with coastal protection, it's difficult to stop," says Ben. "When you protect one beach, you push the problem farther along. It's all about longshore drift—remember that from school?"

"I don't think I grasped geography, being a city kid."

"The point is that once you start interfering, you're committed. And it's difficult to undo."

They make their way, half walking, half sliding, down three distinct levels of shingle to the shoreline and head off westwards in the direction of Brighton.

"It must feel good living somewhere like this, at the edge," says Toniah. "Look," she says, sweeping her hand around the land horizon. "You can't see any houses along the coast. There's only the power station, way off. All we can see is beach, water, sky and clouds."

"Talks to your inner hermit, hmm?"

Ben takes binoculars from his pocket and stops to scan the sea. Toniah walks on. She stoops to pick up a lump of old, weathered wood, almost black, with a neat circular hole worn through, as though a nail had once skewered it. Similar fragments are scattered along the line of high tide. It must be something peculiar to this area—from an old sunken ship? Or from old timber groynes?

He's probably right; she does have hermit envy. She knows she likes to focus on one thing, one project. So when her attention is drawn away from that one project, she feels panicked, and that's when she fantasizes about sitting by a window in a quiet, uncluttered room. She wouldn't want a view out to sea. She suspects a seascape would induce sleepiness, with the soporific effect of one wave crashing after another, after another.

She told Ben about Maximillian last night. She needed someone to talk to, someone who understood the peculiarities of her home life. He's pretty astute, she thinks. He said, "I'm not sure you're ready to settle back home."

She turns the driftwood over in her hands and lifts it to her face, as though its smell might yield the secret of its origin. Stupid, really.

Since talking with Hildi at the nursing home, she has reached a conclusion. It was a pure accident that she and Poppy were raised in an all-female household. Nana couldn't bear to have another boy. It almost seems that a small boy—a long time in the past—was loved too much, and as a result, Toniah finds herself in a partho family. Is it possible to love a child *too* much? she wonders. She throws the driftwood into the sea. Nana Stone *would* have loved a second boy just as much as the first. Toniah's sure of it. But then, if her mother hadn't been born . . .

She recalls the conversation she had with Poppy after they left Hildi's nursing home. They walked to a coffeehouse, and by the time they'd finished their coffees, Poppy seemed satisfied that the puzzle was solved; she was ready to shelve the matter. "I'll tell Eva one day about Maximillian, but there's no point telling her about Pieter. His name isn't on the birth certificate, and he didn't form any attachment; that's clear enough. Anyway, it's too complicated. And for Eva . . . Well, it's ancient history, isn't it?"

Ben catches up with her, and they hold hands. A large blue plastic glove lies ahead of them, washed up. Toniah stops and twists around to look back along the beach. "We passed the other blue glove, didn't we?"

Ben turns around and looks through the binoculars. "It's there."

"What's the chance of that? Two blue gloves lost at sea and washed up on the same stretch of beach."

"Maybe they weren't washed up. Someone might have left them on the beach. A dog might have picked one up."

She looks out to sea, and after a few moments, she laughs.

"What's so funny?"

"We'll never know, will we? How the blue gloves were lost and became separated. It's like my job—trying to reassemble the past. And like Nana Stone's secret. I'll never have all the answers."

"If it's helpful . . ." He pauses, eyebrows raised.

"Go on."

"As an engineer, I think about tolerances when something shocking happens—like discovering your nana's secret. When something in your immediate environment changes, you need to ask yourself if you can live with it. If not, then that implies that your environment has changed beyond your tolerance limit. Which begs the question: Is the tolerance limit you've set . . . actually incorrect?"

She casts a puzzled look at him. What an alien, but intriguing, way of seeing things, she thinks.

He continues. "In *other* words, is this new knowledge about your nana too much to cope with? Or should you change your world view to accommodate this new knowledge, this new environment?" She screws up her face as though she's struggling to translate his words.

"In other words," he repeats, hands outstretched, "is the system broken, or should you change your tolerances?"

She puts her hands on her head. "I can't think straight. I think I've too much on my mind, Ben."

"Like what?"

She slips her arm around his waist. "Sorry. I'm talking too much about me. Let's have a run." She sets off and jogs ahead of him. She uses her hands to vault over a set of timber defences and sprints ahead, then waits for him by the next set of timber posts. He reaches her and stops, panting. "Come on . . . What else is . . . bothering you?"

"I've seen a job I fancy, and I don't know what to do."

"And you can't think straight because of Maximillian."

"And I daren't discuss the job with Poppy. She'd freak out."

She explains that her job at the Academy has taken a sour turn. The Gauguin project, which she didn't want to be involved with in the first place, has leaked. Found its way to the Ministry of Culture in France, no less. And now she's been told to drop her quattrocento work and join the Gauguin team for the foreseeable future, possibly for the rest of her contract. She's in the rearguard.

"Yesterday, the real meltdown started," she says. "The French ambassador in London contacted our vice president, Elodie Maingey. The French are incandescent that Gauguin's being considered for reassessment. They're threatening to cut off all their funding to the Academy. So, you see, it's all politics in the end."

"Who leaked the report?"

"It hardly matters now. It could have been anyone on the Gauguin team. Let's face it: if you've spent a chunk of your career specializing in his work, you're going to be pretty pissed off if his reputation is butchered."

"So what's the other job? It's within the Academy?"

"No. It's a university posting. Not as prestigious as the Academy, but . . ." Her face is alight. "I actually feel the job was created for me. It's a perfect match with my doctorate, and I'd have my own budget for the first time. But the thing is . . . it's in Beijing."

"So . . . ? Beijing isn't Mars."

Ben sticks his head around the door of the New Inn in Winchelsea and reports back. "Looks good. Serves Abbot Ale and Old Speckled Hen, and they do food."

"Beer first? Or the church?" says Toniah.

"Let's do the church."

"Save the best till last?"

"I like churches. And let's walk around the village. I've never seen a place like this—not in this country."

They turn away from the pub and face the thirteenth-century church dedicated to Saint Thomas the Martyr of Canterbury. It stands at the centre of an expansive grassy square with a random scattering of graves. To the left of the square, looking down the village's main street, there's a fine view over marshland to the waters of the English Channel.

Winchelsea has none of the higgledy-piggledy streets typical of settlements dating back hundreds of years. It's laid out on a grid pattern with wide streets. In the tradition of appropriating good ideas from elsewhere, Edward I copied the street pattern from the bastide system in France, from his lands in Aquitaine.

"Saint Thomas the Martyr? That's Thomas Becket, yes?" says Ben. "Slain at the altar."

"'Will no one rid me of this turbulent priest?'"

"One of the history lessons I do remember."

They walk across the square towards the church, which—from the outside—seems to comprise a main nave and two large side chapels, with ruins either side. Toniah comes to halt by a memorial set into the exterior wall. It's the date that pulls her up—1888, one of those marker years that stand out on Toniah's art history timelines. The year that Émile Bernard painted his *Breton Women in the Meadow*. The year that Bernard and Gauguin exhibited with the French avant-garde at the Salon des Indépendants in Paris—when the critic Édouard Dujardin coined a new term for the two men's departure from impressionism. Cloisonnism, referring way back to Byzantine jewellery making, when wires were used to separate areas of colourful enamel. And memorialized here in Winchelsea—in that same year—the twenty-four-year-old son of the local surgeon, who died "after a few hours' illness from cholera at Rawal Pindi, East India." Chiselled in marble. If she were to have a memorial stone, she'd want her name to stand in relief, to have substance.

She adds Rawal Pindi to her timeline marker for 1888. This is how Toniah absorbs world history.

Ben has gone ahead into the church. She makes her way around to the church porch and feels that familiar thrill of anticipation. This is the moment she adores—she turns the circular iron handle and pushes the heavy oak door. What will she find? And in this moment, when the door is open by a crack, she brings to mind, as she always does on the threshold of a church, the marble statue of the Virgin Mary in Venice—she can't remember the name of the church; she should note these things down, but it was *such* a hot day—a statue dressed in real white robes. Adding another layer of macabre gothic, the Virgin Mary's robes were greying.

Today, however, Toniah steps into a field of colour. Ben is already standing at the altar rail, and he slowly turns around, mesmerized. Toniah has never seen so much stained glass in a church of this size, or even in a church *twice* this size. The stone walls seem to melt away. And from the bold geometric style and the intensity of the colour, she guesses the glasswork is a twentieth-century addition.

Three altars are visible from the entrance, plus three ancient tombs, which are set into the wall below three large expanses of stained glass. She and Ben are the only people present. They take separate paths around the church, and Toniah finds herself in front of a window with both swirling and geometric waves, and a boat. For a moment, she interprets the scene as the biblical story of Noah's Ark, but then she realizes it's a more modern scene. It's a sea rescue. Women and children stand on a harbour's edge looking out to sea. Across the bottom panes of glass, there's text painted in black capital letters. It's partly obscured by the window's stonework, but she gets the gist of the story:

> *MEN OF RYE HARBOUR, CREW OF THE*
> *LIFEBOAT MARY STANFORD . . . QUICK TO*
> *HEAR THE CRY OF HUMANITY ABOVE THE*
> *ROARING OF THE SEAS . . . STAYED NOT*
> *TO WEIGH DOUBT OR DANGER BUT . . .*
> *THEIR PORTION IN THIS LIFE FOR THE*
> *RANSOM OF MEN WHOM THEY HAD*
> *NEVER KNOWN . . . WENT BOLDLY INTO*
> *THE LAST OF ALL THEIR STORMS.*

Ben strolls across to stand beside her. "You know, this church is one huge war memorial."

"Except for this window. Look, it's the story of a local lifeboat disaster."

In the pub, over cheese sandwiches and beer, they compare notes; they're each scanning the history of Winchelsea.

"Hellfire. It's been one disaster after another," says Ben. "I didn't realize. All the holidays we had along this coast . . . Listen to this trail of mayhem: French raiding parties, burning and pillaging, the Black Death, drownings—"

"And when you were dead, that was it. No avatars, no photographs. You know, I sometimes feel that Poppy should get an avatar of Mother."

He drains his glass. "I'll get another round."

———

"So what about this job?" he asks when he settles the pint glasses on the table. He sits and knocks the table leg with his knee; beer slops onto the table.

"It's a full-time senior lecturer's post in a new European Studies department, focusing on early women artists and writers. I don't want to apply unless I'm prepared to go. I honestly think I've a good chance of being appointed."

"Would you go if you didn't have to consider Poppy?"

"That's a big *if*."

"It wouldn't be the end of the world. It's not like going to war. Look at those poor sods listed in the church."

"That's what I was thinking. I do feel ready for an adventure."

"If you're asking for my opinion, I'll say this: you're a long time dead."

CHAPTER SEVENTEEN

London, 2015

Fourteen of Toni's friends have each sent her a photograph of a dead relative. She now reckons she'll get an A-plus for her history project. So there's no point in doing any more work on it; she can't do any better than A-plus. She's disappointed that twelve of the fourteen dead relatives are men, though, and only one died outside Europe. She'd like a better spread of photos across the map. And, she admits to herself, she had hoped someone would send her a woman who died in childbirth—to make the point that in the old days, young women didn't have to go to war to end up in a coffin.

From the desk in her bedroom, she looks out onto the back garden. It's a warm evening, and the door to her dad's shed is open—he refuses to call his shed a *studio*. There's a green flag in the beer bottle on his windowsill. A green flag means he can be disturbed. A red flag means don't disturb him unless it's an emergency. A yellow flag means if anyone's going over to see him, bring a cup of tea. Toni suspects he's forgotten his flag system, because the green flag has stood in the bottle for months. In any case, they send texts to one another.

She scrolls through the causes of death: seven died in action in World War I, three in World War II. One drowned in a canal—a woman. One fell from scaffolding. One drowned at sea. One died of diphtheria—a girl, in India. All these deaths happened more than fifty years ago, so she wonders if she could slip in some historical figures; it would be easy to find the names of famous people who died in disasters like the sinking of the *Titanic*. That would give her a pin in the North Atlantic.

But the deaths of her friends' relatives would then seem less important, so she ditches the idea. Her teacher, Mrs. O'Brien, also sent her a photo—it showed her great-uncle in his Royal Navy uniform—and she remembered to write an interesting thing about him: he was the fastest runner in his school. He died in World War II.

Last week, Mrs. O'Brien stopped Toni in the corridor at school and remarked that her history project was "very engaging" but asked if Toni didn't find the subject matter upsetting. Caught off-guard—Toni wasn't sure what Mrs. O'Brien was implying—she blurted, "I'm going to be late for French." Mrs. O'Brien blocked her way and said that anytime Toni wanted a chat, she'd be happy to spend some time with her, maybe during lunch break.

Toni prayed no one overheard this remark and, in desperation, backtracked; she said she found it sad about the little girl in India who died of diphtheria. The last thing Toni wants is anyone in school thinking she's teacher's pet, because someone will *then* call her a bitch. So there's no way she's going to meet Mrs. O'Brien for a lunchtime chat, even though Mrs. O'Brien is her favourite teacher in the whole school. Toni doesn't want to tell her anything private. She reckons all the teachers gossip about the kids when they're in the staffroom.

There's a familiar clattering outside as her dad locks up his shed. He slides a big bolt and fastens the padlock. Toni likes this sound. She jumps up, leans out of her window and shouts, "Want a hand with dinner?"

"No need. I'll barbecue."

That's enough schoolwork for one day, she thinks. She opens her desk drawer and brings out Mr. Lu's aphorism cards and a red notebook, the first page of which is titled "My Life in Aphorisms by Toni Munroe." None of Mr. Lu's cards capture her most recent revelation; namely, that since she started "Toni's History Project—Persons Unknown," she hardly ever stresses about her dad having an accident.

She's struggling to write her own aphorism, and the best so far is this: *Do not waste time imagining improbable disasters, for the worst disasters are always a surprise.* She reckons she can do better; she wants to write something more poetic. She tries again: *Do not waste time imagining improbable disasters, for the worst disasters are beyond imagination.* And again: *Premonitions of disaster are never as shocking as the real thing. To make a premonition is to waste . . .* She doesn't know how to finish that one.

It's far more difficult to write an aphorism than she expected. She writes: *The sign of true genius is making an incredibly complex task look ridiculously easy.*

She hears her dad press the ignition button on the barbecue, and she hopes he makes some veggie skewers; he cooks more red meat than her mum ever did. In fact, she'd like to go vegetarian, but she's holding back from mentioning anything to her dad. What's that phrase she heard recently? Taking . . . ownership. Next time they have a barbecue, she'll tell her dad she'll make veggie skewers.

With her homework finished, she pulls out a plastic storage box from under her bed. She discards the lid and slides her hands under a neatly folded denim jacket—a surprise present from Natalie. She lifts the jacket onto the bed. It's vintage; it's an absolutely brilliant find. Natalie found it in the charity shop near her office. She'd spotted a tangle of unsorted denim in the chaotic sorting room at the back of the shop, and she had the cheek to ask if she could have a rummage.

Toni reckons that Natalie must be psychic, because this jacket's the perfect colour, and it's exactly what she wanted. She smooths her hand across the denim and pokes her little finger through each of the buttonholes in turn. She's going to take her time with this jacket. Not like her first one, which was a size too big in the first place. She didn't realize how much time she'd spend on the project, how much work it would involve. So this time, she's making sure she has the following: the right jacket—cropped and *not* unisex; the right shade of blue—the lightest; the right kind of wear—mainly on the cuffs and collar. And she wants all her ideas sorted out in her head *before* she begins. Because she'll never be happy with the end result if the starting point isn't right. For sure, she'll cut a strip off her mum's psychedelic dress and stitch it to the underside of the collar.

Mainly, though, she wants this jacket to be a memento of her trip to China, so cherry blossoms will have to figure in the design. When she asked her dad if pink and purple embroidery would work against the pale-blue denim, he suggested she do some colour tests with pastel sticks. It wouldn't be his style to say, simply, *yes* or *no*. And her pastel tests are now pinned to her corkboard. She stands in front of them, closes her eyes and counts to sixty in her head, hoping that when she opens her eyes, the best colour combo will jump out.

She opens her eyes and glares at the gaudy, pulsating colours. Purple—it's clear now—is too close to the denim colour, because purple is made by mixing blue and red. But *pink* on pale blue looks a bit flat. She rummages in her box of pastels, finds the purple stick and cleans the end on a piece of scrap paper. She adds a few specks of purple on top of the pink. That's probably the answer, but she'll do some more tests. After all, it's going to take at least a month to embroider a branch of blossoms across the jacket, so she's determined to get it right. The blossoms, she reckons, will start on the back by the waistband, and one branch will curve around and stretch along one arm, and another branch will reach across to the shoulder and curl over, to end roughly by her collarbone.

Her dad whistles from the garden. Her mum would never do that. Instead, she'd call Toni's name up the stairs and shout, "Set the table, please." Toni admits she prefers the whistle; it never sounds impatient. She lays the jacket face down on the bed and imagines the whole design. She fancies sewing a Chinese sword from cloth scraps, and she thinks she'll position it vertically from the collar to the waist. It's likely to look more like a dagger than a sword, but that's all right, she thinks. And she'll embroider birds and musical notes along the blossoming branch to remind her of the music in the trees of the hotel garden in Suzhou. Everyone will think that's cute, but Toni and her dad will know it's a joke. The question is: What species of bird?

Her dad whistles again.

———————

"Sadly, Anna took the hint," says her dad. "So there's no pudding this evening."

"Very funny," says Toni.

He laughs softly, and Toni's smirk softens. There's nothing better than a barbecue before the beginning of true summer.

"Maybe, Dad, you should bake something for Anna. Then she'll know you were serious."

"Serious about baking?"

"What else?" She pulls a face. She can feel herself blush—not because her dad is embarrassing; that's *a given*. She's blushing because whenever she's at home, she imagines her mum can hear everything they say to one another. She's always wondering if her mum thinks they're doing the right or wrong thing. Like, for example, her dad joking about Anna Robecchi. If her mum were standing next to them, would she be smiling about the puddings, or would she think they were being rude and ungrateful? Her mum and Anna were pretty good friends.

"Listen, Toni. I might rent a studio for a month, because this painting for Mr. Lu will be a tight squeeze for the shed. So . . . the point is, I might not be home when you get back from school."

"I'll get on with my homework."

"Good girl. I'll have his painting finished before the summer holidays. Talking of which . . . I have some news."

Toni puts down her knife and fork, sits back and frowns. "Good or bad?"

"I've booked a ferry crossing to France for the first week of your summer holidays. And . . . I've booked a small hotel near Arras."

"Where's Arras? Is there a beach?"

He shakes his head and laughs. "It's near the war graves. I thought we should look for Arthur."

He opens out the map of France and spreads it across the kitchen island. On his laptop, he opens a folder of bookmarked links: several pages on the Commonwealth War Graves Commission, a map showing Arthur's grave with coordinates, hotels in the area, cycle routes between the cemeteries, the Canadian war memorial. He also opens a bunch of files: the cemetery's historical information, the route from the ferry terminal to the small hotel, the hotel's details.

Toni stands with hands on hips. How did he keep all this preplanning to himself? she wonders. She looks at him. Sometimes grown-ups are a real surprise.

"I thought we'd have an adventure instead of going to a beach. We can make picnics and cycle around the countryside."

"Is it hilly?"

"Rolling countryside. Not too hilly. I reckon we'd have a great time."

"But your bike is better than mine. I won't keep up with you."

He taps the side of his nose. "How would *you* . . . like an early birthday present? I thought we could sell your old bike, and"—he looks at her, eyebrows raised—"maybe we should sell your mum's bike, too."

"Would she mind?"

He throws open his hands. "Honestly? What do *you* think?"

She puts her arms around her dad's waist and hugs him tight. "Mum never really liked cycling."

He kisses the top of her head. "And I've taken some books out of the library, novels set in the war—*All Quiet on the Western Front, Birdsong.*"

"So, you're the official tour guide. That makes a change."

———

Dominic can sense that the time is fast approaching when, even on a school night, Toni will no longer go to bed before him. He's looking forward to that particular change in their family dynamic. But at least for now, it's easier to keep a secret. He stands at the bottom of the stairs and listens. She's probably asleep. He goes out into the garden and, as quietly as he can, unlocks the padlock and slides the bolt on his shed door.

In the storage area of the shed, he peers closely at three small oil paintings. They're paintings of the bamboo graffiti that Toni photographed in the Master of the Nets Garden. They're painted on wood panels, and each is the size of a hardback book. Dominic folds his arms, leans back and smiles. It's a long time since he painted something for himself, or at least for someone who wasn't paying. He found them refreshingly quick to paint, because he worked in thick impasto. He *cut* the graffiti with a palette knife, cutting through one layer of paint to a lower layer of a different hue, as though repeating the graffiti artist's cuts. He gently finger-taps a glob of paint. He feels a slight plasticity below the paint's surface skin, but he decides the paint is sufficiently dry to bring them into the house.

In turn, he carries the paintings across the garden. He knows exactly where to place them. In fact, the bamboo paintings will solve the problem of what to do with Connie's shelf by the kitchen table—the shelf that's now bare. It was Connie's shelf from the day they moved into the house; she piled it high with magazines and newspapers, articles she said she'd get around to reading. Dominic would have preferred to put their small collection of Johanne Gerber ceramics on the shelf—the Blue Forest design was his favourite among all the Royal Copenhagen range.

He never actually explained to Connie that the Blue Forest design reminded him of his early days as a painter, when he learned to paint tonally using just two colours—French ultramarine and burnt umber. A small step from drawing towards painting, always a difficult transition. Connie said if she didn't keep the articles handy, she'd never read them. And where better than by the kitchen table, where she could catch up on a bit of reading and relax with a cup of tea?

Now that Dominic has recycled Connie's magazines and newspapers, which he did one evening when Toni was in bed, he can't bring himself to commandeer the shelf for his Blue Forest.

He lifts each bamboo painting into position, sitting them directly on the shelf and leaning them against the wall. He won't construct any frames for these paintings; that wouldn't seem appropriate for the subject matter, for something as informal as graffiti. The middle painting is a close-up of the graffiti; the paint is lumpier. He stands back and decides it dominates too much, so he shifts it to the left. He stands the other two paintings, butted against one another, a few inches to the right. That works, he says to himself. He'll ask Toni for her opinion in the morning. He feels warm because he knows that he and Toni will look at these paintings every morning over breakfast. Even when they're too sleepy to talk to one another, the bamboo paintings will steer their thoughts. Or if not their conscious thoughts, the paintings will steer their *feelings* in a positive direction and remind them that the past is a safe place to visit.

He goes to the fridge, takes out a bottle of beer and sits at the end of the kitchen table. He gazes at the paintings and sips the beer. An hour later, he goes to bed.

CHAPTER EIGHTEEN

Florence, 1469

Gazing at the three portraits, which stand on the narrow table in her bedchamber, Antonia sees it instantly—her skills have improved since her first attempt at her mother's portrait a month ago. She is mixing the pigment and egg binder more consistently, and her brushwork is far more assured; there's less overworking. She sits cross-legged on her bed, her elbows on her knees, her fists planted in her cheeks. She wishes she had painted her mother's portrait last of all, for this is the painting her father will attach to the dowry chest, and to her mind, she should have done a better job. The other two portraits on the table are of her mother's friends, who, on seeing her mother's half-finished portrait, pleaded to have their portraits painted, too. Her father agreed, saying there would be no fee for Antonia's time—the practice would be welcome—as long as they paid for the materials. Neither woman had a portrait of herself; this was an opportunity they couldn't resist.

Antonia can't look at anything in her mother's portrait other than her mother's hand, which rests on the prayer book. It's so frustrating. She painted the prayer book so well, but her mother's fingers look like sausages. For a moment, she considers asking her father for a new wood panel so she might start again, but she knows there isn't time. Instead, she decides she'll block out her mother's hand and repaint it.

Antonia hasn't felt bored for a single moment since she began these paintings. Her aunt's words are even beginning to make sense; maybe she won't notice the simple food if her talent is put to work. In fact, she has already learned that a day spent painting is a day that flies as fast as a sparrow chased by a hawk.

She is keeping the three paintings in her bedchamber, on her father's instruction, until she leaves for the convent in August. She should study the paintings, he said, and learn to be critical of her endeavours; her mother's friends could wait for their portraits. "If they grow impatient, your mother must tell them you're still making subtle adjustments." That, he explained, was another piece of artistic trickery; artists should hold on to their work as long as possible.

When her father listed the necessary materials and quantities—and neither of the women dared to question his estimates—he included a new set of paintbrushes for Antonia. One of the brushes is so fine—with two or three hairs at most—that she can now adjust the hues and tones with great subtlety. Areas of flat colour are brought alive by tiny, thin strokes of paint. From a distance, the strokes are invisible. And much to Antonia's delight, she has pigments to spare. Her father told her to keep them, that she needed to practise with good-quality materials before entering the scriptorium.

Antonia stands up and drags the blanket off her bed. She folds it in half—one, two, three, four times—and places the folded blanket on the floor. She looks up to assess the width of her mother's portrait, which will form the end panel of her dowry chest. How many blankets will the dowry chest take?

Last night in her dreams, she packed and unpacked the chest, time and time again. She woke sweating in the middle of the night with a throbbing head. She struggled to shake off the dream: Jacopa grabbing her arm and shouting, "Where's *my* blanket?"

——————

The smell of beef basted in orange juice and rose-water pervades the house, yet Antonia thumps her growling stomach in annoyance; she wants no distraction. The three portraits now lie on her bed. She moved them from her table so she wouldn't accidentally splash them. Arranged around her on the table are mussel shells containing her ground pigments, a small bowl of egg yolk, two bowls of water, a cloth and a paintbrush. She has set herself a task: to paint each of the colours, as well as she can recall them, from Sister Battista's Book of Hours. Specifically, the colours in her painting of Saint Anthony tortured by devils. Two days ago, Antonia found a poplar panel—no bigger than a prayer book—seemingly discarded in the study. When she asked her father if she could take it, he handed it to her, saying the panel, being so small, was useless to him.

So Antonia prepared the panel with gesso, scraping it back after each coat dried, and this morning, she drew a grid on the beautifully smooth white surface. Each of the squares is about twice the size of her thumbnail. The question is whether she can match the intensity of Sister Battista's colours with the materials at hand. Or does the scriptorium have its own secret methods? She dips her brush in the egg yolk and then in the azurite blue. She mixes them on her palette with a touch of water, then strokes the four sides of a square and infills. In the heat of summer, the paint dries quicker than ever. One perfect square of blue to match the blue bodies of Sister Battista's demons.

Before the pigment dries on her brush, she fills another square. And she repeats this once more to use up the egg and pigment mixture, at which point she washes the brush and moves on to verdigris and malachite for the trees, lead-tin yellow and yellow ochre for Saint Anthony's bell and the demon's clubs, burnt sienna earth for Saint Anthony's robes and vermilion for the demons' wings. Though the paint dries quickly, she paints random squares to avoid two wet squares coming into contact.

An hour later, she cleans her paintbrush, sits back and admires the panel with its twenty-one squares of bright, unmuddied colours. She feels proud that, like her father with his perspective drawings, she has performed her own first experiment.

She hears a familiar sound from the sala. Clara is ringing the triangle with its metal beater—the meal is ready.

———————

"Is this a special occasion, Mother?" says Antonia when she enters the sala. Her mother is already seated. Her father is stood at the head of the table, ready to carve the joint of beef, which Clara has dusted with sugar and herbs.

"It's your father's idea. He sent a message to the workshop telling Donato to eat with us today. He shouldn't be long."

"So, what . . . ?"

"Wait and see," says her father.

Clara brings a steaming bowl of pasta to the table and a platter of boiled capon.

Antonia has noticed over the past two weeks that Clara is making at least one extra dish for each meal. Although Antonia assumes this is for Donato's sake, it now dawns on her that her mother may have another motive—she may be fattening her up before she begins convent life. Her life as a novice will be harder than as a boarder. She'll have more duties, and she'll have to wake for matins in the middle of the night.

She says, tentatively, "Mother, have you decided what you'll pack in my dowry chest? Will there be room for an extra blanket?"

"I've discussed the matter with my aunt—she knows best."

"And I've been thinking, Father. Could you order some poplar panels? I could prepare them and wrap them up carefully in the chest."

He doesn't look up from the carving. "I'm putting a few things aside for you."

Considering that her father has planned this family gathering—assuming Donato turns up—he seems subdued. Antonia looks from her mother to her father, but neither seems eager to have a conversation. So she tries again to engage them. "I've decided to repaint Mother's hand. It's not very good. It spoils the painting."

"Well, you'd better hurry up with it," he says.

It's a curt response, and she blinks away reflexive tears. She wonders if her parents have argued. Silence settles between the three of them, relieved by Clara banging around in the kitchen, and then footsteps on the stairs.

Donato rushes in. "Am I late? What have I missed?" He drags back a chair and sits. He looks ready to arm-wrestle, his legs wide apart, one hand on his hip and an arm resting across the table.

"Antonia is saying she needs to change her mother's portrait," says her father. "I suspect you haven't even started your painting. So, you'd better hurry up, or you'll be racing up the road to Pistoia with your painting as she enters the cloister."

Donato winks at Antonia, but she can't bring herself to smile. Her brother has been in high spirits since his return from Urbino. He has taken on two new assistants, and just last week, he secured a commission from Maria degli Albizzi's husband. It's a fine commission for a set of decorated bedchamber furniture.

He stabs some capon with a fork and looks up, almost triumphant. "I've been thinking, Father. Would you like to visit Urbino with me at the end of summer? You could manage the journey in cooler weather, if we took it slowly."

He replies with a grumbling sound. It comes from deep in his chest. He wipes his hands on his cloth and stares at Donato. He takes several moments to reply. "I'll think about it. Maybe I'll be ready for a change of scene come the autumn."

Antonia looks down into her lap, and the tears well up again.

At the end of their meal, her father stands up from the table and tells them all to follow him to the study. He has something to show them.

His study is tidier than usual. There appears to be a painting on his easel over by the window, covered by a clean sheet. It's clear from the shape of the painting that this is the large panel for the dowry chest. Antonia's heart races. Her father has never unveiled his work to the family before. She glances across to her mother and wills her to smile, but her mother's face appears drained.

Her father walks over to the easel, leans on his walking stick and announces, "This will be my last painting. From now on, I'm devoting all my time to my studies and my drawings. Antonia will take this painting away with her, and I hope she will regard it as my final instruction. Close observation, remember, is the best teacher."

He pulls the cloth to the floor to reveal his hunting scene, and Antonia's first impressions are of colours—bright, shimmering colours that catch the midday light. The flashing red of the riders' fashionable tunics, the yellow-white of the hounds and the exquisite ultramarine of a summer sky.

"Father, it's better than a dream," she says.

Donato folds his arms and grins. "I wouldn't have thought it possible . . . It's better than your night-time hunting scene. And I see you haven't stinted on materials."

For once, her father seems to ignore Donato. "Antonia, tell your mother and Donato how to read this painting, as I've taught you."

She takes a step closer to the painting. She closes her eyes and reminds herself of the elements she must consider. When she opens her eyes, a full minute elapses before she speaks.

"This painting is very wide, and first of all, I notice the hunter on the white horse near the left-hand edge of the painting. And I follow the same white colour across the picture because most of the hounds are also painted in this yellowy white. It's a colour you like, isn't it, Father?" She doesn't wait for an answer.

"A white bird on the right-hand edge is flying up into the oak trees, which form a backdrop to the hunting scene. All these trees have white berries." She takes a deep breath. "The horses and the hounds are much smaller at the far end of the forest than the ones in the foreground. And I feel I am standing in the woodland next to you, Father, with your easel and paints." She peers closely at the foreground. "There are little flecks of blue in the flowers that match the colour of the sky."

"So, in other words, Antonia, I have used colour to unify the painting. In a painting of this shape, it's important to establish order."

She steps back and reassesses the whole. "And now I see—you placed the biggest horses at the edges of the painting." She looks at him, unsure. "Like bookends?"

"Well spotted," says Donato.

Her mother steps forward and points to a figure in the midst of the hunters, who is riding side-saddle. She laughs softly. "It's Clara."

———

Paolo checks through the items spread across his desk. A walnut palette, a mahlstick, a divider, a pestle and mortar—Paolo's *second* largest, since the largest would be too heavy for Antonia—a porphyry grinding slab with a flat-ended muller, three bowls and a handful of mussel and clam shells for holding pigment, an inkpot, and the ivory rack on which he has rested his paintbrushes for all the major commissions of his career. He has selected what he regards as essential equipment; barring breakages, the collection should last Antonia through her time at the convent of San Donato in Polverosa.

The everyday materials she'll need—enough for a year or two's work, he guesses—are piled at the end of his desk: charcoal, chalks, quills, reed pens, ink, lumps of pigment, a selection of papers—mostly undyed—and a sponge for spreading varnish. He adds the small rag cloth he used when painting the hunting scene. It's the cloth he kept for wiping his brushes, now washed, dried and ready to be used again. He turns it over in his fingers, brings it to his mouth and kisses it. And, finally, a small piece of soft leather for erasing chalk and charcoal, though he prefers to use pellets of soft bread, himself. He takes a length of old cloth to wrap up five small poplar panels, coated in gesso, scraped smooth. He feels an ache in his chest, a weariness caused by weeks of stiffened resolve.

Antonia trips into his study. "What's all this? What are you doing, Father?"

"With luck, your mother will make room for all this in your dowry chest. If need be, we can carry it separately to the convent. I've already written to the abbess, and she knows you'll be bringing some items from my workshop. So I don't anticipate any arguments at the gatehouse."

"So will I be allowed to draw and paint whenever—?"

"Antonia, it's a condition attached to the dowry. So don't be apologetic about the time you spend painting. The convent will own your dowry chest one day. I've explained to the abbess that for an artist, the act of painting is a form of meditation. I believe she accepts that notion. Anyway, show me what you've been working on."

"I think it's an experiment." She holds out the painting. "I've painted the colours, from memory, of Sister Battista's Book of Hours."

He takes the painting. His face is a blank. "You should have used a scrap of paper for this."

"I just wanted to paint the colours. Didn't you say I should forget the subject?"

He sighs. He feels deflated. "It was a faulty panel, so there's nothing wasted. But, less of this playtime. Go and work on your mother's portrait, and bring it to me when you're happy with it."

She reaches to take the painting, but he waves her away.

A painting of squared colours, he says to himself. What was she thinking? Maybe this is the way with girls. He shakes his head. She's a clever child, but she should work only on assigned tasks at this age. He takes his quill, dips it in ink and begins a letter to the abbess. He must impress on her that his son will visit the abbess twice yearly for a formal account of Antonia's work. Donato must check that she doesn't lapse into playful ways. And Donato must vet any commission she undertakes before her work leaves the convent. He must safeguard the Uccello name.

This will be his final letter of negotiation with the abbess. He reminds her that the dowry chest will be bequeathed to the convent on Antonia's death, provided that a number of conditions are met during the girl's lifetime. The abbess will allow his daughter to practise her art in her cell without requiring permission from the sister in charge of the scriptorium or from the novicemistress. She will be allocated a cell with sufficient light for this purpose, and all reasonable demands for the supply of pigments and other materials will be met. Antonia must not undertake any silk spinning or help with the production of gold thread, and she must certainly do no gardening or laundry work or any other manual duties that might damage her hands. He recommends, for he must not assume the abbess will reach this decision unprompted, that Antonia should be allowed, when her skills are sufficient, to teach drawing and painting to the boarders and novices.

To sweeten the letter, he points out that the dowry chest will be bequeathed to the convent regardless of how long his daughter serves as a nun before her death. He also states his intention to donate a plot of farmland to the convent, so that Antonia will receive a lifetime annuity based on the land's rental income. He signs off with a final warning:

One day, my daughter will bring prestige to your venerable institution at no substantial cost, but if the conditions of the dowry are not met, I have instructed my son, in the event of my death, to take every measure to retrieve the girl and bring her back to the family.

CHAPTER NINETEEN

Bologna, Italy, 2113

The barista in the corner coffeehouse greets Toniah in Italian and casts a friendly wave.

Toniah stalls. "Wrong language. Won't be a moment."

"Nessun problema. Posso aspettare," says the barista. Unhelpfully, the translation still flashes up in Latin: "Bene est. Possum demorari." Two seconds later, Toniah's retinal translator relaunches with a prompt: *Start anew* or *Return to last spoken*. She chooses *Return to last spoken*, and the English translation appears: "No problem. I can hang around."

Toniah orders her vanilla latte. The barista looks at her suspiciously. "Are you lost? We don't get many tourists around here."

"No. I'm in the right place. I'm here for the church." She twists around and points at the monolithic structure standing diagonally opposite the coffeehouse, across the busy intersection. The church of Corpus Domini is part of a religious complex that spans an entire block in this otherwise unremarkable district of Bologna. Somewhere within the high stone walls—as solid as castle fortifications—lies the convent of the Poor Clares.

"So, you've come to see our mummified saint?"

She nods. "Maybe you can help me. My train leaves in three hours. I've already been to the saint's chapel, and it's locked. I can't see any notice inside the main church about the chapel's opening hours."

"It should open soon—around four o'clock. In fact, when Signora Martelli crosses the road at the pedestrian crossing, there"—the barista points at the side window—"you'll know the chapel is open. She's been praying for years for a miracle cure. It's her legs." She leans across the counter and says, "I don't think Santa Caterina is impressed that she's praying for herself." She turns away, busies herself making the latte and calls over her shoulder, "I'll tell you when I see her."

Toniah sits at a table with a clear view of the pedestrian crossing. She taps the table with her nails. It's so frustrating—to come all this way, and the saint's chapel is closed. On a five-day stopover en route to Beijing, where she'll start her new job, an extra day in Florence might have been more sensible. But Toniah fancied playing a wild card, and so she researched this side trip to Bologna before leaving London. She made the single, *incorrect* assumption that the saint's chapel and the church of Corpus Domini would have the same opening times. It's curious, she thinks. The tourist office doesn't promote the mummified nun—there's barely a mention anywhere. Maybe they think it's ghoulish.

It's evident from photographs that the church authorities have not taken the best care of their saint. Although she's now protected under a glass case, for over six centuries, Caterina was displayed upright in a chair, wearing her nun's habit and surrounded by devotional candles. The candles burned day in, day out, and her exposed skin became blackened by candle soot.

It's Toniah's theory that Antonia Uccello was familiar with the story of this saint—the high-born Caterina dei Vigri as she was then—and that Antonia might have studied her theological writing. Their lives even overlapped, albeit briefly. Caterina's essays—*The Twelve Gardens*,

Treatise of the Seven Spiritual Weapons, The Rosarium and *The Sermons*—
established her reputation as a theologian even among her male peers
in Bologna's professional elite. She was a painter, too.

That would be something, Toniah thinks—to establish that connection; that Antonia was inspired by Caterina. Did Antonia, during
her years in the cloister, read any of Caterina's essays? How unsafe would
it be to assume so? Toniah rechecks the dates on her timeline.

In 1431, Caterina dei Vigri established a convent in Bologna for the
Order of Poor Clares.

In 1463, Caterina died. Antonia was seven or eight years old then,
but she might have heard about the miracle cures at Caterina's graveside. She surely heard from the pulpit that Caterina's body had been
exhumed and found to be incorrupt.

If nothing else, Toniah reckons this visit to Bologna will provide an
entertaining tale for her students in Beijing: a mummified nun in a glass
case. And it takes the edge off her overarching disappointment; she still
hasn't seen the blue-petals painting with her own eyes. She knew before
she left London that the painting had been temporarily withdrawn from
display. It's undergoing forensic examination to confirm the age of the
pigment, and to check for any underpaintings. There's a suspicion that
the sitter's hand has been repainted at least once.

Next time, she'll definitely get to see the painting. If she brings a
group of students back to Italy, she'll also take them to Antonia Uccello's
convent at San Donato in Polverosa, which stands a mile or so north of
the main rail terminus in Florence. There's little of the actual convent
to see; the nun's cells, the scriptorium and the kitchen were redeveloped
for apartments a century ago. But the convent's church is still there. It's
light and airy, simple. At some time in the past, the interior walls were
stripped back to the brickwork, though several sections of fresco were
conserved. These sections were transferred to panels and reattached to
the bare walls. Toniah browses through her images to find one particular detail from the nativity fresco, which she knows Eva will love. She

laughs quietly and sends the image to Eva. It's a close-up of the bottom right corner, and it shows a sleek white hound greeting a rabbit.

"There's Signora Martelli," shouts the barista. "Believe me, the chapel will be open by the time she gets there."

The entrance lies two hundred yards away on the church's windowless edifice on Via Tagliapietre. Toniah brushes her fingertips along the grey stone surface as she follows the limping form of Signora Martelli.

"Splendid isolation," she says under her breath. What a perverse term. She can remember times during her postgraduate studies when a month's isolation might have seemed a blessed gift. But *decades* of incarceration? It's impossible to grasp in today's world. She'll fly around the planet tomorrow, and as soon as she lands in Beijing, she'll contact Poppy and Eva; no doubt she'll chat with them from the airport shuttle. She makes a mental note not to mention the saint's chapel while Eva's within earshot; she might have nightmares. She's upset enough already.

Poppy took the news about Beijing fairly well. She even offered her congratulations. It helped that by the time Toniah received her job offer, Carmen was pregnant, or at least her remote bottle was pregnant. Poppy had something else to latch on to—a new baby to make the household feel more substantial. It was Eva who took the news hard.

The night before she left London, Toniah read a bedtime story to Eva. She felt a wave of regret crash over her as Eva snuggled into her and gripped her arm tight; she'll never forget it. Then Eva buried her face in her pillow. For a young girl who normally had a good deal to say, she seemed at a loss. Maybe, in a crisis, a child can't put the words together. So the following morning, over breakfast, Toniah told Poppy and Eva that she'd pay for them to visit her in Beijing. They must visit during the cherry blossom season, she said, before Carmen's baby is birthed. So now the household has two distractions: a baby and a journey.

In fact, the trickiest conversation Toniah had to broach with Poppy arose from Carmen's pregnancy. Toniah pointed out that she wasn't happy that Poppy had taken a share of legal responsibility for Carmen's baby, as the standby guardian. "God forbid, but if you ever became the child's guardian, where would that place me if you were then to die or become seriously ill?" Toniah explained that although she'd always take care of Eva, Carmen's child was another matter. Poppy simply said she hadn't thought about it, but it was unlikely to come to that. She said, "How many disasters can happen to one child?"

At the church entrance, decorated by a surround of terracotta reliefs, she takes a photograph and messages Ben: *Visiting the mummi-fied nun. I guess . . . you wish you were here!* She smiles. Ben has a month's leave coming up, and he's joining her in Beijing. Initially, she resisted the idea of Ben visiting so soon, but she'd relented; it made sense. He said he'd help with the practicalities while she settles in to the new job. If she's still in temporary accommodation when he arrives, he'll hunt for an apartment—at least do the initial search. And if she's busy with classes, she won't have time to find the best shops and street markets. He has time on his hands, he can afford to visit and she'll be glad of a familiar face.

Inside the church of Corpus Domini, she heads to the side aisle and slips through an open doorway following a small sign: "Santa Caterina." She rushes along a spartan corridor and joins the end of a queue; six adults are filing into the saint's chapel behind Signora Martelli. Three of the visitors are carrying bags of groceries. Toniah shuffles into the back of the small, dark room. There are no pews; it's a shrine rather than a chapel. She immediately feels embarrassed, in this intimate, claustro-phobic space, because she knows she's the only person with no intention of saying prayers. She takes a step back and bides her time. Surely, they'll leave after a few minutes.

Signora Martelli has taken the single-supplicant kneeler at the iron altar rail. Within inches of the rail stands the glass case with the small, seemingly miniaturized, figure of Caterina dei Vigri, her hands in her lap holding upright a silver crucifix. Toniah stands with her arms by her sides.

Caterina dei Vigri—Toniah prefers her secular name—has a sweet face, framed by a white coif below a black veil. What kind of miracles occurred by her graveside? Toniah wonders. How were they attributed to Caterina?

She glances to her right. There's a woman in a blue suit, probably Toniah's age. What on earth is she praying for? A sick relative? A promotion? She seems too young to be asking for a miracle. Not too young to *need* a miracle, but too young to *believe* in them.

Toniah bites her lip to stop herself grinning. Signora Martelli is hamming up her supplication. Her head bows and lifts, bows and lifts, as though her mouth is straining towards the surface of a pool to catch her last breath. She's a distraction, kneeling as she is directly in front of the saint.

After several minutes, one of the standing visitors makes the sign of the cross, picks up his grocery bags and leaves. Toniah steps forward to take his place. She's impressed that these parishioners make time in their days to retreat from the world. Maybe people come to this shrine because it's a place where they can calm their thoughts, a place where they can anchor themselves.

It occurs to Toniah that the closest she ever comes to actual meditation is when she visits a museum. Specifically, there's a painting in Tate Britain that she can't resist. It's a private form of adoration, one she doesn't share—especially not with colleagues, for it's the type of art, dangerously close to sentimental, that lost favour a long time ago. When she sits in front of this painting, she can't find the words to match its emotional pull—it's something about love, tied tightly to the fear of loss. But it's more exalted . . .

Signora Martelli struggles to her feet with the aid of her walking stick. No one steps forward to help. It seems to Toniah they all recognize that Signora Martelli welcomes the pain; she offers her suffering to the saint in the hope that she will intercede on her behalf.

Toniah takes a short step. She falters. There might be a code of etiquette regarding who may kneel at the altar. But she's come a long way for this encounter. She walks forward, kneels at the altar rail and puts her hands together. Slowly, she makes the sign of the cross—Get it right, she tells herself—forehead, stomach, shoulder, shoulder. Amen. She lowers her head and closes her eyes.

Art history has brought her to many strange places, but to date, this is the strangest of all. She takes this moment to formulate a request, but she can't think of anything that requires an actual miracle. It's all a matter of luck, she feels. When she opens her eyes, she finds herself staring at the hem of Caterina dei Vigri's habit. Toniah can't stop herself; she reaches with both hands and presses her fingertips against the glass case, close to Caterina's blackened, sandalled feet.

CHAPTER TWENTY

Fontaine-au-Bois, France, 2015

Long car journeys used to be Toni's pet hate, but it's different now that she sits up front. Driving through France side by side with her dad, with bikes on the bike rack, she feels like an equal partner in a Continental escapade. According to her dad, she's the copilot.

"Man with baguette," says her dad. He points.

"That's four this morning, but we've only spotted one beret."

The window is down, and Toni splays her hand to catch the breeze.

Neither she nor her dad trusts the sat nav to find their destination—a small cemetery in the middle of nowhere. So Toni has a road map in her lap and a printout of the road junction in detail. It's called Cross Roads Cemetery, and it's two or three miles away.

She twists around suddenly, stares out the window behind them. "You've got to stop—"

"I can't just stop—" But he brakes hard, swings the car into the side street on the right and pulls up in a residential parking place. "We're almost at the cemetery. What's so important?"

"You'll love it." She opens the car door. "Come on."

She's well ahead of him. He calls out as he locks the car, "Give me a clue."

"It's purple," she says over her shoulder, and she waves for him to follow.

She turns left at the main road, past a forecourt stacked with marble gravestones, and she heads towards the road junction. Arthur will wait another ten minutes, she thinks. What's ten minutes as a fraction of ninety-seven years?

They're in the small town of Landrecies, the last urban area before the war graves cemetery at Fontaine-au-Bois. She's a couple of paces ahead of her dad when she reaches the junction. She points to the right. He lunges and grabs her shoulder to stop her stepping off the pavement. When he looks along the side road, he sees it, the third house on the right. An advertisement, the kind that covers the entire side of a house. Expanses of purplish-blue and ghosted-white lettering, with burnt sienna brickwork showing through. Evidently delighted, he reads the sign aloud, "DUBONNET."

"I want a close-up photograph. It's the perfect purple."

He keeps his hand on her shoulder as they cross to a triangular traffic island.

"I'll take a snap from here, first," she says.

They cross the road and walk towards the house.

"People collect photos of these ghost advertisements. They'd love this one," he says.

"Ghost advertisements? That's a *thing*?"

He laughs. "They're a leftover from the early days of advertising, before billboards came along. Companies leased the sides of houses and painted their adverts. And when the lease ended, they either repainted the original or painted a new advertisement on top. These days, they're left to the elements, and you sometimes see older advertisements showing through."

They reach the house. The strongest patch of colour on the brick gable end is conveniently close to the pavement, and Toni takes a close-up snap.

"In fact, I think the colour is lapis," her dad says. "Lapis lazuli. The ground pigment is called ultramarine." He leans forward and rubs the paint surface with his index finger. "It's lasted well; the pigment content must be high." He looks at his fingertip, and there's a hint of the lapis. "You could go online and search for the Pantone colour of the old Dubonnet adverts. Some nerd will have blogged about it."

Toni knows about Pantone. Years ago, her mum bought a set of mugs with coloured stripes and Pantone numbers—an arty birthday present for her dad. He liked them, but now everyone's got them.

She stands back and photographs the full gable. The word DUBONNET—in faded, stretched white capitals—is repeated three times at different heights. Two are stacked close together, high on the wall, while the third almost sits on the ground. And each DUBONNET stretches the full width of the brickwork.

"It looks like three different adverts," says Toni.

"It's one advert. I'm sure of it."

"But why did they paint the name Dubonnet three times?"

"It's an old advertising trick. Reinforcement through repetition. Your brain registers the word three times."

"The more you hear a name—"

"The more you remember it. I think the same company made Cinzano, and I've seen one of its adverts. It says, 'Cin Cin Cinzano.' Same kind of idea."

She offers him her phone to see the photos. He swipes through them. "That's a good one. Email it to me, will you? Full size. I'll play around with it."

They walk back to the car. Toni does a skipping walk. Her dad puts his arm around her and kisses her head. She doesn't mind; they're in France—no one knows her. That's the best thing about holidays.

"I have a plan." He slows down and takes a left turn off the main road. They're driving along a country lane that's hardly wide enough for two cars to pass. Toni looks at him, sceptical. "I'm going to park in Bousies. Last year, it won the competition for best-kept village. We can take a look around and then cycle to the cemetery; it's a mile or so from Bousies." Toni wonders if she can trust her dad's estimate of distance. He says, "I thought . . . instead of driving straight to the cemetery, it might be nice if we approached it, you know, at a slower speed." He glances at Toni to gauge her reaction.

"You want to sneak up on it?"

"I've had this image in my head . . . We're cycling around a bend in the road, and we come across the graves in the middle of a field, almost by accident."

Toni nods her head, though she wishes he hadn't used the *accident* word.

"Arthur must have walked around all this area," he says. "He died in the Forest of Mormal, but I can't work out where that is. It can't be far away."

They sit quietly for the rest of the journey to Bousies. Toni looks out across fields planted with maize. She finds it difficult to imagine trenches and bomb craters. She can't picture the mud. She sees a farmhouse in the distance and wonders how it survived. Had other buildings surrounded the farmhouse before the war?

The road through Bousies is lined by hanging baskets heaving with flowers, which reminds Dominic that next year, he'll make more effort with the garden and particularly the patio. He feels he let Toni down this year. Connie always replanted the tubs and baskets during May, but he was too busy when they arrived home from China. Toni hasn't passed comment; maybe kids don't even notice these things. Still, he can't keep everything the same. In one or two ways . . . Hell, he won't say *anything* is better than before, but he's relieved they're finding their own ways of doing things.

Case in point: since he bought the new road bike for Toni, they've been out cycling three Sundays out of the past four. They headed off through the suburban back streets to a different park each Sunday. He's wondering if he and Toni might have regular biking holidays—a fun way for a dad and a young teenage girl to spend time together. And, God knows, he has to look after his health, more so than ever. For Toni's sake.

He lifts the bikes down from the bike rack and checks the contents of his backpack: camera, maps and the basic picnic he bought near their hotel this morning—four croissants plus two fruit tarts, which he hopes will survive intact. As an afterthought, an attempt to elevate his picnicking standards, he grabs some paper tissues from the back seat of the car.

"Sunblock?" he asks. She nods.

Toni stands astride her bike frame. He smiles. She looks the part—cycling shorts, breathable top with reflective strips. He passes her a water bottle to slot on her bike frame. She tightens the string keeping her sunglasses in place; fastens her helmet and tucks in the dangling strap; puts on her fingerless gloves and checks the Velcro fastenings. She's in the moment—he can see that.

"Let's head out, then," he says.

———————

A mile out of town, it dawns on Toni that she's about to do something remarkable. She's only thirteen years old, and she's the one who started this adventure. This was her idea in the first place, even if her dad was the one who made the travel arrangements. If it wasn't for her history project, Arthur would remain stuck in the middle of nowhere, *unvisited*. And now, they're nearly there.

She shifts down a gear for the long, slow incline ahead; the gears are so smooth. She shifts again, and again, as she feels pain rising in her thighs, and then she changes down to her easiest crank gear. She's halfway up the incline, and she still has three gears to spare. Until her dad bought this bike, she thought she was a crap cyclist; she always had to dismount on long hills. Clearly, she needed a lightweight frame and road tyres. Her mum had the wrong kind of bike, too.

Her dad is slowing down. When she reaches him, they cycle side by side. "Got a problem?" she says.

"I want you to see it first, so you go ahead. It's not far. When you come to the junction, there's a house on the right, but look over to your left across the field, and you should see the cemetery."

Within a minute, the house comes into view. She catches sight of the top of a memorial. Then, as she approaches the junction, she sees a low, neat wall around the cemetery and the curved tops of the headstones.

They stop at the junction; the road is narrow, and a muddy quad bike splutters towards them. The driver is a middle-aged man wearing rough clothes and heavy boots. He passes and gives them a barely perceptible nod. Toni sets off, standing on her pedals. At the cemetery, she leaps off her bike.

There's no boundary wall at the front of the cemetery—just a newly mown grass verge, which is inset with wide stone steps leading up to the graves. It's so unlike English church cemeteries, with their weathered and leaning headstones. The headstones here are a yellowy white; the lettering and insignia are sharp, as though carved yesterday. And a neatly clipped, flowering shrub, tended by the war graves' gardeners, nestles in front of each headstone. A wide, grassy path separates two sets of graves.

Toni looks across the cemetery to the surrounding fields and to a far distant horizon. She turns, and her dad is fishing a piece of paper from his backpack. "Where's Arthur?" she calls.

"Row H."

She finds the row and walks slowly along the line of graves: Lancashire Regiment, Royal Army Medical Corps, Coldstream Guards, New Zealand Rifle Brigade, Lancashire Fusiliers, Royal Field Artillery, Essex Regiment, Gloucestershire Regiment, Somerset Light Infantry, Royal Welch Fusiliers and then Manchester Regiment. Not the first one, but the third Manchester Regiment headstone: "PRIVATE A. GEORGE." At the foot of the headstone is a small rosebush with orange buds.

Her dad joins her. "You found him," he says.

———————

Toni and her dad have walked along every row of graves. In case, as Toni said, there was another soldier who had never had a visitor. Toni tried to speak the name of each soldier in her head, but there were so many—over six hundred.

Her dad says this is small compared to most of the war grave cemeteries. What stabs Toni's heart is that all these soldiers died within a month of one another, between early October and the eleventh of November, 1918, when the armistice was signed. Arthur died on the fourth.

She's pleased Arthur has a beautiful resting place, though she knows it's a stupid thing to think; it's not as though he can see this lovely view. A tractor trundles past. She likes the idea that the soldiers have some company; everyday farming chores are going on around them. And she wonders if the tractor driver's family has lived in this area for a long time. Maybe they farmed this land before World War I. They'll have different stories to tell, she thinks, but she can't imagine how they would start or end.

Toni wanders to the end of the cemetery to a small brick shed. She looks through a grill and sees garden implements. She turns, and at the end of a line of headstones, set against the back boundary wall, she notices two that are slightly set apart. "Dad," she shouts. "You've got to see this."

Chinese characters are carved into the two headstones. English words, too. At the base of each: "CHINESE LABOUR CORPS." But each one has its own epitaph: "A GOOD REPUTATION ENDURES FOREVER" and "THOUGH DEAD HE STILL LIVETH."

Her dad stands beside her.

"Isn't that sweet?" she says, pointing at the miniature bamboo planted between the two graves. "Isn't that kind?" She doesn't understand why her eyes are filling with tears. It seems she's more upset about the dead Chinese labourers than about her own great-great-uncle.

"It's a shame we can't read their names. And look at the dates," says her dad. "They died after the war ended. This one died three days after the armistice, and this one died in the following year. I suppose they died in accidents."

"They're such a long way from home. Photograph them, Dad, and send the photos to Mr. Lu. Send them home that way."

They sit cross-legged on the grass in front of Arthur's headstone, and her dad lifts the bag of croissants from his backpack.

"Do you think anyone will mind?" says Toni.

"No one's going to see. Anyway, Arthur wants us to stay awhile. He can join our picnic."

"Next time we come here, we should bring a little flag and put it in the ground by his grave," she says. "Like other visitors have done. I didn't think about leaving something."

He pulls a face. "It seems a shame to leave anything plastic. I'll paint a flag on a stone."

"You know what's amazing? If we drove away from our house immediately after breakfast and drove straight to Dover, and straight on a ferry, we'd be here by early afternoon."

"We've actually driven within half an hour of this spot in the past, on our way south. It's a real shame we didn't come with your mum."

"We can tell Natalie how to get here," says Toni immediately. It's sad enough without bringing her mum into it.

Toni takes a selfie in front of Arthur's headstone. Her dad picks up his camera. "Let's do this properly. Stand behind the grave." He stands and frames the picture. "That's great. I've got you and the headstone, most of the cemetery and a long view towards the woods in the far distance."

Toni places her fingertips on the top of Arthur's headstone, and her dad takes the shot.

———

Rolling countryside isn't the right description, Toni decides, because the hills are nothing like a roller-coaster. The inclines are ridiculously long, but they're gentle. And she loves the French country lanes—they're far better than English ones, because she can see for miles; there are no hedges to block the view.

Since leaving the Cross Roads Cemetery, they've cycled to three more war grave sites. She made her dad put a circle on the map for each cemetery so that when they return to London, she can start a new history project with exact location details.

They stop for a breather, and Toni takes a swig from her water bottle. Her dad opens out the map across his handlebars. Then he lifts it up for a closer look. Toni knows he's looking at the contour lines. He doesn't want to put her off cycling by choosing a tough route. He needn't worry so much. She reckons cycling is going to be her next big hobby, and she's considering a new embroidery project, too. This time, she'll pimp up a sleeveless denim jacket, which will be easier to wear when she's cycling.

Her dad says that when they reach the top of the hill—the one with the wind turbine—they'll eat the fruit tarts. She reads the implication: it's a killer hill.

Refreshed, they mount their bikes, and Toni sets off ahead of her dad. She prefers to lead. But on the long rise, he overtakes her and steadily pulls away. The wind turbine isn't far now. Toni is cycling slowly on her lowest crank gear.

She tightens her grip on the handlebars and tucks in her chin. She breaks into a sweat. Her dad's so much stronger; it's no effort for him. She looks up. She can't bear to see her dad so far in the distance. If he were to have an accident, she'd see it happen right in front of her eyes. There'd be nothing she could do. She could shout to warn him, but he wouldn't hear. Her French isn't good enough to call for an ambulance, and in any case, her phone won't have a signal. And she doesn't know the password for her dad's phone.

There's a pothole in the road, and Toni rides straight into it, jarring her arms; her teeth nip the side of her tongue. Her eyes fill with tears, but she blinks them away. She wipes her face with one hand and keeps pedalling. Don't be stupid, she thinks. She looks up again; her dad has stopped at the top of the hill. He rests his bike on the ground and waves. The wind turbine towers above him, and the blades sweep through the perfect blue sky.

It's not going to happen, she tells herself. The turbine blade will not shear off and fall on him; he won't step on an unexploded mortar shell; a tractor won't come over the brow of the hill and flatten him. Everything is normal. Totally.

CHAPTER TWENTY-ONE

Florence, 1469

With heavy hammer blows, Donato nails his panel into the dowry chest; his self-portrait faces *into* the chest. Antonia reaches to grab his arm. She tries to call out: Don't be a fool, Brother. The words stick in her throat. She awakens and realizes that one of two knocking sounds has prompted her dream; loose roof tiles are clacking in the wind, and there's a tapping on her cell door. She leaps out of bed and opens the door by a crack, though she knows the visitor must be Jacopa.

"I can't believe you've slept through this din. You'll be late for lauds," Jacopa whispers. She waits on the threshold of the cell while Antonia throws on her robe, then eases the door open and squeezes into the cell. The cell is cramped, because the abbess decided last week that Antonia needed a desk. She instructed Antonia that any commissions should be painted in her cell, in isolation, away from the prying eyes of other novices and the servants. Portraits, she said, were too personal to be kept in the workroom for all and sundry to see.

Even in the early-morning gloom, a spillage of paint-stained water is visible on the floor by the side of her desk. Above the desk, new paint flecks have appeared on the wall. Papers, chalks, shells and bowls are scattered across the desk's surface. Jacopa steps up to Antonia and straightens the young girl's robe. "You've been working half the night, haven't you? You'll lose your eyesight before you take the veil. I'll mop up the spillages after lauds."

Antonia smiles at the realization that one blanket, one act of kindness, has forged such a friendship, such loyalty. Jacopa checks her cell every morning to see if Antonia has heard the chapel bells and is dressed and ready for daybreak prayers. Antonia is grateful. She loves to sleep until Jacopa's tapping at the door; if she wakes beforehand, unwelcome thoughts creep into her mind. About home. She imagines that Clara will be starting the fire in the kitchen. She imagines the sparrows and blackcaps warbling in the honeysuckle in the courtyard.

"I like working at night," she says. "The abbess told me it's God's gift . . . that I need so little sleep."

Jacopa listens at the door. She looks over her shoulder at Antonia. "If it's such a gift, why do you have dark rings around your eyes?"

Antonia slowly pushes her fingers through her short-cropped hair, hoping to discover that during the night her hair had regrown. She ties her novice's headscarf. "I get so much done in the night—when I'm not jumping up every five minutes to say prayers. I wish I could do all my praying in the morning and then paint for the rest of the day." She turns to her desk, gathers her night's work and takes it over to her dowry chest, which is covered by a cloth for protection. She pushes the cloth aside, lifts the lid an inch and slips the papers inside. She doubts the abbess would approve of these colour exercises any more than her father did.

"You weren't working on the girl's portrait, then?" says Jacopa.

"The candlelight's too dim for that."

Jacopa puts a finger to her lips, and they leave the cell. They make their way, in step, swiftly and silently, downstairs to the Great Cloister, on to the small courtyard and towards the chapel, which forms the segregated choir of the public church. Antonia has walked this same path with her great-aunt, hand in hand, so many times at daybreak. As a young boarder, she often crept to her aunt's cell in the night and shared her bed. At first, it was homesickness that kept her awake in the dormitory, but as time went on, her sleeplessness became fixed, unshakable. She always found sleep in her aunt's bed, and during the darkest hour of the night, when her aunt slipped away for matins, Antonia kept the bed warm.

As a novice, Antonia has learned to embrace her sleeplessness. She feels free to dabble with her own experiments using the pigments and papers provided by her father. After all, if God expects their community to sleep between evening compline and matins, she feels she may spend the time as she pleases. She tells herself she is painting as a form of meditation; it's something she recalls her father once saying. And during her painting vigils, she finds the convent's silence perfectly natural. It's the daytime silence she finds oppressive, when the noises of the outside world penetrate the convent, teasing and tempting her to cough, to hum a tune.

So the pattern of her night-times is established; she works until matins and sleeps for three hours between matins and lauds.

As they reach the chapel, Jacopa pushes Antonia ahead of her, so that if anyone gets the blame for being tardy, it will be the servant and not the novice.

Though she's bone-tired, Antonia prefers these daybreak prayers to any later in the day. With her mind still lingering at the edge of her dreams, and before the duties of the day invade her thoughts, she finds that the questions she took with her to bed tend to answer themselves, as though an angel listens to her thoughts as she falls asleep, and whispers a resolution in her ear at lauds.

This morning, as she recites familiar psalms that require little concentration, she reflects on the coloured grid she painted last night. A moment of clarity seems within reach. The angel whispers: there's no reason she should only paint squares. She may paint any shape she likes. Odd shapes. Like the glass artist who pours colour and then binds his pools of pure vermilion, pure azurite, with lead strips. She holds this thought and hopes she won't lose it before nightfall.

Following noon prayers, the convent community gathers in the refectory for the main meal of the day. It is the turn of Sister Innocence, the novicemistress, to read a religious text.

"Beloved sisters, open up your hearts and take heed of the holy teaching of Caterina dei Vigri, abbess of the Poor Clares in Bologna, God rest her soul. Allow Caterina to guide you towards sanctification, today and through all your days, through quiet contemplation of her *Seven Spiritual Weapons*.

"One: always take care to do good.

"Two: remember that we can never achieve anything truly good by ourselves.

"Three: trust in God, for we should never fear the battle against evil, either in the world or in ourselves.

"Four: meditate frequently on the life of Jesus.

"Five: remember that we must die.

"Six: remember the benefits of heaven.

"Seven: let the Holy Scripture guide all our thoughts and deeds."

None of the weapons sound remarkable to Antonia, and she wonders why Caterina should need to write them down. She looks up from her broth, but Sister Innocence sees her and with a scowl instructs her to look down. She immediately bows her head, but the table seems to shift sideways. Her head swims. Too little sleep, an empty stomach.

"Today, we will consider Caterina's fifth spiritual weapon," Sister Innocence continues. "Remember that we must die." She continues to recite Caterina's lengthy exposition on death and dying, but Antonia concentrates on her bean broth, which is thick, and hot, and contains large chunks of carrot. If she eats quickly, she'll feel better, revived, and she'll be less likely to faint.

Her tiredness has already landed her in trouble. For last week, she confessed to the abbess that she had catnapped in her cell while working on the portrait of Maria degli Albizzi's granddaughter. Her tiredness was the result, she told the abbess, of concentrating so hard on drawing the outline of the composition. She confessed, specifically, that she sat back to assess the outline and allowed her eyelids to close, and that she awoke because of her own loud snoring.

She made the admission out of anxiety—that someone had heard her snoring and might denounce her to the abbess. Rather than rebuke her for the catnap, the abbess inquired if she was satisfied with the composition. As an afterthought, it seemed, the abbess punished her for succumbing to tiredness, instructing her to attend early prayers before vespers.

Sister Innocence is evidently inspired by the fifth spiritual weapon. She adds great emphasis to each of Caterina's shorter sentences. Antonia stalls, her spoon almost touching her lips, as Sister Innocence announces, "Let us do good while we have time." Antonia's heart beats hard. Yes, she wants to do good. Good *work*, that is. Good *painting*. The refectory table seems to shift again. She drops her head low as if in prayer, and she breathes deeply. She must not faint.

"From my memory of the girl, it seems a fair likeness," says the abbess. She peers down at the portrait on Antonia's desk. "Is it finished? The girl's grandmother grows impatient."

"I'm sorry, Mother Abbess, but I still have work to do. The final adjustments . . ." She feels herself blush. "My father taught me not to rush."

"Then I shall tell Maria degli Albizzi that the portrait is progressing well. Before I release the portrait to the family, I will need your brother's approval. I shall write to him and request his attendance in the parlour in . . . ?" She looks to Antonia and raises her eyebrows. "Surely, two weeks will give you sufficient time."

Antonia nods, embarrassed to be in negotiation with the abbess.

"If everyone is happy with your work, I will invite other parents to commission portraits. If their daughters are boarding here, it would be a convenient opportunity for all concerned." The abbess turns to leave, but hesitates. She looks back. "Antonia, have you slept at all this past week?"

She sits in the candlelight in her cell and casts her thoughts back to her father's lessons. Colour is such a puzzle. She wishes she could ask her father for one more lesson. She closes her eyes and tries to tease out from all his lessons the specific points he made about colour.

He told her that terre-verte created a muted effect in his painting of Noah and the flood, that terre-verte unified his entire fresco cycle in the cloister of Santa Maria Novella. And he often painted elements in his composition in a white colour tinged with yellow; in *The Battle of San Romano*, he used this colour for the horse, the lance, the soldiers' hose. It emphasized his composition. And he used this same colour, as well as blue, in the same manner for the hunting scene on her dowry chest; it unified the composition of a long panel painting.

She can't remember her father ever talking about colour for its own sake. With hindsight, she sees that the composition always came first for him. The composition, and the story.

She spreads out her five small paintings. Since her angel whispered to her a week ago, Antonia has worked hard each night, and now she assesses the results. She touches the paintings, lightly, as though her fingertips might divine some insight. In one painting, she created a twisting pattern of coloured shapes. In another, she made triangular shapes of colour. And in another, she combined circles of different sizes. The coloured shapes touch without any paint bleeding across to infect their neighbours. Each colour is pure. In the last two of the five paintings, she repeated the twisting pattern, using different combinations of colours.

Antonia tidies her mussel shells of pigment into a neat row. She notices she's running low on vermilion and azurite—she'll need to pound and grind some more tomorrow. There's still a full shell of boneblack; she picks it up and cups the shell in the palm of her left hand. She frowns and looks back at her paintings. Her favourite paintbrush is propped against her father's ivory rest. She picks up the brush, mixes some of the pigment with egg yolk, adds a touch of water and strokes a thick line of boneblack around the edge of a vermilion triangle. She continues to stroke the paint until the painting becomes a black swamp with isolated, shimmering pools of pure colour. She repeats this for a second painting, and as she does so, she smiles and recalls her father's warning: *First and foremost, you must enjoy loading your paintbrush with paint.*

She sits back in her chair. She feels tired, ready at last to slip into sleep. In this muzzy state, she takes hold of the two paintings transformed by the black lines, and it strikes her that one of the paintings makes her feel sad, whereas another makes her feel joyful. She wonders if colours are like letters; they spell out a word, a feeling, if arranged in the right order. This thought creeps into bed with her, and as she drifts into sleep, she wonders if she'll glean an answer to this question in her dreams, or if a revelation might come during lauds.

It seems only moments later that she hears the tapping at her door. She wakes in the morning gloom, reaches for her robe and whips it around to throw it over her head. But the action is too hasty, and the edge of the heavy material catches the water bowl on the edge of her desk. The bowl smashes against the wall; paint-stained water splatters across the white plaster and falls in long drips to the cold stone floor.

The cell door opens; it's Jacopa. At the sight of a spectacularly drenched wall, she clamps her hands over her mouth to smother laughter.

Antonia, stupefied, slowly straightens her robe.

Jacopa says, "Leave the mess. I'll clean it up after prayers. Come, let's not be late."

Antonia pushes her fingers through her close-cropped hair, ties her novice's headscarf. She turns to her desk, gathers her small paintings, unscathed by the disaster, and takes them to her dowry chest. She lifts the lid an inch and slips the papers inside.

"Hurry, now," says Jacopa.

Antonia takes three quick steps across her cell but falters as her hand touches the door. She looks over her shoulder and stares, transfixed by the glorious drips and splatters.

AUTHOR'S HISTORICAL NOTE

Antonia Uccello, the daughter of Tomasa di Benedetto Malifici and Paolo Uccello, was born in Florence in 1456. Her older brother was named Donato. Antonia entered the convent of San Donato in Polverosa outside the city walls of Florence, most likely before her thirteenth birthday. The painters' guild recorded Antonia as a *pittoressa*—a painter—on her death certificate dated 9 February 1490. This is all we know about the life of Antonia Uccello. None of her work is known to have survived.

Paolo Uccello was an innovator in creating the illusion of three-dimensional space through the use of linear perspective, and he became well known for his depictions of storms, battles, dragons and wild animals. Antonia was born when Paolo was aged around fifty-nine. His last known painting is a night-time hunting scene, *The Hunt in the Forest*.

It was commonplace for wealthy Italian families to board their daughters at convents for their education. The high cost of marriage dowries in Renaissance Italy often resulted in fathers allowing only their eldest daughters to marry. Such was the fear of any gossip being attached to younger daughters that they were packed off at an early age to convents to become "brides of Christ." I was fascinated to learn that convents were important civic institutions and took a decisive role in the commercial life of Florence. The abbess of a convent was a key player in a complex web of social and power-based relationships within the city. And families vied to place their daughters in convents with high status so that important family connections in the outside world were mirrored and enhanced within the cloisters.

It took me several years to work out how to combine my interests in art history, science and fiction writing with my experience of actually making art; this novel is my first published attempt. With hindsight, I realize that the exhibition *Maurice Denis, 1870–1943* at Liverpool's Walker Art Gallery in 1995 sparked my enduring fascination with those painters at the end of the nineteenth century who rejected realism in art. Subsequently, I researched how some of those modernists (Émile Bernard, Maurice Denis, Paul Sérusier, André Derain) were influenced by the early Italian painters of the quattrocento. I visited Italy as often as possible, and naturally, it was no hardship when I felt obliged to return to Florence for this novel. I had to visit Antonia's convent—the location of which I discovered in the tiniest of footnotes in Sharon T. Strocchia's *Nuns and Nunneries in Renaissance Florence*.

Although the convent of San Donato in Polverosa has recently been converted to apartments—and a large H&M store now stands opposite—the public church attached to the convent is still a place of worship. Cenni di Francesco's nativity fresco, *The Adoration of the Magi*, adorns the nave. It's in a good state of preservation, considering it was painted almost 750 years ago—in 1383, to be precise. I like to imagine that Antonia Uccello herself spent many hours in quiet contemplation of this truly engaging fresco.

Few women painters are known from the early Italian Renaissance in Italy, and most were nuns, including Maria Ormani, Caterina dei Vigri, Barbara Ragnoni and, of course, Antonia Uccello. Plautilla Nelli is the best known of the nun painters of the Renaissance, and her astonishingly modern *Lamentation with Saints*—restored in 2006—is now on display in the great refectory of San Marco Museum in Florence.

I visited Bologna to see the remarkable saint's chapel that displays the mummified remains of Caterina dei Vigri. Respected in her own lifetime as a writer and painter, she became the abbess of the convent of the Poor Clares in Bologna. Later in the Renaissance, a few Italian women artists did gain public recognition. In some cases, these painters were the daughters of male artists, and they worked within their fathers' studios. Among the best known of these Italian artists are Fede Galizia, Sofanisba Anguissola and her sister Lucia, Marietta Tintoretto, Lavinia Fontana, Artemisia Gentileschi and Elisabetta Sirani.

On a personal historical note, my great-aunt's fiancé died during the final days of World War I, and he is buried at the Cross Roads Cemetery at Fontaine-au-Bois in France. It has always struck me that there is a missing side to our family, since my aunt did not marry until later in life, and she didn't have children. I visited the cemetery for the first time while writing this novel, having just delved into the family archive. In the row of graves farthest from the cemetery entrance, there are headstones for two men of the Chinese Labour Corps. Miniature bamboo is planted between their headstones. Both men came from the modern-day Chinese province of Shandong.

ACKNOWLEDGMENTS

I take great pleasure in thanking Alexandra Jungwirth and Robert Charnock for their kindness in helping me to plan my research trip to Shanghai and Suzhou, and for making my stay in China so enjoyable. My thanks also to Wang Yu Hong and Wang Xingyi for their generous hospitality and assistance. I am also grateful to friends and family who read my manuscript at various stages of completion. In particular I thank three members of the Charnock family—Garry, Robert and Adam—Andrew Fletcher, Neve Maslakovic and Jacqui Nevin.

During the development of this novel, I received invaluable guidance from my editor, Jason Kirk, at 47North. I am immensely grateful to Jason for his sustained support and enthusiasm for this writing project. My thanks also to Britt Rogers, Ben Smith and each member of the 47North publishing team; they are all delightful.

I always enjoy the research element of writing fiction, and I'm pleased to thank Aarathi Prasad for our fascinating conversation about the future of human-reproduction technologies. I heartily recommend Aarathi's fascinating book *Like a Virgin—How Science Is Redesigning the Rules of Sex*.

This novel makes some sense of my meandering career, which has taken me from science journalism and photography to a fine art practice. I'm grateful to my former studio colleague Fiona Curran for encouraging me to start this novel at a time when I was hesitant.

Thanks to the many enthusiasts who write excellent websites and blogs on subjects as diverse as medieval writing, ghost advertisements and the customization of denim jackets. And thanks to Lise den Brok of Historypin.

The extract from Laura Cereta's "A Letter to Bibulus Sempronius: A Defense of the Liberal Instruction of Women" (in *Her Immaculate Hand, Selected Works by and about the Women Humanists of Quattrocento Italy*, edited by Margaret L. King and Albert Rabil Jr.) is reproduced by kind permission of the Arizona Center for Medieval & Renaissance Studies.

My thanks also to Cheng Jia Wen for her translation of the Chinese inscriptions on two headstones at Cross Roads Cemetery.

My special thanks are reserved for Garry—always my first reader and my travelling companion on every journey.

BIBLIOGRAPHY

Painting and images referred to in this novel can be viewed on Anne Charnock's Pinterest page: www.pinterest.com/annecharnock.

Bartlett, Kenneth. *The Civilization of the Italian Renaissance: A Sourcebook.* 2nd ed. Toronto, ON: University of Toronto Press, 2011.

Burke, Peter. *The Italian Renaissance: Culture and Society in Italy.* 3rd ed. Cambridge, UK: Polity Press, 2014.

Cennini, Cennino d'Andrea. *The Craftsman's Handbook—The Italian "Il Libro dell' Arte."* 2nd ed. Translated by Daniel V. Thompson Jr. New York: Dover Publications, 1954.

Cereta, Laura. "A Letter to Bibulus Sempronius: A Defense of the Liberal Instruction of Women." In *Her Immaculate Hand: Selected Works by and about the Women Humanists of Quattrocento Italy,* edited by Margaret L. King and Albert Rabil Jr., 81–84. Asheville, NC: Pegasus, 2000.

Chadwick, Whitney. *Women, Art, and Society.* London: Thames & Hudson, 2012.

Cogeval, Guy, Claire Denis, and Thérèse Barruel. *Maurice Denis,*

1870–1943. Ghent: Snoeck-Ducaju & Zoon, 1994.

Currie, Elizabeth. *Inside the Renaissance House.* London: V&A Publications, 2006.

Evangelisti, Silvia. *Nuns: A History of Convent Life.* Oxford: Oxford University Press, 2007.

Ferrier, Jean-Louis. *The Fauves: The Reign of Colour.* Paris: Pierre Terrail, 1995.

Frèches-Thory, Claire, and Antoine Terrasse. *The Nabis, Bonnard, Vuillard and their Circle.* Paris: Flammarion, 1990.

Gauguin et l'Ecole de Pont-Aven. Edited by Catherine Puget, Denise Delouche, Richard Robson Brettell and Ronald Pickvance. Pont-Aven: Musée de Pont-Aven, 1997. Exhibition catalog.

Gayford, Martin. *The Yellow House: Van Gogh, Gauguin, and Nine Turbulent Weeks in Provence.* London: Penguin Fig Tree, 2006.

Hudson, Hugh. *Paolo Uccello—Artist of the Florentine Renaissance Republic.* Saarbrücken: VDM Verlag, 2008.

Hughes, Robert. *Nothing if Not Critical, Selected Essays on Art and Artists.* London: The Harvill Press, 1995.

King, Margaret L., and Albert Rabil Jr., eds. *Her Immaculate Hand: Selected Works by and about the Women Humanists of Quattrocento Italy.* Asheville, NC: Pegasus, 2000.

Niccolini, Sister Giustina. *The Chronicle of Le Murate.* The Other Voice in Early Modern Europe: The Toronto Series, vol. 12. Translated and edited by Saundra Weddle. Toronto, ON: Iter and the Centre for Reformation and Renaissance Studies, Victoria University in the University of Toronto.

Perry, Gill, Charles Harrison, and Francis Frascina. *Primitivism, Cubism, Abstraction: The Early Twentieth Century.* New Haven, CT: Yale University Press with The Open University, 1993.

Pope-Hennessy, John. *Uccello: The Complete Work of the Great Florentine Painter.* London: Phaidon, 1950.

Prasad, Aarathi. *Like a Virgin—How Science Is Redesigning the Rules of Sex.* Oxford: Oneworld Publications, 2012.

Saville, Malcolm. *The Story of Winchelsea Church.* Lewes: East Sussex County Library, 1986.

Stevens, MaryAnne. Émile **Bernard** 1868–*1941: A Pioneer of Modern Art.* Zwolle, Netherlands: Waanders Publishers, 1990.

Strocchia, Sharon T. *Nuns and Nunneries in Renaissance Florence.* Baltimore, MD: The Johns Hopkins University Press, 2009.

Tillotson, Dianne. Medieval Writing: History, Heritage and Data Source. Last modified November 22, 2014. http://medievalwriting.50megs.com/.

Vasari, Giorgio. *Lives of the Artists: Volume 1.* Translated by George Bull. London: Penguin Books, 1987.

Welch, Evelyn. *Art and Society in Italy 1350–1500.* Oxford: Oxford University Press, 1997.

Whistler, Catherine. *Paolo Uccello's The Hunt in the Forest.* Oxford: Ashmolean Museum, 2010.

AN EXCERPT FROM ANNE CHARNOCK'S

A Calculated Life

CHAPTER ONE

The second-smallest stick insect lay askew and lifeless on the trails of ivy. Jayna lifted the mesh cover, nudged the foliage with her middle finger, and the corpse dropped to the cage floor. It made no sense. The smallest of the brood, the outlier, should have died first. Why this one, the second smallest? She glanced at the temperature monitor. Surely, it wasn't her fault? And it couldn't be the food—she turned over a leaf—or they would all be ill by now. So what exactly . . . ? The surviving insects shuddered indifferently.

Jayna placed the cover back on its base. One thing was certain. An autopsy was out of the question; she had no scalpels. In any case, she thought, it was a fact: in the normal run of things, people had autopsies; insects did not. She pushed a hand through her hair. One dead stick insect and now she was running two minutes late for breakfast. That's all the death amounted to—a slight delay in her morning routine. The death would remain a mystery. No ripple of concern, no cascade of grief. She peered into the cage at the still-smallest stick insect.

"Maybe you're . . . just lucky," she murmured.

* * *

Jayna left Rest Station C7 with her friend Julie and together they headed towards the tower blocks of downtown Manchester. They looked like schoolgirls, holding their packed lunches and wearing identical office garb.

"Why would the smallest, feeblest one survive longer?" said Jayna.

"Was it feeble? Perhaps it was just . . . small," said Julie.

By the time they reached the Vimto sculpture on Granby Row, Jayna had scanned through the data she'd compiled over the past three months on the eating habits of her stick insects, their rates of growth, their response to stimuli—light, heat, and touch—morning and evening activity rates . . . thirteen variables in all. She plotted against time, overlaid the graphs, and compared. No help at all.

"I kept a close eye on them all but I only took measurements for two—the two closest to average size," said Jayna.

"Hmm. Mistake."

The morning street projections let rip with the usual inducements— half-price breakfast deals, lunchtime soup 'n' sushi specials. Julie peeled off northwards. Jayna, still perplexed, pressed ahead and pulled up sixteen data sets culled over recent weeks from a slew of enthusiasts' forums and from academic studies by the Bangalore Environmental Research Institute. Rates of growth, population size, mortality figures; it was all there. She plotted the longevity of stick insects against their size at death, and regressed the data. The correlation with size was . . . heck, weaker than she'd imagined. She tripped on a raised paving flag. And as for luck, she thought, the tiniest survivor in mind, that was without doubt a dumbed-down term referring to randomness.

On entering the high atrium of the Grace Hopper Building, she walked under the turquoise-leaved palms and bit her lip. She pushed the Bangalore data from her mind and considered her Monday schedule as she stepped to the back of the elevator. The doors closed with a whoosh-chang! and she tapped the back of her head against the elevator panel.

Time to think straight. How should she handle her entrance? Act as though nothing had happened on Friday? Walk straight past Eloise? Or should she apologize without any delay? It was just too awkward . . . and confusing. She hoped Eloise had calmed down over the weekend. According to Benjamin, it was a simple misjudgment. "A minor faux pas"—his exact words. The elevator doors opened and she stepped out. She was relieved Benjamin had said minor. A bit of a faux pas would be worse, definitely.

Pushing open the office door, she came to a decision. She would keep quiet, hope for the best.

Eloise jumped up, lifted a hand—not exactly a wave—and scuffled across the analysts' floor at Mayhew McCline to intercept Jayna. "Tea!" she said, and pulled Jayna towards the kitchen galley. "Listen, I'm sorry about Friday."

"No. I'm the one who's sorry, Eloise. How was your father?"

"You were right. No real panic. He was comfortable and sedated when I got there."

"You were worried. I wasn't—"

"I overreacted. I didn't mean it."

"Is he still in hospital?"

"Yes, should be home tomorrow." She cocked her head to one side. "It was a very nasty fall, you know . . . but nothing's broken. They're running tests, giving him a full check."

"That's—"

"I shouldn't have barked at you."

Jayna raised her eyebrows fractionally. She didn't disagree. What had she said that was so bad? "Don't forget the monthly figures before you go. Only take a minute." It hadn't exactly been a quarrel; too brief and one-sided. Jayna reassessed the incident: Eloise pushing things into her bag, one arm in her coat. She'd barged past and barked so the whole department heard, "You really are the bloody limit, Jayna." The emphasis still caught her by surprise. And then Eloise had thrown open the office door. Her coat belt got caught on the handle. She'd yanked at the belt and shoved the door, which had slammed back against the wall.

"Darjeeling, black, isn't it?" Eloise turned and hit the kettle switch. "Jayna, you have to understand. We can't all be as calm as you."

Jayna shook her head, "Nothing for me, thanks," and turned to leave but Eloise touched her arm. "Listen, to be honest, I wanted to clear the air quickly. Something serious . . ." She hesitated. "You'd better see Benjamin, now. It's about Tom Blenkinsop." Eloise frowned at Jayna's blankness and, as if spelling things out for a child, "It's . . . not . . . good."

* * *

A bugbear, that Tom. She should have told him; if he needed so much help he should have asked through proper channels, booked some extra training, some official mentoring time. Maybe Benjamin had found out about his off-loading. It had started two months back when Tom sent her a research report before submitting it to Benjamin, with a request: Cast an eye over this, will you, Jayna? An aberration; an extra step in the accredited process. On the first three occasions the amendments had taken less than ten minutes but, from that point on, Tom's requests had landed every few days and the reports had become weightier. She hadn't complained because once she'd corrected the first report she hadn't liked the idea of Tom's errors reaching Benjamin. He might have missed them. So Jayna had developed the habit of charging the time to her own jobs; five minutes here, ten minutes there. She finessed his arguments, improved his executive summaries—his weakest area—and, when essential, she hunted down additional data sources to "beef things up," as Tom himself would say.

Benjamin usually worked in the middle of the analysts' floor on the thirty-first but this morning he summoned staff to the thirty-second, to his so-called quiet room.

"About Tom?" she said, poking her head around his door. Benjamin, slumped in his sofa, looked up at Jayna and seemingly had no inclination to say anything. She felt hot. "I thought his last report—"

"It's not about his work," he said, and gestured to the armchair. "You know he's . . . he was on holiday?"

She did. Tom had dropped another tome on her before he left, with a brief note: *Check and forward. Thx.*

"Was on holiday?"

"Tragic accident," he said. "I want to tell everyone individually."

"Tragic?"

"Swimming in the sea . . ."

Benjamin, she realized, had already told the story several times. He didn't continue. So she prompted: "Drowned?"

"His wife and kids were on the beach. Couldn't do anything about it."

"That's terrible."

"Swept out. His brother phoned me last night at home. He's flying out today."

Another silence. What was she supposed to say? She recalled a drowning incident reported in the news. What did the journalist ask . . . ?

"Have they found his body?" she said with precision.

"No. Not yet. Only happened yesterday."

"That's terrible."

"And it's going to be a long time before there's a funeral. There'll be an autopsy when they find the body . . ."

Stumped.

"Jayna, can you help me out?" Benjamin, gray-faced, pulled himself up to sit straight-backed. Was this one problem too many for Benjamin, she wondered, or was he upset? Tom had only joined seven months ago. "Can you go through his files? Finish anything that needs finishing. I think the others might find it too upsetting, so soon."

"Okay. I'm familiar—"

"Thanks. Don't tell the others. Just fit it around your own work. Let me know if I need to do any firefighting."

A secondary post-mortem, she thought. "Fine."

* * *

Jayna stepped along the corridor's repeat-pattern squares and dipped into the washroom. Inside the end cubicle, she leaned back against the door.

Such bad timing! Rebuffing Tom . . . of all the opportunities I could have taken, Jayna reproached herself. He didn't bother to explain . . . just assumed. She flushed the toilet unnecessarily as though eradicating her response to his request: Tom, I can't possibly find time until the end of the month. Send it to Benjamin, as is. He'd retorted: FU2. Thanks for nothing, wonder woman.

I didn't know he was in a rush, going on holiday. How stupid of him to drown!

What, she wondered, were the chances of Tom's death? In the entire working population of the Grace Hopper Building she'd expect a premature fatality . . . once a year? But at Mayhew McCline, with only forty-five employees, the chance of anyone drowning was so small it was technically . . . She stopped herself and opened the door.

It was never negligible, it was always there. She turned the tap, too far, and water shot out from the basin. Accidents simply happened.

* * *

The kitchen became the unofficial, designated space for commiserations and the occasional sobbing over Tom as though the analysts were protecting their office space from permanent stains of association. Jayna observed Eloise zigzagging through the department with a condolence card. She averted her eyes as each person hesitated with pen poised. Eloise didn't bring the card to Jayna. Hester, chief analyst, announced she was installing herself for the morning in Benjamin's quiet room and they all knew what she'd be doing— she'd inform colleagues in London about Tom's death and speak to his personal business contacts, get them reassigned to other analysts. Jayna imagined ripples of concern of varying magnitude spreading from all these subsidiary nodes. No such after-effects from her stick insect's demise.

She brought up Tom's files on her array. And immediately closed them. Instead, she pulled up her own studies and began drilling through her energy data sets. Hydrogen, she decided, was worth a closer look. She interrogated the data on hydrogen car ownership, rotated the charts and geographical visuals—global, continental, and regional— and calculated a trend for global hydrogen car ownership over the past five-years. Next, she searched for a correlation with individual variables in other data sets: disposable income for the same period, fresh fruit exports, per capita holiday spending, a host of commodity production figures, wholesale energy prices . . . thirty-seven variables in all. Her array flashed, cycling through regressions and wildly fluctuating figures for statistical significance. She brushed twenty-one possibilities aside. Playing with combinations of the remaining variables, she derived seventeen relationships. A fair start, she thought. By instinct, she assigned a weighting for each variable and began her quest for the perfect curve, one that matched the five-year historical trend. And as she adjusted the weightings, the curves began their shape shifting. Benjamin appeared at Jayna's shoulder. "How can you take it all in? I feel sick just watching."

But Jayna refused the interruption. She was closing in but the match simply wasn't good enough. There was nothing to flag up, as yet, for Benjamin. Definitely needed more variables. She could, at this stage, submit a bland sector summary on hydrogen, but anyone could do that. No, she wanted nothing less than a full investment strategy. Worth spending the extra time. She checked her own performance statistics. On average, over her six months' service to date, she'd concluded three projects a week, quadruple the frequency of anyone else in the department. Yes, she could afford to spend more time on hydrogen.

* * *

Sitting in the park, as she always did after work on Monday, she threw crumbs to her left and right and occasionally ahead of her. Such simple creatures. Each time she flicked her wrist, she reckoned only one or two pigeons espied the flight of stale scraps. She tested her theory by throwing crumbs to her far right. One pigeon twisted around, reacting in the instant. Correct. The other pigeons followed as though a switch had been thrown in each of their tiny brains. Jayna threw to the far left. Again, a single cadger tracked the new trajectory. Leading one minute, subservient the next.

Bother! Maybe she should have rewritten Tom's report. She shook out the remaining crumbs from her paper bag. But she'd been right to consider her own productivity. It was all getting way out of hand. I know now what I should have done. She flattened the paper bag against her thigh and made quarter folds. From the outset I should have allocated the time I spent on his jobs to his timesheet, not mine, without asking him. He'd have thought twice, then, about asking for help.

The birds were in a frenzy. Their heads jabbed, jabbing the air as they jerked along, jabbing at the crumbs on the ground. Jayna examined the evidence of their mishaps—empty eye sockets, stump feet, trailing feathers—and noticed that two of the birds were verging on obese.

And as for Eloise and her father, she rolled her eyes to the treetops, I still get it wrong.

* * *

On the way to her residence in Granby Row, she stopped by the garish menu boards at the Jasmin Five Star Tandoori Restaurant and examined the names of the dishes: King Prawn Vindaloo, Aloo Methi, Bindi Bhaji, Baroa Mozaa. A waiter hovered in the doorway, so she turned away before he could begin his entreaties. No point wasting his time. And, rejoining the mid-afternoon crowds ambling in the hot spring breeze, she thought about her work colleagues who went back to their own kitchens in their own homes at the end of each day. She wondered if they, too, gave names to all their meals.

The incessant street projections begged the city workers to delay their journeys home. They showed trailers for the latest films intercut with clips of star karaoke performers, all aimed at sucking the more impressionable commuters towards the downtown Entertainment Quarter and the Repertory Domes. As the crowds neared their metro stops, high-kick dancers were scorched across the city skyline in a last-ditch attempt to prevent anyone leaving. Jayna lowered her gaze and scrutinized the footwear worn by pedestrians who rushed towards her or cut across her path. Today, she looked for shoes that demanded attention; shoes that demanded she look up to see the wearer's face. And in these faces she searched for any indication that they returned her curiosity. It didn't happen. So she stared directly into the eyes of oncoming pedestrians but she failed again; she couldn't force any connection.

She entered her residence by the side door and climbed the scrubbed stairway to her single-room quarters on the second floor, just as she had done every working day for the previous twenty-six weeks. She changed into her loose clothes and hung her suit in the narrow, open-fronted wardrobe by the sink. Dropping onto her single bed, she closed her eyes. A difficult day. She assessed her options beyond the routine of taking a shower and dining with the other residents. She could (a) chat in the common room with her friends; (b) relax alone in her room until lights out; or (c) continue her private studies. She admitted that (b) and (c) amounted to pretty much the same thing.

* * *

"How rare is drowning at the age of thirty-four?" Jayna said as soon as Julie seated herself at the dining table. With Julie's job at the Pensions Agency, she'd know the figures.

"Confidential . . . but not as rare as you might think."

Harry and Lucas briefly looked up from their meals to acknowledge Julie's remark. These four were the only diners. They ate one hour earlier than the rest of the residents at C7 because their working day was shorter by one hour. Jayna explained about Tom.

"If you consider all accidental deaths between ages thirty and thirty-five," Julie continued, "the figures are also far higher than anyone would guess. We've done a study. It seems people's natural instincts on risk are very poor."

"Care to disassemble?" said Harry.

"I'm talking historically . . . When primitive man lived on the savannah, the risk of accidental death was high but the types of risk were limited in number. Our intuition on certainty and uncertainty was formed then. Totally inadequate now. Life's too complex."

"Is that a problem?" said Lucas. He was the new boy.

"Yes and no. Obviously, if people underestimate certain risks they'll make decisions with unfortunate outcomes. But—" she paused and looked around her friends "—if everyone could grasp their true exposure to negative events there'd be . . . ramifications. People have to get on with life as though the risks aren't there. That's why everyone anticipates an average lifespan. I assume you all caught the latest news from National Statistics—ninety-nine years."

"So, in theory, your colleague lost two-thirds his due," said Lucas.

"I didn't understand the media's reaction," Jayna said. "What's so special about living to one hundred rather than ninety-nine?"

"Teasing failure from success," said Harry.

"Anyway, I don't believe they should massage the figures to achieve an extra year," said Julie. "They were even suggesting taking deaths through natural disasters out of the statistics. The facts are the facts."

"Well, I can tell you one thing," said Jayna. "I don't think any massaging would keep Tom Blenkinsop out of the statistics."

The group of friends fell quiet. Jayna took a piece of bread from the platter at the center of the table and chased the remaining traces of a thin gravy from her plate. Her companions registered her eagerness and, in turn, they too reached towards the bread.

* * *

With barely two hours of her evening remaining, Jayna returned to her small room and, prompted by Julie's remark about the savannah, she downloaded a wildlife program on the Serengeti. She turned to the cage on her bedside table. Hester had given her a branch of privet last week and it was now stripped almost bare. Observing her insects, as she always did in the evening, she jotted a note: Leaves are consumed by an insect that looks like a twig. So what is the difference between a leaf falling and a stick insect dying?

Out on the Serengeti, a lioness pounced at the flanks of a bolting zebra. Jayna had watched hundreds of similar murderous sequences over recent months and she recognized that only a few animals were immune to the carnivorous advances of others. She decided to formalize this thought by writing an essay on food chain hierarchies and biomass diversity. There were plenty of learned treatises already on the subject but she wouldn't consult them. She preferred to work it out for herself; it all came down to basic mathematics.

The lights in her room dimmed and she prepared herself for a twelve-hour sleep. As she lay in bed she looked into her little wildlife park and, in the remaining half-light, could just discern her twiggy roommates from their twiggy habitat. She knew Hester would bring another privet branch from the suburbs. With family to take care of, she had plenty to think about other than stick insects. And she might be preoccupied over Tom's death. But she simply wouldn't forget.

Anne Charnock's A Calculated Life *is available from 47North.*

ABOUT THE AUTHOR

Photo © 2013 Yvette Owen

Anne Charnock's writing career began in journalism. Her articles have appeared in the *Guardian, New Scientist, International Herald Tribune* and *Geographical*. She has travelled widely as a foreign correspondent and spent a year driving overland through Egypt, Sudan and Kenya.

Although Anne's education initially focused on science—she studied environmental sciences at the University of East Anglia—she later attended the Manchester School of Art, where she gained a master's degree in fine art. At the end of her art studies, she began exhibiting her work internationally, and on the quiet, she started writing a novel. Her debut novel, *A Calculated Life*, was a finalist for the 2013 Philip K. Dick Award and the 2013 Kitschies Golden Tentacle award for a debut novel.

Anne is an active blogger, and she contributes exhibition reviews and book recommendations to the *Huffington Post*. She splits her time between London and Chester, and v[...]-band, Garry, take off in their little [...] y travelled as far as the Anti-Atlas Mo[...] d they next plan to drive from Londo[...]

Learn more at www.annech[...] t @annecharnock.